# RISE OF THE
# GOLDEN COBRA

# RISE OF THE GOLDEN COBRA

A NOVEL FOR YOUNG ADULTS

## BY HENRY T. AUBIN

annick press
toronto + new york + vancouver

©2007 Henry T. Aubin (text)
©2007 Stephen M. Taylor (cover and interior illustration)
Edited by Barbara Pulling
Copyedited by Barbara Hehner
Map by Justin Stahlman
Cover and interior design by Sheryl Shapiro

Annick Press Ltd.

We acknowledge the support of the Canada Council for the Arts, the Ontario
Arts Council, and the Government of Canada through the Book Publishing
Industry Development Program (BPIDP) for our publishing activities.

**Cataloging in Publication**

Aubin, Henry, 1942-
    Rise of the golden cobra : a novel for young adults / Henry T. Aubin.

Includes bibliographical references.
ISBN-13: 978-1-55451-060-3 (bound)
ISBN-10: 1-55451-060-0 (bound)
ISBN-13: 978-1-55451-059-7 (pbk.)
ISBN-10:1-55451-059-7 (pbk.)

    1. Piankhy, King of Kush, fl. 720 B.C.—Juvenile fiction. I. Title.

PS8601.U25R57 2007          jC813'.6          C2006-
906264-1

Distributed in Canada by:      Published in the U.S.A. by:
Firefly Books Ltd.             Annick Press (U.S.) Ltd.
66 Leek Crescent           Distributed in the U.S.A. by:
Richmond Hill, ON         Firefly Books (U.S.) Inc.
L4B 1H1                  P.O. Box 1338
                            Ellicott Station
                            Buffalo, NY 14205

Enthroned monarch on map: Photograph © 2007 Museum of Fine Arts, Boston

Printed in Canada.

Visit us at: www.annickpress.com

To my children Seth, Nishi, Nicolas and Raphaëlle.
—H.A.

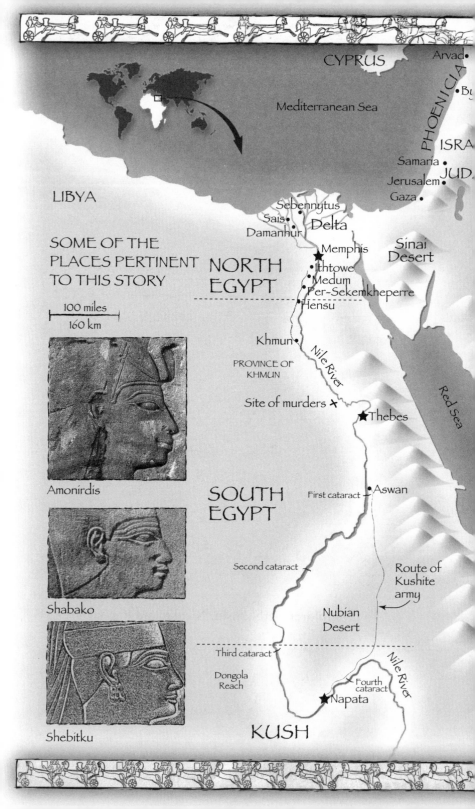

SOME OF THE
PLACES PERTINENT
TO THIS STORY

100 miles
160 km

Amonirdis

Shabako

Shebitku

CYPRUS

Mediterranean Sea

Arvad

PHOENICIA

By

ISRA

Samaria

Jerusalem

JUD.

Gaza

LIBYA

Sebennytus

Sais

Damanhur

Delta

Sinai
Desert

Memphis

Ithtowe

Medum

Per-Sekemkheperre

Hensu

NORTH
EGYPT

Khmun

PROVINCE OF
KHMUN

Nile River

Site of murders

Thebes

Red Sea

SOUTH
EGYPT

First cataract

Aswan

Second cataract

Route of
Kushite
army

Nubian
Desert

Third cataract

Dongola
Reach

Fourth
cataract

Nile River

Napata

KUSH

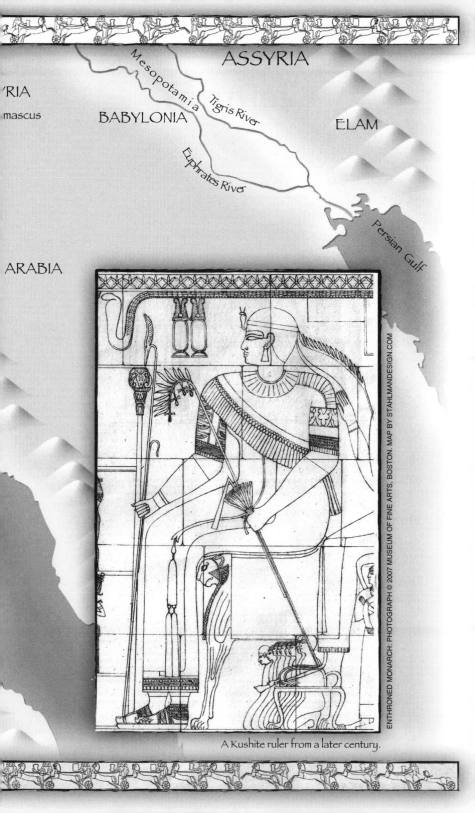

ASSYRIA

'RIA

mascus

BABYLONIA

Mesopotamia

Tigris River

ELAM

Euphrates River

Persian Gulf

ARABIA

A Kushite ruler from a later century.

# CONTENTS

# AUTHOR'S NOTE

This novel dramatizes a true event: the great invasion of ancient Egypt by Piankhy. He was king of the African nation of Kush, sometimes called Nubia. It was located in present-day northern Sudan and southern Egypt.

The invasion took place around 734 BCE. The flowering of democracy in Athens was then three centuries away, Jerusalem was the capital of the modest kingdom of Judah, and Rome was but a village.

In addition to Piankhy, many characters in the novel correspond to real people who appear either in the king's own account of the war or in other ancient records. They include Nimlot, Tefnakht, Amonirdis, Shebitku, Shabako, Purem, Lemersekeny, and Khaliut. To make the geography easier to visualize, the novel replaces the usual terms Lower and Upper Egypt with North and South Egypt.

For more information on the characters, please see the Afterword.

# CAST OF MAIN CHARACTERS

*Ameye*—a Kushite colonel who loses an eye early in the campaign

*Amonirdis*—Piankhy's sister, the symbolic wife of the god Amon and the ruler of South Egypt

*Khaliut*—Piankhy's son, the titular commander of the First Division and one of the candidates to become king someday

*Khuit*—the daughter of the mayor of Damanhur, Nebamon's home village

*Lemersekeny*—a Kushite general and the leader of the First Division

*Nebamon (Nebi)*—a young native of the Delta, the northernmost part of North Egypt

*Nimlot*—the young ruler of the city of Khmun and the province of the same name, located in South Egypt

*Piankhy*—at the time the story begins, he has been king of both Kush and South Egypt for 20 years

*Purem*—the commanding general of all three of the Kushite army's divisions, with direct personal responsibility for the Second Division

*Setka*—Nebamon's Kushite master and, many years before, Piankhy's tutor

*Shabako*—Piankhy's younger brother, Shebitku's father, and a leading candidate to someday succeed Piankhy as king

*Shebitku (Sheb)*—a precocious young horseman and building designer who is Piankhy's nephew

*Tebey*—a distant cousin of Shebitku. As a lieutenant, his role is to deal with army supplies and assist General Purem.

*Tefnakht*—the ruler of Sais (one of the Delta's numerous fiefdoms) and the leader of an alliance of North Egypt's leaders that seeks to conquer all of Egypt

*Wosmol*—a Kushite army captain whose father and grandfather had earned military glory

# PART I

# CHAPTER 1

# THE ATTACK

No one saw the riders gallop over the grassy ridge. No one saw them pause and draw swords.

The three picnickers lay on their elbows in a meadow overlooking the Nile River. They were feeling contented after a dessert of honey pastries. A blue cotton canopy, held up by poles, shielded them from the scorching Egyptian sun. A hound proudly watched as her puppies raced after sticks the picnickers tossed. Even she did not notice the riders.

A servant spotted them first. He had been gathering the remains of the picnic, stacking the earthen dishes in a cart. He was a slim 14-year-old, with the sharp features and mellow tan skin of most Egyptians. "Master Setka!" he said. He jerked his head toward the ridge.

The master, heavy-set and balding, stopped his arm in midthrow. Like his host, he was bare-chested and dressed in a white linen kilt and sandals. Unlike the others, his skin was deep brown, the color of mahogany. What remained of his wiry hair was gray. His brow furrowed with concern.

"They look like the Mesh," said Setka. He spoke in Egyptian, so that the others could understand, but his accent and dark hue marked him as a visitor from Kush. That prosperous land lay just to the south of the Two Lands, as North and South Egypt were often called.

The Kushite sprang to his feet with agility uncommon for someone of his girth. His companions, a stiffly moving Egyptian and his petite wife, also rose. From the Egyptian man's neck dangled a bronze medallion indicating his rank as the province's chief of police.

"Mesh?" said the woman. "That can't be."

"We never see them this far south," said the police chief.

The boy-servant saw the chief grope for a sword at his hip. But it was not there. Earlier in the day, the boy had heard the chief brag to his Kushite guest that there was no need to bring weapons. After all, they were in young Count Nimlot's province, a part of South Egypt that lay in and around Khmun, where Nimlot's family had ruled for generations. The family had long protected its subjects from the Mesh, known for their appetite for war. Originally from arid Libya, the Mesh had drifted into North Egypt's lush Nile Delta centuries before, enlisting as soldiers in pharaohs' armies. Because of their fighting skill, they had eventually become a power in their own right.

The 10 riders approached at a trot. All but one had the pale skin and brown or reddish hair of the Mesh. Their unshaven faces and unkempt tunics showed they were not soldiers but either brigands or swords-for-hire. They rode mules rather than horses, a sign they had yet to make their fortune.

The tenth member of the group was in the center. He was about 16 years old, an Egyptian with close-cropped black hair. Elegantly groomed, he rode a magnificent white stallion. Like the male picnickers, he wore a white linen kilt, but also a vest of black leather with bronze studs and shoulder pads, as if to try to conceal his leanness. A cape striped in green and yellow billowed from his shoulders.

"Count Nimlot!" exclaimed the police chief, recognizing the family colors.

"I don't understand," said the woman. "Why is he with these thugs?" She looked anxiously at her husband.

"He can mean no harm," said the police chief. After all, Count Nimlot of Khmun employed him to keep the peace, just as the young lord's late father had done until his death six years before. But no sooner had the chief spoken than the hound's barking stopped. An arrow had pierced her chest. She lay in the high grass, whimpering. The intruders laughed. Next to Nimlot was a fleshy, red-bearded archer with a peculiar tattoo—some kind of greenish design stretched uninterrupted across both his arms and his beefy chest. He raised his bow in mock triumph.

"Perhaps if I give them my jewelry they'll leave," said the woman. Her necklace and three bracelets were gold.

"It's our lives he wants," Setka said matter-of-factly. Though a stranger to the region, he was the first to grasp the situation.

"Our chariot!" shouted the police chief. But the chariot, parked beside the cart that had brought the servants, was useless. Both horses were unhitched and grazing. Harnessing them would take too long. The chief cursed. "And no weapons either," he said. "Unarmed, an officer cannot die in battle with honor!"

It was then that the chief noticed the boy-servant. He was pulling the squeaky-wheeled cart behind him and ambling toward the three picnickers, a long blade of grass in his mouth. The boy appeared unconcerned about the riders, now a stone's throw away.

As the boy reached the picnickers, he bent to pick up more plates. Furious that a servant should be preoccupied with a petty chore at this moment, the police chief kicked the dishes, sending them clattering to the ground. "Idiot!" he said.

The servant's master pointed to the cart. "No—look!"

In it lay two hunting javelins and a skinning knife that the party had brought along that morning. The boy-servant lackadaisically folded the picnic cloth and placed it in the cart, hiding the arms.

The riders pulled their mounts up short. In the fashion of Mesh fighters, most boasted sidelocks—braided side-burns, glistening with oil, that hung to their shoulders.

The servant shuffled behind the picnickers and started taking down the four tall poles that held up the canopy. He struggled to maintain a dull-eyed appearance while a year-old memory flashed before him.

*Sitting high in the palm tree overlooking his house, hidden in its fan-like leaves, he hears hooves and the jangle of weapons. He is picking the dom nuts his little brother has begged him to get. Three Mesh riders enter the village, a cluster of sun-dried mud-brick houses. They ask directions from a frightened neighbor, then dismount. Never looking up, they tether their mules to the palm. Sidelocks swinging, they stride toward the door of one house—his.*

*From his roost, he can see into the courtyard of his house. His mother is stirring supper. Smoke from the charcoal burner curls upward. Wia, his three-year-old sister, sits on her lap, playing with her mother's braid. When the strangers burst in, Mother clutches Wia and runs out through the same door the men have entered.*

*He raises his eyes to the field beyond the house. Unaware, his father is pulling the wooden plow.*

"Whoa, you dumb beast!" Count Nimlot jerked his large stallion to a halt in front of the picnickers.

As he tugged at a canopy pole, the servant sized up the young noble. He had a hatchet nose, and since his skull was long and narrow like his body, his whole head gave the impression of an ax blade. His eyes, cold and hard, bored into the group like drills.

The police chief sought to put the best face on things. "Your Grace!" he said, bowing. "It gladdens us to see you. Come and dismount, My Lord, and your companions as well, and join us in our meal with my wife and our honored guest, a merchant from Kush."

Nimlot smiled coldly. "I know all about your guest. He is no merchant."

At this moment, Nimlot saw something that made him frown. One servant—a slope-shouldered, middle-aged man—had untethered one of the horses. As the man frantically galloped away bareback, the count turned to the red-bearded archer beside him. "No witnesses," he said.

The tattooed man nodded. He nocked an arrow on his bowstring.

The boy-servant, still picking up the poles, glimpsed the older servant dropping into the grass.

Nimlot returned his gaze to his police chief. "As you see," he said, waving his arm toward his companions, "I am with the Mesh. Our old enemies are now my friends."

"This is treason!" hissed the woman, eyes afire.

Nimlot steadied his prancing stallion. "No, it is wisdom," he said. "The Mesh are strong. And now, with Lord Tefnakht as their leader, they are unbeatable. The other lords of the Delta have now joined him. And so have I. I am no longer King Piankhy's vassal. Should I resist Tefnakht and his allies, and see them destroy my city and my people? No, I must think of my people."

"But, your Grace," blurted the chief, "under Tefnakht, your people would have no police, no courts, only brutes like these"—he motioned toward Nimlot's companions. "Tell me, with what riches has Tefnakht bribed you to betray King Piankhy?"

"Speak to me and my men with respect," Nimlot snapped. He drew his sword.

The gray-haired man from Kush addressed the count for the first time. "Where is your respect for your own lord, King Piankhy, he who has allowed your family to rule this region?"

"I respect only those who can defeat me. Piankhy is too far off to do so."

"Only months ago you swore allegiance to His Majesty," reminded Setka. "You even sought to wed his niece. The king knew full well what he was doing when he scoffed at your bid." He smiled at the fury in Nimlot's eyes. "Ah yes, there is no anger like that of a rejected suitor."

"Enough!" cried Nimlot. He turned to his companions. "Kill them all!"

The Kushite was ready. He plunged both hands into the cart. With one, he tossed a hunting javelin to his host. With the other, he passed the knife to the woman. He then grabbed the other javelin and, with an easy motion, hurled it into the chest of the rider nearest him.

"Master!" It was the voice of the boy-servant. Setka turned, and as he did so the boy flung him a canopy pole. The foreigner used it to knock a second warrior off his horse.

One of the riders raised his bow toward him. The chief sent his weapon into the man's shoulder.

Nimlot, startled by the picnickers' resistance, had by now nocked his arrow. He aimed at the least mobile target, the woman. The boy-servant clenched a second canopy pole and swung. It struck the hand that held the bow. Yelping in pain, the young noble dropped the arrow.

Nimlot drew a new shaft from his quiver and aimed at the boy. The servant dodged, trying to lose himself in the confusion of horses. As the count aimed at him, his stallion reared. Instead of striking the boy's torso, the arrow pierced his lower leg.

He fell. He found himself in the grass next to his Kushite master.

Setka lay on his back with a gaping sword wound in his heaving chest. He turned his head to the boy. Eyes that had been bulging with pain softened with affection. He uttered several hoarse, urgent words.

"Nebamon," he whispered, calling the boy by his name. "You tell ... tell *all* to the king."

The boy could only nod. The weight of the commission rendered him speechless. His face contorted by his own stabbing pain, he craned his neck to see that the arrow had struck just below the right knee, in his calf. When he turned again toward his master, he saw that his eyes were open— unblinking and lifeless.

Hooves trod heavily all around him. He lurched from one side to the other to avoid them.

Within moments the turmoil was over. The boy, his naked back skyward, strove desperately to lie motionless among the three lifeless picnickers. Yet his gasps from pain were impossible to conceal.

"On your feet, cur!" someone commanded. A spear poked his side. "Up!"

Next to him lay a canopy pole. Holding it vertically to the ground, he grasped it with both hands and, swaying, hoisted himself to his feet. He found himself facing a chest sprouting reddish hair and reeking of putrid sweat. Seeing the tattoo close up, the boy shuddered. It was of a python—Apophis, god of darkness and strife. The serpent's scaly tail began just above the man's left fist and stretched up one arm, across his powerful chest, and down the other. Its fangs covered the back of his sword hand.

Huddled on either side of the boy were two frightened men—the servants who had not tried to flee. The chubby one was the cook. The other was a horse groom, tall and thin. They worked for the police chief and his wife, and the boy had never seen them before this day.

Their mounts stamping the ground, the warriors encircled the three prisoners. Nimlot advanced to the center of the ring, eyed the servants, and said loudly, "As I said, no witnesses." He paused. "But how shall they die?"

His men eyed him, waiting for his word to finish them off.

Nimlot raised his left arm, the uninjured one. "Hold!" he said. "It is no sport to dispose of them as lambs at the slaughter. Let us amuse ourselves with a little game."

The warriors' sneers became grins.

Nimlot addressed the three servants. "You there," he said. The cook and groom looked at their feet for fear of offending their captor. The boy glared at him with fear and hatred. Nimlot circled them once with his stallion, looking them up and down. "You have lived dull, stupid lives, but I will do you a favor. I will not let you die dull, stupid deaths. Your lives will end with excitement."

His teeth flashed as he smiled. "We will let you go. Run as fast as you can. While you run, we will drink." He pointed to a goatskin container that hung behind the tattooed warrior's saddle. "When the beer is gone, we will come after you."

The men grunted their approval.

"And," Nimlot added, turning to them, "there will be prizes. Our picnickers here had five horses. I will choose two of them for myself, but the others can be claimed by those who slay these nobodies."

Horses were in short supply in Egypt. Only the army and the rich had them. The men's eyes shone.

Nimlot seized the skin container and held it over his head while squeezing beer into his mouth. He tossed the container to another man, then turned to the trio.

"What are you waiting for?" he shouted. *"Run!"*

# CHAPTER 2

# THE "GAME"

The plump cook ran east through the waist-high grass. The land sloped slightly downhill, but even so, he could not continue for long. He stopped to catch his breath, then continued at a walk, peering fearfully over his shoulder every few steps. When he saw that none of the drinkers was looking his way, he flopped into the grass to hide.

The second servant was in better physical condition. He ran north through the grass. He never stopped.

The boy was by far the slowest. He limped toward the low western ridge. He knew it was useless to hide, since he was leaving a clear trail of trampled grass. The grass brushed against the arrow in his leg, making it wobble and causing spasms of hurt.

*His mother's screams. She stands in the road, her normally rosy, good-natured face twisted into blanched despair. The crackle of flames. From inside come the frightened wails of Mosi, Wia's twin. As Tefnakht's riders gallop off, he shinnies down the tree. Smoke churns from the doorway. He enters, but the reed floor mats are aflame. Heat and smoke drive him back. He lies gasping on the road.*

If he fainted from the pain, he would be found at once, he knew. He would have to do something about the arrow. With sobbing breath, he threw himself on the ground, grasped the arrow's shaft with both his hands, and yanked. He yelped in agony. But it would not come out. Instead, its jagged metal barbs tore into his flesh when he pulled. He waited until the pain subsided a little, and then did the next best thing. Clenching the arrow's shaft in his fists, he snapped it off as close to his leg as he could.

He ran, faster than before, toward a ridge. At the skyline were scraggly trees growing among reddish boulders the size of elephants. By the time he reached the rocks, the men were just finishing their beer. He slipped in between two boulders. As he caught his breath, he saw that hiding there—or anywhere—would be futile, since the track of blood that dripped from his leg would give him away.

Should he run on? He looked about him. The Nile River valley, where he was now, was a slim green band of fields and groves. Beyond these, all was yellow—the Sahara Desert. It started with rocks and a few outcroppings of grass and brush. Then came the dunes. Enter them and the riders would catch him in no time.

From the meadow below, he heard a cry of anguish. Peering between the boulders, he could see five riders surrounding the cook and brandishing spears.

To the north, another five riders were pursuing the other servant. He was racing through the grass ever more desperately. The men had stopped and were laughing as they took turns shooting at him. Target practice didn't last long. The tattooed man shook his bow above his head.

Now he was the only prey left. The boy's eyes darted leftward, where a horse and rider approached. Even from afar the servant could see his pursuer's lean outline. The Count of Khmun.

The boy knew what he had to do.

He was crouching between two boulders an arm's breadth from each other. Between them stood two young trees. His trail of blood led to the space between these saplings.

What he needed was a vine. He looked behind. There were only thorn bushes. The next best thing was the thongs on his sandals. The rawhide strips criss-crossed up past his ankle.

He tore off both thongs, then tied them together. He tried yanking them apart with all his strength and was relieved when they held. He hitched one end around the left sapling at knee level.

The clopping sound of Nimlot's horse grew near.

He tied the other end to the other sapling at the same height. The rawhide, nearly the same color as the saplings' bark, would be hard to spot.

The plan was for the stallion to trip and cause the rider to fall. The problem was that a walking horse would never stumble.

The boy scooped up a rock the size of a plum. As soon as Nimlot came into range, he threw it.

It struck the noble on his leather shoulder pad. As the startled Nimlot looked around for his attacker, the boy stood up between the saplings.

For a moment the eyes of the two Egyptian youths locked. Then, remembering how his master's remark about Piankhy's niece had so angered Nimlot, he yelled, "What girl would want a sissy like you!"

The taunt worked. Holding the reins with his injured hand and grasping a whip in the other, Nimlot thrashed his horse forward.

"You're mine, cur! Mine!" he shouted above the clatter of hooves.

The boy ducked back behind a boulder. Nimlot spurred the stallion into the opening. The horse's right foreleg hit the trip line. He buckled, and his head and neck came down. The lurch caught the rider by surprise and sent him flying over the horse's neck. His head, bare except for his green and yellow headband, struck a limestone boulder. He lay on his back, motionless but breathing.

Before the horse could bolt off, the servant seized the reins and tied them to a sapling. He'd have little time before the other riders rejoined their employer.

He grabbed the fallen spear and held its point close to Nimlot's belly. Without touching the flesh, the boy slashed through the young noble's fine linen kilt. He ripped off a large strip and wrapped it tightly around his leg, letting the arrow protrude. That, he hoped, would slow the bleeding and deny searchers a further trail.

Through the gap in the boulders he now spotted two riders ascending the slope. Unaware of their leader's mishap, they were taking their time.

The servant yanked off the rest of the lord's kilt. He removed both the quiver of arrows slung around Nimlot's chest and the sleeveless vest. He looked down at the unconscious form, now naked except for headband and sandals. "I'll need these more than you," he muttered.

He limped toward the horse, who was eying him nervously. It backed away, the reins bending the sapling. The boy had ridden sway-backed burros and donkeys before but, like most Egyptians, he had never been on a mule or horse. It would often be months before a horseman passed through his village.

As the boy got close, the stallion, nostrils flaring, jerked his head away, almost uprooting the small tree. Showing he meant no harm, the boy held his palms out the way he did with a dog so the animal could smell them. "Easy, easy," he murmured, trying to keep his voice calm. He ran his hand softly over the horse's flank. The big white head swung around to look at him. He caressed the animal's neck. "I'm Nebi," he whispered, using his nickname.

He stuffed the clothes and the quiver into the saddle-bag, then bound the spear to the saddle with a piece of thong. He led the skittish horse to a rock that was almost as high as the saddle. Wincing, he climbed the rock and carefully eased himself onto the seat. The wary animal tensed at the unfamiliar rider.

Astonishment at being so high off the ground took the boy's mind off his pain. So did the empowering sensation of the great lathered flanks beneath him. He clasped the reins with one hand as he had seen Nimlot do, but nearly fell off when the horse lurched forward. He had to clutch the saddle with both hands while still holding the reins.

The stallion clambered over the rocks. Once, its front hoof slipped on a tippy rock and Nebi again almost slid off his back.

When they reached the desert floor, he guided the animal south along a course parallel to the ridge from which he had come and which separated the Sahara from the valley. By now, he guessed, the warriors would have found Nimlot. The pursuit would soon begin. With his bare heels, he nudged the stallion into a trot. The saddle, like all in those days, lacked stirrups, and his wound made it impossible to grip his mount firmly with his legs.

He was beginning to breathe more easily when, looking back, he saw a glint of light somewhere in the rocks—the sun reflecting off a spear.

"Come on," he pressed. He eased the horse into a canter and found the rocking motion of the faster gait more comfortable than the bouncing of the trot. But the riders' jeers grew louder behind him.

He saw he had three choices. He could keep heading south along this rocky edge of the desert. He could turn east, back up the rock-strewn slope, and then try to make it into the fields and orchards of the valley. But in either case, the riders would easily catch up to him.

His third option was to turn west and enter the immensity of the desert. He saw the rolling dunes stretching to the horizon like waves on a lethal, limitless sea. He closed his eyes.

*Lying in the road, he sees that the doorway has become a rectangle of roaring fire, plainly impassable. Suddenly a man's face stands between him and the doorway. The sturdy back and legs are bare and belong to his father. His father arches his back as he takes a deep breath, then—impossibly—runs through the flame.*

The boy stared at the dunes. "I'm going," he said aloud.

Hanging from the saddle was the goatskin container. He lifted it to see if anything remained inside. It still felt about half full. So Nimlot and the others had started the blood hunt before finishing the beer.

"Thank you for cheating," he murmured.

That fast start was now to the boy's advantage—at least a gallon of precious liquid remained inside.

"There he is!" cried one voice behind him.

"We've got him!" shouted another. The voice was high and youthful. Nimlot's.

Soon the boy would be in reach of their arrows. He knew what he had to do. A gully lay ahead and he descended into it, dipping out of his pursuers' sight. Because the gully's floor was limestone, the horse would leave no hoofprints. He swung the horse to the right, and cantered around a bend to the end of the gully and the beginning of the desert.

Before his pursuers could know what had become of him, he was into the wilderness of the dunes.

CHAPTER 3

# ALONE IN THE DESERT

Nebi zigzagged, keeping to the hollows between dunes, where he was out of sight. A stiff breeze arose. He whispered thanks to the great god Amon: the wind was covering the stallion's tracks with sand.

Count Nimlot would expect him to head back to the balmy valley, but he would not. Instead he would keep heading toward the afternoon sun, farther into the desert.

The horse slowed, needing rest. It was time to stop and look back. At the foot of a particularly lofty dune, Nebi dismounted on one foot. He eyed the stallion. "If you run away, I die," he said.

He untied the spear from the saddle, stuck it deep into the sand like a stake, and tied the reins to it. His hands burned from the sand as he crawled up the dune. He squinted in the direction from which he had come. Still visible, shimmering in the heat waves, was the long dark ridge. To get back to the valley beyond it he would need to pass those immobile, ant-like riders.

Nimlot's crew was no longer chasing, but waiting.

The boy heaved an anxious sigh. The Count of Khmun would spare no effort to silence the sole witness to the killings. The noble could not allow King Piankhy to hear he had joined Lord Tefnakht in an attempt to conquer all of the Two Lands. For Piankhy, King of Kush, was the only one who could try to block them.

Nimlot would also know roughly how much beer remained in the goatskin. That would tell him how long the witness could survive. For someone resting in the shade of a tent, the beer could last for perhaps four days; for someone traveling, three. The count would likely post patrols along the desert's edge for four days, possibly five or six. After that, Nimlot could breathe easy. He could assume the vultures were at work.

Nebi gritted his teeth at the searing pain in his right leg. He slid down the dune, holding the leg stiff in front of him. He hobbled to the stallion from the side. Best not to let the horse see his vulnerable state.

As he made his way around the ivory-colored horse, he examined his flank. Nimlot's animal was superbly muscled, but signs of mistreatment were everywhere. Long scabs on his rump indicated brutish whipping. Scars on his sides told of his master's gouging spurs. No wonder the horse at first had been mistrustful.

Nebi ruffled the long white mane. "The future of the Two Lands rests with you, big fellow." He forced himself to adopt a confident tone. "You're taking me to Thebes." The animal bent his powerful neck in response.

"Thebes," he said again. The word gave him a shiver.

Everyone said it was the grandest city anywhere. It was one of Amon's two holy cities. It was also the capital of South

Egypt, which belonged to King Piankhy. However, the king himself did not live there, preferring to remain in Napata, Kush's capital. Napata was Amon's other holy city, but it was impossibly far from the South Egyptian capital—100 *iteru*, or 700 miles, up the Nile. Piankhy had therefore entrusted South Egypt to his sister, Princess Amonirdis, who ruled from Thebes.

"We'll be safe if we can reach the princess," he assured the stallion, stroking his forelock. "But here's the trouble. We can't reach Thebes by the valley—your old master has blocked us off. So we'll go that way—" he jerked his head toward the dunes. "It's shorter than the winding valley, but it's still far, maybe ten *iteru*."

In the desert, Nebi knew, it is as important to avoid sweating as it is to have drinking water. He used the spear to cut a slit through the cotton saddle, poked his head through the hole, and let the material drape over his chest and back, poncho-style. Then he ripped Nimlot's kilt into strips to cover his head and neck. He wrapped the extra pieces around his arms and thighs. The last piece became a fresh bandage.

"You'll need protection too, big fellow," he told the stallion. He fixed the leather vest over the horse's bowed head and neck. The ears, pointing out of the same armhole, helped keep the sunshade in place.

Only the quiver remained on the sand. He frowned, then brightened. "I know," he said. He cut out the bottom of the leather cylinder and sliced it lengthwise. Then, biting his lip, he fitted it over his lower leg so that the arrow protruded from the slit. It would keep his calf from rubbing against the horse.

"We're all set."

His shoulder rose barely above the horse's back. He led him to a large weathered rock at the base of a dune. He used that as a perch from which to swing his bad leg across the animal's back.

Nebi directed his mount west until the ridge was out of sight, then turned left and headed southeast. As the sun set, the air became chilly, then goosebump cold. But the boy kept the North Star over his left shoulder and kept going.

His calf no longer had the same sharp, stabbing pain. It had become a dull, throbbing ache, more hurtful if anything. Thinking about it made it worse.

Dwelling on the temperature had the same effect. He'd heard the desert could be cold at night, but he'd never imagined it would chill his bones.

Nebi forced himself to keep his mind on good things. "I'm lucky. I'm alive." He repeated the words aloud. In the vast stillness, a voice—any voice—was reassuring. "Your master was generous. Look at all that he gave us—linen, equipment, drink. And you're the most welcome present I've ever had." He thought a moment. "Friends need names. I'll call you Hotep"—Gift.

He warmed himself by picturing his mother with her ever-gentle features and her tawny braided hair. He saw her holding a twin by each hand. There was Wia, her dark bangs and greenish-blue eyes an echo of her mother's. And at the other hand, squirming mischievously, was Mosi, head shaved except for his topknot. The two would tease Nebi about his secret admiration for the neighbors' daughter. He still didn't know how they'd guessed.

The sun rose. Horse and rider left the sand and entered a wasteland of boulders. They had to make as much progress as they could when the desert was not unbearably hot. That would mean traveling constantly except when the sun was high.

At midday, they spotted precious shade next to a tall rock.

Hotep fell to his knees. Nebi rubbed the horse's forehead. He had no sweat. Nor did the boy himself. He reached for what he'd been craving, the goatskin. So far, he'd resisted taking even a swallow. He sat behind and downwind from Hotep so that the horse couldn't see or smell what he was doing. Hotep's body was many times heavier than his own; if the liquid were to do the horse any good, he would have to drink the entire amount. Nebi popped the stopper and breathed in the sweetish odor of fermented barley—the soupy, only slightly alcoholic beverage that everyone drank not just for pleasure but also nourishment. He swished half a mouthful of the hot, lumpy liquid into every parched corner of his mouth, then swallowed.

Early that night, the boy dozed briefly as he rode. When he awakened, he realized the North Star was behind him. Hotep must have strayed wildly off their southeasterly course. How much time they had lost he could not tell. Fear kept his eyes open from then on.

The first red sliver of the sun brought hope as well as warmth. "We're going to be lucky today, Hotep. This is our third day. Three is lucky for me. What do *you* think we'll find? An oasis? A caravan?" But he was not really surprised when the only semblance of life they saw was a mirage of shimmering pools, palms, and buildings.

On the fourth day, Hotep could no longer plod in a straight line. "Are your eyes all right?" Nebi asked in a sun-parched whisper. As soon as the boy dismounted, the horse lay down on his side.

Hotep's pupils were glassy. Nebi sat on the sand and carefully placed his legs tent-like over Hotep's head to give him shade. Then he too lay down, covering his own face with the goatskin to block the sun.

When Nebi awoke, it was twilight. He stroked Hotep's head, but the horse's eyes had a vacant look. "Come on," he urged the horse, "you can't leave me stranded here."

Hotep seemed to try his best, moving into a crouch. Nebi sat on his back, but the animal lacked the strength to rise. He sat and sat. Finally, Nebi said, "Since I'm too heavy, I'll walk next to you."

He tugged at the horse's bridle until he rose. Then, wrapping his arm around Hotep's neck, he coaxed his friend forward, using him like a crutch. Awkward as this was, it took enough weight off his bad leg to allow him to walk at about half the normal rate.

"This is good, Hotep, this is good. We must have done three-quarters of the way. Three more days at this pace—we won't keep those Theban mares waiting much longer!"

All night he hobbled. His leg by this time was numb. He would be barely aware of the wound until the broken arrow touched something. Then he would gasp.

In the morning they entered an area of red rocks. When Nebi awoke in late afternoon, he tried to rouse Hotep. The animal did not move.

Nebi clung tightly to the great horse, his arm around Hotep's neck in desperate hope of detecting a pulse. There was none. Nebi tightened his embrace into a hug.

He cried for the first time in years. He was now alone.

# CHAPTER 4

# THE BURNING DOORWAY

As Nebi's eyes dried, the world became clearer. Propped up against the dead stallion's back, he stared southeast at the red emptiness.

"You're lucky, Hotep," he whispered. "You died quickly. I need your luck." Speaking aloud gave comfort in the solitude of the desert.

"You were lucky too, Master Setka. You died even faster." He felt too discouraged, too weak, to make the effort of crawling into the shade.

"The more I broil, the faster I'll die."

He imagined his master looking down on him disapprovingly. "I'm sorry, Setka. I can't go on. Don't you see? It's futile. There are no oases here, no caravans."

The more he pleaded, the more the frown deepened on Setka's round, mahogany face. "Don't ask me to go on!" Nebi murmured angrily. "Even on two feet I couldn't make it."

The sympathy he sought from his master did not come. Setka looked him squarely in the eye.

Nimlot had been right, of course: Setka had been no merchant. He had been a spy for King Piankhy.

Nebi had two messages to deliver. One was that Setka was dead and that Nimlot had betrayed the king. The other message was the one that Setka had planned to deliver himself and that dwarfed the other in importance. It was surely why Nimlot had tracked Setka down and killed him.

In the picture in Nebi's mind, Setka's frown had disappeared. His master's face had now taken on a look of encouragement. Nebi remembered Setka's three-word rule for dealing with peril: "Calm, courage, confidence." And the most important of these, his master had said, was calm. Calm made it easier to find the other two within yourself.

Nebi closed his eyes. It made thinking easier. He waited until he could breathe slowly.

"There are two lives here: my life and the life of the message. If I die, my family would care—no one else. But if the message dies with me—many, many people could suffer."

He opened his eyes and stared at the vibrating horizon. "So there's no choice."

He reached for the spear. He grabbed the blade, then dropped it. It was too hot. After the iron had cooled in the shade, he cut dripping strips of meat from the horse's flank. Raised as he had been on a farm, it was hard to feel sentimental toward animals; still, Hotep had been no ordinary beast. Shuddering, Nebi cupped his hands where he had cut a vein and drank. He ate two of the strips and attached the rest to the reins. Then he looped the reins over his shoulders so that the meat would dry and stay edible. Now he had energy. But where could he find courage?

The memory that was so often at the edge of his thoughts returned.

*As he lies in the road, he waits an eternity for a sign of his father. Finally an unrecognizable form staggers from the doorway. It carries Mosi, rolled in a blanket and unconscious. The form falls and thrashes about on the road, a skinless mass of red tissue. To reach the goal, pain had not mattered.*

"My turn."

Nebi grasped the spear in both hands, using it half as a crutch, half as a walking stick. He found he could plant the spear in front of him, then hoist his body forward.

After one night's march, the spear technique proved exhausting. At dawn he dug a hole in the sand, rolled himself into it, and covered his body with the sand. He slipped his unburied arm under the saddle.

He dreamed of home, but this time it was of Khuit, the girl across the road. He had known her all his life, and yet still did not know her well. She was the mayor's daughter. Once, they and others had played tag and started beehives. At about the age that he became aware of her beauty, he took an oral test—neither he nor anyone else in the village could read—and, miraculously, the school for scribes admitted him. He was the first boy from his village in living memory to have that honor. The school was in Sais, the nearest city, and when home on holiday he found he could hardly talk to Khuit. She had grown taller than he. He wondered whether she thought he was indifferent, or whether she understood that he was simply shy.

In his dream that night, she filled a clay jug at the village well. She looked at him with large dark eyes. They flashed a hint of flirtation. When she offered him the dripping jug, he awoke with a start.

Liquid. That afternoon of the fifth day, he could think of nothing else. He eyed the goatskin. He was dizzy. It was time. If he were to keep moving, he must drain the beer.

Using the spearhead, he cut the goatskin container open and licked the last drops. Then he wore it on his head like a sun helmet. But as he grew weaker, he put more and more weight on the spear. Finally, it snapped in the middle. As a crutch, it was now useless. There was no way to walk.

From where he had fallen, he watched the sun set for the sixth time. He ate, but without saliva the meat was as hard to chew as rawhide. As the stars came out, a last plan began to form in his mind.

He sliced the goatskin vest in half. He used strips of the bridle to tie one swatch of hide to each of his forearms. The pads protected them from the roughness of the terrain. Sharp pebbles scraped his unprotected belly, but his weight was mostly on the arms.

He concentrated only on making it to the next bluff, the next dune, the next crag. Somewhere beyond that burning doorway lay his goal.

To save strength, he changed his way of crawling. He lay on his left side and, with his left arm reaching forward, he hauled himself across the gravelly sand. He imagined swimming in the creek next to his village, doing the side-stroke—and Khuit watching him. He would show her he could do it.

It was now the seventh day. Or maybe the eighth. Nebi's mind was as numb as his leg.

Just before the next dawn he crawled up yet another knoll. From the summit he expected to see the rising of the cursed sun. He did, but he saw something else as well.

Stretching below him lay a canyon. A band of shining water ran through the center. Next to that sprawled buildings so spectacular that he knew it must be the cruelest mirage so far. He cursed Amon for mocking him, then fell unconscious.

When, much later, the first great vulture flapped down beside him, he did not move.

# CHAPTER 5

# THE PRINCESS

An old goatherd found the messenger by the cliff overlooking Thebes—or rather, the goatherd's mangy dog did, barking fiercely until the waiting vultures flew off.

At first, as the goatherd later told him, he did not think Nebi was alive. Wrapped in strips of rags, he looked from a distance like a disheveled mummy, many of which were buried in nearby sacred cliffs. The old man carried the stick-like body to the village below.

Nebi awakened to a wonderful sound—the murmur of human voices. They spoke Egyptian with an unfamiliar accent, a strong twang. He was certainly far from home.

And yet not so far. He lay on a straw mat in a room whose earthen walls, single narrow window, and perfectly cubic shape reminded him of his own former home.

The next day he smiled back when the goatherd's wrinkled wife leaned over him. To begin with, she gave him only a few sips of water. Later that day she fed him goat's milk and dates. She gently smeared a salve of honey and goat grease on the wound in his leg.

On the morning of the third day, Nebi startled everyone by sitting bolt upright. Wincing from his split lips, he told the goatherd, "I must see Princess Amonirdis. Bring me to her."

The goatherd's wife chortled.

"I can hear from your accent that you are not from around here. That must be why you can't get it through your head—the Holy Princess is like a goddess." Her voice fell to a reverential whisper. "She is like Mout herself." Mout was the goddess who was Amon's wife.

"I know," Nebi whispered back. Amonirdis was the earthly incarnation of Mout, whose name meant "mother." Each of the many gods and goddesses represented a different aspect of Amon's nature, so that really there was only one universal god. Amonirdis, the Divine Adoratrice, or priestess of Amon, was, like her brother the king, a bridge between her subjects and nature's divine forces. "Bring me," Nebi repeated.

The old woman shook her head. "You don't just walk up to the princess. She oversees fifty towns besides Thebes. Tens of thousands of people work on her Temple estate—farmers, tradesmen, slaves."

"*We* work for her," put in her raspy-voiced husband. "She has a hundred thousand goats, and three times as many cows."

"But does she rule well?" asked Nebi.

"The dikes are kept solid," the goatherd said. "Our taxes are fair. Few robbers remain. Since the Kushites came when I was a lad, life has been better." A generation before, the Theban priesthood had urged the Kushites to come north to take over Thebes and all of South Egypt to protect it from invasion from the north.

"Then if she is as good a ruler as you say," said Nebi, "she will see me."

The couple saw his determined eyes. "All right," sighed the goatherd. "If the Divine Adoratrice won't see you, at least the palace doctors might. If we wait much longer, you'll lose the leg."

The goatherd and his neighbor, a tomb-worker, slung the youth in a blanket and brought him to a ferry. Then the little barque with the lateen sail skittered across the river toward Thebes.

Nebi took in the spectacle through half-closed, feverish eyes. Thebes had few fortifications, yet its appearance from midriver awed him even more than North Egypt's capital, high-walled Memphis, which he had sailed past with Master Setka. Here, signs of great wealth were everywhere. Estates and villas spread out from the city. Obelisks towered over the center. As the Temple of Amon at Karnak came into view, his eyes widened. It was said to be the biggest building any-where. Monumental pylons rose above a protective wall. In the rich afternoon light, the yellow stone looked golden.

The villagers lugged the boy through streets lined with open-air stalls and teeming with farmers, slaves, civil ser-vants, and children. Nebi's deprived senses sprang back to life. Aromas of spices and flowers filled his nostrils. He bathed in the sounds—snatches of animated banter, the cries of vendors, and the giggling of girls. From knee level, he could see swirling about him tan Egyptians, black Kushites, pale traders from the Middle East, and, here and there, still paler traders such as he had seen in the Delta. He had heard they came from a thickly forested area emerging from barbarism—Europe.

The peasants wove their way up an avenue lined with stone sphinxes the size of horses. It led to the entrance of the Karnak temple's outer walls. Carved in limestone above the gate was one of the symbols of the faith, the disk of the sun carried on two great wings. Guarding the immense bronze doors, eight times a man's height, were a few bare-chested soldiers in red kilts, their number evenly divided between Kushites and Egyptians. At the ends of the tall pikes they held upright, red pennants drooped in the breezeless heat.

The villagers set Nebi on the dusty ground. Bowing and stuttering, the goatherd timidly asked for the captain of the guard.

It took so long for the Kushite officer to emerge from his little office that Nebi wondered if he had to be awakened. But he was a striking, large-boned man, fully a head taller than his soldiers, and broad-shouldered as well. He wore an officer's standard kilt of white pleated linen; two red stripes down each side denoted his rank. His eyes turned downward at the outer corners, giving him a melancholy expression.

Hands on hips, the big man examined the humble trio but said nothing.

Nebi propped himself on an elbow. "Please, sir, get word to Her Holiness the Divine Adoratrice that a messenger from His Excellency Setka is here to see her."

The captain cocked a skeptical eyebrow at the scrawny, blistered speaker. To be a messenger, and particularly a messenger for the royal family, was as prestigious as it was demanding. It was not a job for a ragamuffin.

"Setka?" drawled the captain. "Who is Setka?"

"Her Holiness will know."

The captain looked him in the eye. Nebi held his stare. And held it.

"I'll see," the captain finally said.

When the lanky officer returned, he was striding

quickly. He clapped for the guards. "Pick him up and follow me," he told two of them.

Nebi put one bony arm over each guard's shoulders. When he turned to thank the goatherd and his neighbor, their mouths were wide open with astonishment. The guards followed the captain through the gate.

Inside the wall, it was Nebi's turn to gape. After passing through courtyards and corridors, they entered a hall into which his whole village of 80 houses could have fit. Here, all was dim, cool, and restful. The guards followed the captain through a forest of pillars, each adorned with colorfully painted carvings of gods, lions, lotuses, and past pharaohs. Nebi craned his neck to look up. Each of the pillars was the equivalent of seven stories high. The sweet haze of incense made this colossal scale seem dreamlike.

They entered a smaller, ornate chamber off to one side. On a raised platform in the room's center, a woman sat on a throne. Next to the platform, with their backs to Nebi, stood three men and two women. A shaft of sunlight angled down on them.

The guards halted in front of the seated princess. She was middle-aged and sturdy, with earnest eyes. Hand cupping her chin, she was presiding over a discussion of some affair of state. A bejeweled collar of many colors spanned her shoulders, and a blue sheath dress left her ebony arms bare. But what caught Nebi's eye was a peculiar gold ornament over her forehead that glinted in the sun shaft. Attached to the gold band encircling her head, it looked rather like a curled index finger.

The guards placed Nebi in a chair in front of the princess. Desiring privacy, she waited until both guards and their captain had departed. Then she said, "What is this about Setka?"

"Most Holy One," Nebi said, "His Excellency Setka's last words were that I should see King Piankhy."

"*Last* words!" she said. "Tell me what has happened to the king's oldest friend!"

"Your Holiness, my master was killed by a traitor after his real mission was discovered."

She leaned forward. "We can trust my advisers and courtiers," she told the youth, gesturing to those on either side of her. "I knew of Setka's mission, but I need to know much more. Explain to me who you are and why you have come to me." Her voice was kind but commanding.

"My name is Nebamon. I am from North Egypt—from Damanhur, a village in the Delta. My father was Egyptian, a farmer, and my mother is Mesh. I worked for His Excellency."

"In what capacity?" she asked.

"I was his servant—at first. I felt from the beginning that my master was more than just a merchant from Kush exploring trade possibilities. He came to trust me, and he told me that King Piankhy had commissioned him to uncover what was really happening in North Egypt."

A murmur of interest came from Amonirdis's entourage.

"I know the Delta and its dialect, so I began to act as his guide and interpreter," said Nebi. "I would take him from village to village. He learned that Lord Tefnakht was quietly drafting young men into a large new army."

The princess's eyes widened.

Nebi went on: "Master Setka heard that Tefnakht was meeting other Delta warlords, some of whom had been Tefnakht's enemies until then. He learned that these new allies had amassed a fleet of ships with which they planned to invade the south. In the evening, he would dictate to me his notes for a report intended for the king."

"You can write?" she asked.

"I have received training in writing as a scribe at Sais, Your Holiness. Events kept me from completing my studies."

Amonirdis nodded. "Yes, I thought you sounded well spoken for a peasant." She looked at him with respect. Only one of every hundred Egyptians could read and write. Almost all scribes were from privileged backgrounds; they were an elite group who looked after records, one of the most precious things for any administration. No profession was more exalted—or more challenging. Scribes had to memorize more than a thousand hieroglyphic and cursive characters. Even the powerful viziers, who ran each Egyptian domain on behalf of its ruler, always came up through the scribal ranks.

"Master Setka's report was for King Piankhy himself. He was murdered so that it could never reach the king."

"Who slew him?"

"The Mesh. They attacked him as he was preparing to return to Napata to give King Piankhy his report. The other witnesses were killed, including the police chief of Khmun and his wife."

The princess glowered.

Nebi plunged on. "Lord Tefnakht has North Egypt's lords on his side, and now he has made one major ally in South Egypt."

"Who?" said Amonirdis with alarm.

"Count Nimlot of Khmun." Nebi did not try to hide his bitterness as he almost spat out the name. "He has abandoned King Piankhy and joined Tefnakht. The person leading the Mesh thugs who murdered Master Setka and his companions was Nimlot himself."

A hush fell over the group on the platform. After a

moment a loud sound erupted from among them—a confident, sarcastic cackle.

The source of the laughter had been standing out of the light and behind the others, so that Nebi had been hardly aware of him. Now this slender figure strode forward, hands on hips. A cape embroidered in his family colors, brilliant stripes of yellow and green, hung from his shoulders.

It was Nimlot.

# CHAPTER 6

# PROOF

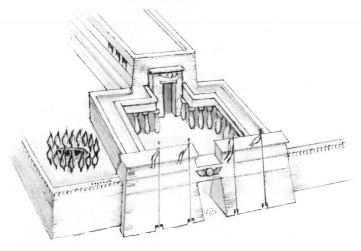

During his struggle for survival, Nebi had not dwelled on his hatred for the Count of Khmun. Now, enmity flooded him. He wished he could grab the stump of arrow from his leg and hurl it through Nimlot's heart.

Nimlot stopped laughing. His eyes drilled his accuser and he curled his upper lip in disdain.

"Most Worshipful Majesty," he retorted, "I have never heard a more absurd lie. Would I have come here, Most Generous Princess, if I were rebelling against you and your brother?"

The Kushite princess frowned. "Why, then, would this young man make up such a story?"

Nimlot waved a sinewy arm toward Nebi. "Tefnakht himself must have sent him. Tefnakht must know that the best way to weaken South Egypt is to spread suspicion and discord among your most faithful allies. This plowboy wants you to think there is treachery where only loyalty exists. He wants to divide us."

Amonirdis appeared to weigh Nimlot's words and his confident manner.

Nimlot pointed angrily at the youth slouched in the chair. On the stone floor, the shadow of a giant finger jabbed the air as the count's voice rose in pitch. "This knave's falsehoods violate this temple's sanctity. He is accusing an innocent person, and there is only one penalty for that. Under centuries-old laws, that penalty is—"

"I know the penalty," said Princess Amonirdis. "It is death."

Her eyes narrowed as she turned her crowned head first toward Nimlot, then toward the young stranger.

"These charges could hardly be more grave," she said. "One of you accuses the other of treason, murder, and plotting to plunder this city. The other is accused of working for the enemy." She fixed her eyes severely on the youth slumped in the chair below her. "What proof have you," she demanded, "that the Lord of Khmun has done these things?"

Nebi tried to sit more erectly. He was becoming feverish again and his head was spinning. "None," he said. "He has killed those who would vouch for me."

"Hah!" said Nimlot. "There can be no proof for another reason: no such event took place."

Amonirdis addressed the four others present. "It is one person's word against another's." She turned to a dignified Egyptian in a shoulder-to-knee white tunic. "What say you, Vizier?"

"It would be wise," he responded without hesitation, "to trust the one whom we know. No one has ever questioned the loyalty of Lord Nimlot's family."

Nebi was filled with desperation. He had sustained himself in the desert with the belief that his message would command the princess's attention. Now, this.

Then Nebi's eyes sharpened. "Your Holiness!" he exclaimed. "I remember. There *is* evidence. Please look at Count Nimlot's left hand. You should find a bruise. I can tell you how that happened. He was aiming his bow at the police chief's wife when I struck him on that hand with a pole."

Nimlot snorted, waving his swollen, purplish hand for all to see. "It is true, Revered Princess, that my hand is hurt. But this traitorous dog was able to see that from where he sits. He's simply dreaming up an explanation for this injury."

"And how, Count, did you come to get this bruise?" asked Amonirdis.

"I was kicked by my horse."

"That is plausible," Amonirdis replied, glancing knowingly at her vizier. "Your rough approach to horses, Count, is well known. They would have no great love for you."

The princess turned to stare at Nebi with piercing eyes, as if looking him over one last time before finding him guilty. In the presence of so majestic a personage, a ruler who reigned in the name of Amon, commoners should lower their eyes. Nebi knew that. But instead, he stared back, his eyes blazing and his head trembling with the intensity of his feelings. Anger filled his soul. He had delivered his message, or at least part of it, but no one would listen.

The advisers and courtiers murmured astonishment. The Divine Adoratrice's eyes opened wide at the sacrilege and held Nebi's gaze. She suddenly rose from her throne and came down off the platform, crouching before Nebi. She frowned as she scrutinized his shrunken form, his cracked, bloodied lips. The most powerful person in South Egypt was so close now he could have touched her. And Nebi could now recognize the finger-like object on her crown: it was a cobra. Its hood was open and its back arched, as if poised to strike.

The princess circled behind Nebi. He flinched as she barked out a command. "Count, come here."

Nimlot hastened to her.

"Hold the stranger's leg up so I can see it closely."

Nimlot wrinkled his nose. Blood and pus stained the bandage the goatherd's wife had wrapped around Nebi's leg that morning. "Revered Princess," complained Nimlot, "I am not a servant!"

"You always tell me that you will do anything to serve me," snapped Amonirdis. "Now hold this wretched leg."

Nimlot flushed. He lifted Nebi's ankle with his good hand as if it were a dead rat.

"Who do you say shot this arrow?" the princess asked Nebi. "A Mesh warrior, or someone else?"

Nebi stretched out his feeble arm until his accusing finger was so close to Nimlot's face that he could feel the count's panting breath.

For a long moment Amonirdis was silent. Then, firmly, she said, "I believe you."

"Revered Princess!" cried Nimlot.

She beckoned to her advisers and courtiers. "Look here," she said when they had clustered around Nebi. "Blood has darkened most of the shaft, but you can still see painted bands. They are green and yellow—the colors of the House of Khmun."

The young noble dropped Nebi's leg. His face was ashen.

Amonirdis ignored his stuttering protest. "What else do you have to report, young man?"

"Much, Your Holiness. The count's treachery is but a small part." His head was swimming. He added faintly, "The information is military."

"Then you must give it to King Piankhy," said the princess. "It is urgent that you go to him in Napata. But if you leave now, that infected leg will kill you." She turned to the vizier. "Call Captain Wosmol and his guards to take Nimlot to his quarters, and keep him locked inside until we can weigh his case carefully."

Tall, sad-eyed Captain Wosmol and his two guards re-entered. Each guard gripped one of Nimlot's arms and they started to lead him away when, showing unusual strength for one so lean, the youth flung his long arms up to free himself. The captain stepped forward. He clenched Nimlot's right wrist, jerked it up behind his back, and marched him out the door.

The princess turned again to the vizier. "See to it that my personal physician attends to this young man," she commanded. "He has served Thebes with courage. Now it is Thebes's turn to serve *him*."

# CHAPTER 7

# ESCAPE

Sheer willpower had kept Nebi alert during the duel of accusations, but as the guards bore his chair from the temple, his head swirled and he lost consciousness. The first thing he heard as he slowly came back to his senses was a voice saying, "Will you amputate the leg, Sunu?" The word meant "surgeon."

The question jolted Nebi to full consciousness. His eyelids snapped open. He was lying chest down on a sheet-covered table. The speakers were out of view.

"He's weak. Amputation might kill him," answered the doctor.

"The palace put me in charge of this young man's security," said the other. "Make sure he lives. They didn't say why, but he's the most important person in Egypt right now. The king has to see him." The speaker's voice—forceful yet genial—sounded familiar. Yet Nebi could not place it.

Fingers probed Nebi's calf. Then the doctor said, "Help me lift him."

Strong hands sat him upright on the table, leaving his legs dangling over the side.

He was in a tidy room. Bottles and basins filled the shelves. Now he could see that the man assisting the doctor was Captain Wosmol.

"Look at me," said the doctor pleasantly to Nebi. He was a plump and elderly Egyptian with a white fringe of hair around his bald head. He studied Nebi's eyes.

When the examination was over, the doctor said,

"Captain, call the orderly who is down the hall. Have him bring a charcoal burner, a reed, towels, and my cauterizing knife."

Nebi breathed easier. A saw was not on the list.

While the orderly made the preparations, the doctor cut off a short piece of reed, then sliced it down the center. "This is sharper than the sharpest iron knife, and it's many times thinner," he explained to Nebi. "Still, the removal will hurt. I'll put this between your jaws." He inserted a roll of soft leather. "When I start work, hold the captain's hands. Keep your leg still. If you make me cut a tendon, you'll be lame for life."

Nebi nodded.

They turned him back onto his chest and the doctor sliced into his flesh. When the reed became dull, the doctor asked for another. He then took an iron blade that had been in the charcoal. There was a sizzling sound as he placed it against the lips of the wound to close the blood vessels. "You take pain well," said the doctor as he worked. "You have not cried out."

The patient hardly heard. As he tightened his grip on the captain's massive hands, he concentrated on the image of his father, lying in the road, a writhing mass of redness, silent except for gasping.

"Here is the final part. To take out the arrowhead, I must twist it around a tendon."

When it was over, the orderly removed the leather roll. "He almost bit through it," he said with wonder.

The captain fluttered his own hands to get the circulation back. "And he never made a sound."

The doctor sealed the lips of the wound with tiny criss-crossed strips of cloth covered with acacia gum to make them stick. Then he stood with arms folded across his chest. "I have two prizes for you, young man. One is my prognosis. In a few months, you should not limp."

Nebi closed his eyes and breathed deeply.

"The other prize is this." He handed over a jagged piece of metal. Nebi fingered it cautiously. The two sharp points at the end of the arrowhead, like the two tips of a V, were what had impeded his own attempts to remove it.

"Vicious, wouldn't you say?" said the doctor.

"Like its owner," whispered Nebi.

NEBI AWOKE to the sound of doves cooing outside an open window. He was in what he later learned was the palace infirmary. For the first time in his life he lay on a bed rather than a straw mat on the floor. He was too weak to get up and his leg ached dully, but he was happy. Time passed peacefully as he lay atop all this fresh softness, sipping the aromatic garlic soup the serving girl brought him, watching the busy river, and basking in the fact that everyone here, starting with the princess, had been calling him "young man." Until now he'd always been called a boy.

When Captain Wosmol came to ask if he needed anything, Nebi had a ready response: "A rawhide thong." After the officer brought it, Nebi tied it securely around the arrowhead and looped the thong around his neck.

Wosmol, like many Kushites and Egyptians, wore an object around his neck too. It was a tiny leather cylinder, half the size of a thumb, that no doubt contained an amulet, a charm that brought the wearer protection.

Wosmol looked puzzled at the arrowhead. "That's no amulet," he said. "Amulets bring good fortune. That"—he gestured at the arrowhead—"has brought you pain."

"It'll remind me that there's evil in the world—and that I've got to keep resisting it," Nebi replied.

"Be careful with it," said the captain seriously. "Evil things have a way of rubbing off on people."

Nebi held the sharp object between his fingers. The arrowhead seemed almost the same shape as the eye of Apophis, the mighty python in the red-haired thug's tattoo. He shuddered, yet the hatred that the memento stirred in his breast quickened his heartbeat. The object felt strangely empowering, as if it gave him permission to do terrible things to Nimlot in his imagination.

DURING THE NIGHT, Nebi awoke to the sound of shouts outside his window. "He's gone! Stop them!" The patient was too tired to take much notice and went back to sleep.

In the morning, Captain Wosmol came to the room. Red-eyed, his face drawn, he stood in front of the bed. "The Count of Khmun has escaped."

Nebi sat up straight. His jaw quivered. "How could he?"

"The guard I posted outside his room fled with him. The count must have bribed him."

Nebi said nothing.

"The vizier says Lord Nimlot was present when it was decided you would save your message for the king's ears. So the count has reason to try to stop you. I've assigned two guards to the infirmary door and two outside your room."

Nebi spent the morning staring at the blank wall in front of him, over and over shaking his head with disgust. Nimlot had thrown in his lot with Tefnakht, the man responsible for the ruin of Nebi's family. The count had also killed Setka, the man he respected most next to his own father, and slaughtered five innocent people. Now he was free to do more harm.

"I'll kill him myself if I get the chance," Nebi murmured through clenched teeth.

THE MIDDAY MEAL arrived late. And instead of a servant, the captain himself carried the tray.

"If you're wondering why an officer is waiting on you," he said, "it's security. The palace says the count has already tried to kill you. We're taking no chances." He pointed a huge finger at the tray. "Look."

A corner of the bun had been torn off. In Nebi's cup, a line indicated that the goat's milk had originally been at a higher level. And the patty of almond butter bore an indentation where someone had spooned off a bit.

"I don't want you poisoned," Wosmol explained. "I gave the job of tasting your food to an old thief who's working off his sentence in the palace kitchen."

The next day, supper did not come. It was midnight when Wosmol finally arrived. "The taster died," he announced bitterly. "He clutched his belly and collapsed on the kitchen floor."

A stranger had inadvertently given his life for Nebi's own. Stunned, Nebi started to whisper a prayer for the old man's *ka*, his life force, but stopped when Wosmol, turning to the door, said brusquely, "Put it here, men." Two guards set down a long narrow cedar chest next to the bed.

"You're not safe here," Wosmol told Nebi. "Hundreds of people work in the palace and temple compound. There's an army saying: 'The third time the enemy tries something, he succeeds.' We don't want a third time. Whomever the count hired to poison your food can try something again, so Her Majesty has put out word that the poison killed you. And I'm taking you to Napata."

"When?"

"Now. You're too weak to travel by the fast overland route—the wagon would shake you to death. So we sail at dawn." His sigh suggested it was a trip he did not want to make. "Get in this coffin," he said, gesturing toward the chest. "We don't want anyone knowing what ship you are on."

Being careful with his leg, Nebi climbed out of bed quickly. He was anxious to resume his journey.

"The king will be expecting you," reassured Wosmol. "The princess is sending a messenger by road to tell him who you are."

The lid came down and Nebi was enclosed in musty, cedar-smelling blackness.

He wondered what the king would be like. The only powerful men he had encountered so far—Tefnakht, the warlords, Nimlot—abused their power. And Piankhy, he knew, had more power than any of them.

# CHAPTER 8

# THE CROSS-EYED LONER

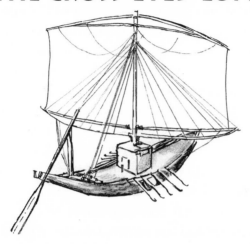

The second day that the ship was on the river, angry words suddenly exploded from CaptainWosmol. They were incomprehensible to Nebi, for they were all in Kushite, but he could recognize an oath when he heard one.

The captain's bowstring had snapped as he tested it, aiming it without an arrow at an imaginary target along the riverbank. From where he reclined under an awning, Nebi could see another string dangling from Wosmol's kilt pocket, and the outburst seemed excessive, given the minor annoyance.

So far on the trip south, Wosmol had scowled at everything in sight, even the elegant ibises as they fished and the agile baboons as they hunted for scorpions on the rocks. Yet the big man had given no clue as to what was bothering him.

"That certainly is an impressive bow," called Nebi, trying to say something positive. He had to speak loudly to be heard above the chanting of the 10 Kushite crew members, clad in kilts and straw hats, who pulled the oars under a broad tangerine sail. They were in high spirits, since they had been hired for the trip at double pay. The rowing was unusually easy, too: for the sake of speed, the ship was empty, its regular heavy cargo of linen bales left behind.

The captain's weapon was a composite bow. Nebi had heard of these deadly weapons but had never seen one up close. Thin layers of different materials ran the length of it. "My grandfather made it when he was a warrior," Wosmol said proudly as he walked over to Nebi. Nebi's interest had returned the captain to his usual geniality. He squatted next to his charge and pointed at a gray layer. "That one is ox horn," said Wosmol. "This one is from tendon. Only this one is wood."

Nebi turned the unusually curved bow in his hands. Its power gave him both a thrill and a shudder. It took a soldier of above-average strength to shoot a composite bow and—unless you had Wosmol's brawn—two men to string one.

"That bow can kill a man at 400 paces," said Wosmol. "That's four times farther than a regular bow made from carob wood."

Nebi gave a low whistle. "How strong is the Kushite army?" he asked, in as casual a tone as he could manage. The question had been preoccupying him.

"The army is small, yet our warriors have experience. When Egypt was master of Kush, centuries ago, we fought in pharaohs' armies as mercenaries. Since then, kingdoms that Assyria threatened have paid us well to fight for them. Those kingdoms all lost to Assyria, so our men have returned. Some are now officers in King Piankhy's army. They've fought against the best, and learned. My grandfather studied Assyrian bows before making this one."

"Has this bow seen a lot of action?" Nebi asked.

Wosmol nodded. "My grandfather used it when Israel hired him as an infantryman. He handed it down to my father, a charioteer in King Kashta's army when we took over South Egypt. Both of them earned the highest award—the Medal for Prowess." Wosmol's tone told Nebi this was a matter of great family pride.

"When have you used the bow?"

Anger returned to the captain's face, and Nebi immediately regretted asking.

"Not once!" Wosmol replied bitterly.

Nebi frowned in sympathy.

"Everyone thinks I'm having a brilliant career." Wosmol spat over his shoulder into the river. "That's because I started as a rigger and carpenter on an army supply ship and worked my way up. But I've never been in combat. I've never shown what I can do. King Piankhy is a man of peace. That's good for most people, but not for a professional soldier."

The words were pouring out of Wosmol now. He was plainly welcoming the chance to unburden himself. "It was hard staying awake in Thebes. And Thebes was exciting compared to what's happening now."

"What—what's happening now?"

"I'm being demoted. Oh, I'm keeping my rank, but I have less responsibility. I've always wanted my son to be as proud of me as I was of my father. Now I'm further than ever from being a warrior." He stopped, as if checking himself from becoming too personal. "I should have posted more guards around Lord Nimlot."

"You couldn't know he'd be so desperate. No one has told you what this is all about."

Something gnawed at Nebi too—the fear that the coffin

trick might not have fooled Nimlot for long. The count might not know which one of the many ships carried Nebi, but he would know that its destination was Napata. Traveling overland, Nimlot's people might get there ahead of him and wait for him.

NEBI FELT WELL enough after two weeks to limp around the deck without a cane, but, still needing rest, he mostly clung to the shade of the captain's cabin, the only object protruding from the deck besides the mast. There, he and Wosmol would while away the time by playing *senet*. It was a popular board game whose pieces the captain—like many soldiers—carried in his pack. After supper, when they had set up camp on shore, the ship's skipper would play the winner. Nebi was rapidly learning Kushite words from both men. He liked trying to wrap his tongue around the unfamiliar sounds.

The changing world also helped distract Nebi from his worry. After the first of a series of rapids, or cataracts, that marked the border between South Egypt and Kush, the valley became narrower and the skin tones of the people darker. Instead of the mud-brick houses familiar to Nebi, the houses were formed from yellow grass into pleasingly round shapes that resembled beehives. The boys that Nebi could see along the riverbanks were doing the same chores he himself had done before he'd gone off to boarding school—planting fields, herding goats, and shoveling dirt into baskets, which they then lugged to the top of the dikes. The earthen dikes had to be rebuilt like this every year in order to keep the annual flood from villages.

Two days after they passed the third cataract, a close game of *senet* was interrupted by a Kushite ship bound for the Mediterranean and laden with ebony logs and ivory from central Africa. The skippers of the two vessels, old friends, paused midriver to swap news. No sooner was that meeting over than the sailors on Nebi's ship began rowing harder. No one had to urge them.

Curious, Nebi asked what was happening.

"We want to get to the race in time," said Wosmol, scarcely disguising his own excitement.

"The race?"

"The Napata championships."

"The Napata championships!" Nebi almost shouted. Kush was famous as a center for chariotry, and he and his friends in the village had always been eager to get news of its yearly race. The Napata contest was a far cry from the Delta's races, in which the chariots were light and flimsy, designed for smooth, manicured racing tracks. The Napata contest was for heavy war chariots on rugged terrain. It was only natural that Kush host such a competition. Its special breed of horses, raised on the Dongola plateau west of Napata, were large and strong. They were ideal for pulling chariots, the most important part of an army on the field of battle. Kushite traders sold the horses at high prices to places as far away as Israel, Syria, and even Mesopotamia—three months away by caravan.

"If we row all night, the skipper thinks we might get there just in time," said Wosmol. "The race starts in late afternoon and—"

Nebi cut in, concern in his voice. "But when we reach Napata, shouldn't we see King Piankhy at once? He'll want my report."

"You're worried about Count Nimlot's men creating some mischief after we arrive?"

Nebi nodded.

"I've thought about that. We'll be arriving earlier than anyone could expect. If the count has men there, they won't be ready. You'll be safe." He patted Nebi's shoulder reassuringly. "Besides," the captain continued, "even if I took you directly from the river to the palace, you wouldn't find the king. He'll be at the race for certain. Horses are what he's known for. He breeds and trains them—and, before he became king, he raced them."

"But no more?" asked Nebi.

Wosmol smiled. He obviously thought it a silly question. "The king is like a god. What would happen if he competed and lost? Besides, he's no longer so young. He's in his late forties."

As the crew rowed that night, Wosmol with them, Nebi sat at the prow, searching for sandbars in the moonlight. In the morning, feeling close to his old self, he took a seat behind Wosmol and grabbed an oar. Finally, as the sun was low in the west, Wosmol pointed. "The Mountain of Purity. We're almost there!"

Napata's revered landmark jutted from the plain. Its sides were almost vertical, a hundred paces high, but its top was flat like an altar. Nebi felt a shiver of awe. Worship of Amon had dropped off in the Delta, but the old people still said that the mountain was where Amon dwelled. Monumental buildings—they could only be temples or palaces, Nebi knew—were nestled in the very shadow of the mesa.

Nebi craned his neck toward the opposite bank. Lining the streets were prosperous one- and two-story houses of adobe, almost the same shape as ones back home. Although Egypt had not ruled Kush for many centuries, clearly its influence on the way of life remained. Beyond the city stretched fields, orchards, and a grid of irrigation channels as far as he could see.

The vessel glided toward the sprawling waterfront, meeting point of trade routes from the Mediterranean, the African interior, and India. Nebi kept his eyes on the mud-brick warehouses lining the river. The docks were deserted. Everyone must be at the race.

Suddenly someone darted across the narrow space between two buildings. At the next opening between buildings, Nebi saw him again. It was a skinny, barefoot man. He seemed to be keeping pace with the ship from behind the warehouses.

With a whoosh of the rudder, the helmsman guided the ship left toward a berthing place. As sailors tied up the ship, Nebi scanned the dock. But now he saw nothing. Wosmol came up beside him. "I think what you're looking for is next to that cart," he said.

In the vehicle's shadow, a narrow-shouldered man studied the ship. Nebi was close enough to see that his eyes were crossed.

The light-skinned passenger was not hard to spot. Upon seeing Nebi, the man smirked, revealing missing front teeth. He then turned and vanished into a tangle of ramshackle buildings.

Wosmol said, "He's an old wharf rat—too feeble to be dangerous. But he might be a lookout."

From the distance came the sound of a ram's horn.

"They're starting!" a sailor cried.

Three of the ship's most muscular sailors gathered around Nebi. They had club-like belaying pins tucked inside their waistbands. Two of them grabbed Nebi's arms and placed them over their shoulders.

Startled, Nebi turned to Wosmol.

"I've hired them to come with us," said the captain.

With Nebi swinging between them, the bodyguards started running up the street toward the sound of the roaring crowd.

Glancing back over his shoulder, Nebi saw the bony man trailing them.

# CHAPTER 9

# FANGS IN THE NIGHT

Through the deserted streets they ran, passing block after block of whitewashed adobe homes, before finally coming to the rim of a saucerlike hollow a quarter-mile wide. On its slopes sat more people than Nebi had ever seen in one place.

Moments before, the crowd had been roaring. Now it was quiet. The racers were out of sight in a broad palm grove on the far side of the winding racecourse. Fast-moving clouds of dust billowed from beneath the foliage.

Wosmol scrutinized the slopes as if looking for something. "Ah!" he said after a moment. He motioned to the sailors to follow, and the party quickly wove its way through the townspeople. Nebi noticed that most were dressed much like Egyptians, although some from the countryside stood out—boys and men with intricately scarred faces wearing only loincloths, bare-breasted women with bright headcloths.

Nebi's eyes widened as they passed behind a reviewing stand. Purple cloth on three sides kept Nebi from seeing inside. *"Qore?"* he asked one of the sailors, using the Kushite word for "king" that he had picked up during the journey. The sailor smiled and nodded.

Wosmol's destination turned out to be a cluster of off-duty Kushite army officers—about a dozen of them—in white-kilt uniforms and sword belts. Though the captain did not seem to know them, he conversed with them easily. Nebi breathed easier in their midst.

While the chariots were still distant, Wosmol passed on to Nebi what he had just learned. The Phoenician team was out with a cracked wheel and—bad news for Nebi—a broken axle had also forced out the Delta team. Now, on this second and final lap, three of the seven remaining chariots were Kushite, while the others came from Thebes, Memphis, Samaria, and an upstart city-state across the northern sea called Athens.

Before Wosmol finished his report, the crowd had risen to its feet. The first five chariots, closely bunched, had careened into view. Nebi stared wide-eyed: if he ever got back to his village, he'd want to tell his friends everything.

The two-horse chariots had wheels thicker than those of farm wagons. Each carried two men, driver and warrior. To keep from losing their balance on the lurching, bouncing vehicle, they held on to the mud-splattered sides.

When a sixth team emerged from the trees, Wosmol said, "Those must be the Athenians—the horses are Thracians." Both steeds were white, the only horses in the race that weren't of the Kushite breed, with black bodies and white faces and legs.

As the chariots entered a final figure-eight circuit, galloping past the reviewing stand, the crowd was roaring so loudly that Wosmol had to shout in Nebi's ear. "That driver's a prince—the king's nephew." The captain was pointing to the team in seventh—and last—place.

Short but broad-shouldered, the driver of that Kushite team was one of the few contestants wearing an ordinary helmet instead of one with a mask to protect against stones that horses kicked up. He was extraordinarily young, not yet a man. Even from a distance, Nebi could see the thrill of risk-taking in his teeth-bared grin. As the prince tried to rejoin the pack, his tall teammate—prudently masked—touched his whip hand to slow him down.

A solitary post the size of a man stood beside the course, about 10 paces away from the racers. The first-place Kushite team never slowed as its warrior cocked his arm then hurled a javelin. The missile hit the post. The crowd's screaming drowned out the hoofbeats.

The Theban team's javelin went wide. The driver braked, semicircled through the scrub-filled terrain, then passed the post again. The missile connected this time, but now the Thebans were next to last. As the prince's chariot neared the post, its warrior again gripped the young man's arm to reduce speed. He then lobbed his javelin with less power than the other warriors, but with such confidence that he did not even turn his head to see that he had connected.

When the chariots reached a tiny marsh, their wheels sank a quarter way into the mud. The last-place team's horses adopted an unusual prancing motion, enabling them to move quickly. They passed the straining Theban and Athenian teams.

Pillow-sized rocks on the track soon forced the horses to weave, and as they neared another post some chariots almost tipped over. The warrior on the prince's chariot again signaled a slowdown as he raised his bow. It paid off: he was the only archer to hit the post on the first attempt.

Astonishingly, the prince's chariot was now well ahead. Some in the crowd were jumping up and down with excitement. Both leading teams were Kushite.

The second-place team in the red chariot took a chance, threading its way at top speed through a copse of acacia trees as if they were harmless reeds. It seemed to work: with barely a hundred lengths to go, that team was but two lengths behind the prince. But the prince's horses seemed far fresher as they thundered down the obstacle-free home stretch. His chariot started to pull farther ahead.

With one hand, the youth held his helmet high above his shaved head, pumping his arms as if to encourage cheers. Two officers in front of Nebi exchanged dubious looks.

Youngsters poured from the hill toward the finish line to greet the winner.

Then it happened.

A sharp cracking sound pierced the din of the cheers and hoofbeats. The red chariot began acting strangely. Though its horses were still galloping straight ahead, the chariot itself swung wildly to the left, almost perpendicular to the horses' path.

"Broken axle!" cried Wosmol.

Both occupants fell, spinning wildly after hitting the ground. The panicked horses kept galloping.

Those on the hill screamed warnings to the youngsters crowding near the finish. But it was too late. As the runaway chariot bore down on them, the children froze in fright.

The prince glanced over his shoulder at the tumult and kept going. His taller teammate elbowed him hard in the abdomen, grabbed the reins, and pulled up short, slowing the big horses and turning them leftward. Returning the reins to the prince, he leaned over the side, seizing the other horses' harness. As the tall man did so, the prince directed his horses sharply to the right. At the last moment, both vehicles veered away from the crowd.

By this time the other chariots had flashed by. The Memphis team crossed the finish line first and came to a halt far down the track. The crowd mobbed them.

The prince's chariot, which failed to finish among the top three, was left to itself.

"The prince should have won," said Nebi regretfully.

Wosmol shook his head. "I've heard he's a hothead, and you could see it in his driving. His teammate, whoever he is, deserves the credit. He paced the horses so that they had strength at the end. And he prevented a tragedy."

Once the medals had been awarded and most of the crowd had left, Wosmol brought Nebi and the sailors to the royal reviewing stand. He disappeared to arrange an appointment for Nebi but came back quickly with disappointing news. "His aides insist the king will be busy the rest of the day with a banquet for the racers and foreign visitors. He'll see you at mid-morning tomorrow."

The delay made Nebi edgy. "Where will I sleep—the palace?"

"No, the skipper's cabin. He won't be using it. You can turn in early. Tomorrow's your big day."

NEBI SLID A HEAVY BOLT across the door of the skipper's tiny cabin. He tugged at the door to test it: it seemed strong. The windows were near the ceiling, so no one could see inside, and though they were wide, they were barely tall enough to slip an orange through. Good. No one could crawl in, either.

Nebi knew that Wosmol and two of the brawny sailors were outside. Despite that, he felt vulnerable. In the infirmary, too, he had been well guarded—and yet Nimlot's people had found a way around that. If not for Wosmol's taster, their plan might have worked.

Wosmol too was uneasy. Nebi could hear him through the door, cursing the continued absence of the third sailor. The man had ducked into a waterfront tavern for what he said would be one quick brew, and had not been seen again.

Nebi lay in the bunk, listening anxiously each time footsteps approached along the dock. Finally, exhausted, he fell into uneasy sleep.

Sharp clanging jolted him awake. He sat bolt upright. It was the sound of sword against sword, coming from just outside the cabin.

Then came shouts, grunts from the other side of the door. The door quivered as someone was slammed against it. Nebi felt helpless. There was nothing in this cabin with which to defend himself—not even a stool.

Suddenly the whole cabin quaked as a heavy body crashed against the door. The faint sound of splintering came from near the lock. But it held.

He was about to chin himself on the high windowsill to see what was happening when, on the other side of that same windowsill, he saw a dark object silhouetted against the moonlight. It appeared to be a basket, of all things. Someone was tilting it up against the window, trying to stuff something in through the slit-like window.

Nebi backed away, staring at the window. Soon he heard a tapping sound, as if the person were knocking the bottom of the container with his hand.

The cabin shook again as someone crashed into the door.

The thumping on the basket became louder, faster.

It was then that Nebi saw something shaped like a rope slide from the basket and across the windowsill, dark against the lesser dark of the sky.

It was a snake, its scales gleaming like oiled leather. When it reached the end of the window, it could go no farther without entering the room. With horror he watched its silhouette turn upward. Its neck abruptly expanded. It was a hooded cobra.

Nebi froze. He had never felt more helpless. If the snake entered the room, it would be invisible to him in the blackness. But he himself could be seen. Cobras could see in the dark.

He decided to take his chances with human enemies instead. At least he could see them. He pushed back the bolt and opened the door.

One sailor was thrashing about on the deck with another man, hands at each other's throat. Wosmol had pinned another man against the mast and was yelling at him to drop his sword.

Nebi peered around the corner of the skipper's cabin. The man with the basket was the cross-eyed man. He held the empty container menacingly, waving it at the cobra and trying to induce it to enter the room.

The snake glared down at this bothersome person.

It was over in an instant. The serpent darted forward, mouth wide open. Its fangs sank into the man's cheek.

So chilling was the man's shriek that the turmoil on deck froze. The man who was backed up against the mast had already dropped his sword. He and Wosmol stared open-mouthed as the skinny man reeled onto the center of the deck, clutching his face.

In the confusion, the other intruders leapt onto the dock and vanished up an alley.

# CHAPTER 10

# THE EAGER PRINCE

In the morning Nebi scrubbed himself in the river, then donned the kilt that Princess Amonirdis's staff had provided for him. It was made of the smoothest linen he had ever worn.

Wosmol, hand warily on sword, escorted him away from the waterfront. Both carried their packs, since neither would be returning to the ship. Nebi hobbled slowly, but with no pain.

Wosmol said nothing. He was brooding again. The man he'd pinned against the mast had turned out to be the same guard Nimlot had bribed in Thebes. If Wosmol had slain or captured him, he could have partly redeemed himself.

Nebi broke the silence. "I want to thank you again for saving my life."

"Thank the cobra. It could have killed you and didn't."

"I detest snakes," shuddered Nebi. "I can't see why Princess Amonirdis has one on her crown, of all places."

"You don't know why?" Astonishment snapped Wosmol out of his moodiness. "I guess it's because your corner of Egypt hasn't had real kings in a long time. Well, royalty always wears the cobra crown—both in Egypt and in Kush."

"I still don't like it."

"Cobras don't attack, pythons do. Cobra are shy. They defend."

They had entered the bureaucratic quarter of Napata by now. Buildings made of pinkish-orange sandstone, three stories high, flanked the broad avenue.

"If a cobra feels threatened," Wosmol went on, "it becomes like the cobra in the crown. It arches its back, flares its hood, and tries scaring you away. Keep coming and it'll try to spit in your eye to blind you. Still keep coming, *then* it'll kill you. Kings are supposed to protect us like that."

As they approached the royal compound, they passed civil servants clutching scrolls. Inside the wall and next to the palace was the Temple of Amon; its pylons rose six stories, standing like sentinels on either side.

The guards at the gate saluted Wosmol smartly when they saw his insignia, bringing their right arm horizontally in front of them, bending the forearm at a right angle, and holding the edge of the palm forward, as if poised to chop. Wosmol returned the salute, then turned to Nebi to say goodbye.

"Where will you be going now?" Nebi asked.

"To the army camp to report. If they tell me I'll be stationed here a long time, I'll send for my wife and boy in Thebes to join me right away."

Nebi thought of the message he was bringing the king. "I wouldn't get too settled," he said.

Wosmol looked at him quizzically.

"The cobra may find he needs every bit of venom up north—soon. That's all I can say."

A smile stretched across the captain's face as he decoded the meaning. "I'll keep my sword sharp, Nebamon," he said. "May Amon bless you."

They clasped hands warmly.

When Nebi identified himself at the gate, the guard replied in accented Egyptian, "His Majesty is expecting you. Follow me."

They walked under a familiar carving above the gate—the sun carried by wings—and passed an invitingly green courtyard where gardeners were cleaning a fish pool and clipping shrubs. The fragrance of lilies filled the air. They wove past servants on their knees scrubbing the black tile floors. Through one open door, Nebi could see a class of a dozen Kushite boys and girls reciting lessons.

The guard turned left, and they came into a broad open-air space. Workers with wheelbarrows were delivering sandstone blocks to a building under construction. Masons were building walls, while others were busy with plumb lines and rulers.

"We're making a new, more comfortable royal stable," explained the guard. He added with a smile, "His Majesty likes to pamper his horses."

Nebi and his escort approached a youth with wide dark shoulders, whose back was turned to them. Tucked behind the youth's ear was a rush pen, and on his hip, attached to a belt, was the kind of slim leather case that scribes carried for their gear. That was curious, Nebi thought: the youth's muscular physique testified to a vigorous outdoor life, something few student scribes had time for. He held a roll of papyrus, and was speaking indignantly to an older man who might have been a foreman. The youth seemed to be insisting that something be done his way.

The guard waited until the older man had inclined his head in a bow and left. He then bowed and said in Egyptian for Nebi's benefit, "Prince Shebitku, here is the visitor you asked me to bring to you."

At the mention of the word "prince," Nebi fell to his knees. But before doing so, he caught a glimpse of the young man's dusty face. The wide nose with the slight bump, the thick lips and bold jaw were unmistakable. He had been driver of the chariot that had come so close to winning. Nebi was amazed. He had known the driver was young, but not this young. Close up, he looked about 15. They were both the same height, despite the year's difference in age.

"Up, up," said Shebitku. He assessed Nebi from head to foot. "Ha, so you're the famous Nebamon my aunt gushed about."

Nebi blushed.

The prince glanced about him to make sure no one was nearby. "You're the one who borrows Nimlot's horse, then takes him for this little joyride in the desert." He smiled. "Famous horse, too," he added.

Nebi stared.

"You didn't know? His name was Akenesh. He was too small for chariotry, but perfect for cavalry—fast and tough and with a heart as big as Egypt. Nimlot's father bred him. The king wanted Akenesh as a gift—as tribute. But Nimlot's father died before he could give the horse to him." Shebitku chuckled. "I would have given anything to see Nimlot's face when my aunt said he was a liar. We went to school together for two years in Thebes. What a scorpion! To think he almost married my sister!"

The prince spoke Egyptian perfectly and with the same lilt as the upper-class boys at scribe school. Nebi was aware his own accent would betray his peasant background.

Shebitku stared at the silent visitor. "You do speak, don't you?"

"I'm—I'm not sure how to address you. Should I say

Your Highness? Your Grace?" Piankhy and Amonirdis were both rulers. But Shebitku, a nephew, where did he fit in?

Shebitku laughed and clapped him on the shoulder. "You're no servant anymore. You're a hero. Call me Sheb," he said. "My classmates at military school do."

"I'm Nebi." Feeling a little bolder, he added admiringly, "That was quite a race yesterday."

The prince's sunny manner vanished from his dust-smudged features. He tightened his lips. "Those wretched little brats. If they hadn't been so close to the track, and if we hadn't slowed to save them, we'd have won."

Nebi looked away to hide his shock.

"I'd have been the youngest driver to have won the championship—ever," the prince said. He glanced at Nebi. As if recognizing that his outburst had taken the visitor aback, he added, "Still, I suppose my teammate did the right thing."

"Who is he?"

"Ah, I'm sworn to secrecy. Only a few people here know." He waved his arm toward the palace and stable. He added mischievously, "I can't tell you who he is, but I'll take you to him. He also bred my horses and showed me how to train them. Come."

"Thank you, but I'm to see His Majesty. I shouldn't keep him waiting."

Sheb laughed. "Come!"

Nebi limped after the prince toward the existing stable, adjoining the one under construction. Inside, all was dim and cool and smelled agreeably of fresh hay and horses.

Three bare-chested men were bent down, inspecting a horse's front fetlock. Nebi was startled by the size of the Kushite steed when seen up close. It was far bigger than Akenesh.

"He will get better with rest," said the tallest of the three men. He had a pleasant face and, rising, he looked the gelding in the eye, rubbing his forehead. "Good race, Jo-at, big fellow. You rest here for a few days and then we'll move you into the best stall in Shebitku's new stable."

Sheb said, "I've brought the survivor of the Khmun killings."

The man looked up, gave the horse a friendly slap on the flank, and walked toward them into the sunlight. His white kilt was no different from that of the others except for the trim—and Nebi caught his breath when he saw it. Its color was purple, the color of kings.

Nebi had already started bending his knees when Piankhy raised his hand with a smile. "No, do not try kneeling." He was looking at the manure on the stable floor near which Nebi was standing. The others laughed.

Piankhy had the same bold nose as his nephew but a higher forehead—and a more relaxed manner. He looked Nebi up and down. "We want you to come to a meeting with my advisers." He spoke Egyptian with the same lilt as his nephew, but with greater formality. Then, turning to Shebitku, he said, "We will want a record of what this messenger tells me, but we do not want a regular scribe. We are dealing here with sensitive matters."

Nebi had to pay close attention to understand Piankhy: although his voice was deep, it was also soft, as if a king did not need to assert himself to be obeyed. Piankhy added, "You already have a scribal kit with you, Nephew, so come along. Take notes." Shebitku's eyes brightened.

Nebi and Shebitku followed Piankhy across the courtyard separating the stable from the palace. Masons, engineers, and grooms leading horses fell to one knee as the king passed. At a well, Piankhy, then Sheb, splashed water on his face and arms.

As they washed, Nebi studied the king more closely. Scrubbing up, he looked less like the chosen of the gods than like a normal person. Wosmol had said Piankhy was middle-aged, and indeed his close-cropped hair was starting to go gray at the temples; yet his face was surprisingly unworn for someone who had run a kingdom for some 20 years.

Nebi knew Piankhy's reputation as a popular ruler and easygoing horseman. He was also master of a bountiful gold-field and the upper Nile Valley's rich black soil. No wonder Piankhy and his Kingdom of Kush were content to be isolated. The kingdom bothered nobody and nobody bothered it. But now the king was about to learn that all this would soon change. Nebi wondered anxiously how he would respond.

The king led them up a narrow stairway to the top of the two-story building, where they stepped out onto a broad, flat roof. It was the place the king preferred for meetings, Nebi would come to understand. It was outside the gaze of servants, civil servants, nobles, wives, and concubines. From one side of the roof was a view of the rest of the E-shaped palace. On the other, just beyond a stone's throw, rose the Mountain of Purity's majestic cliff. Its closeness filled Nebi with awe. He craned his neck to see the top of its craggy heights.

Two Kushite men, also bare-chested, sat on cushions under a canopy in the center of the roof. As the king approached, they rose and bowed from the waist down.

Sheb made the introductions. One of the men was Prince Shabako. Nebi would not have guessed the bald, round-faced man was Piankhy's younger brother and Sheb's father. He had bright, kindly eyes, but his chunky body lacked muscle tone, and it was impossible to imagine him in an athletic contest.

Shabako, as his son told Nebi later, was responsible for managing Napata's Temple of Amon and its vast holdings, which included many towns.

The other man was the Kushite army commander, General Purem. Wosmol had once mentioned him to Nebi in a tone of respect that bordered on fear. Barrel-chested and heavily muscled, he made Sheb's pudgy father seem almost puny. His eyes radiated an air of humorless authority. His shaved head glistened with oil and bore a jagged scar from forehead to ear. On each cheek he bore three horizontal scars. His skin was exceptionally dark. When teaching Nebi some Kushite words, Wosmol had said *purem* meant "black." Like many of the king's soldiers, the general's forebears were from tropical lands to the south.

"Let us start," said the king crisply. The informality of the stable had gone.

Sheb plucked the pen from behind his ear and removed the contents of the leather case. Sitting off to one side, he dipped the pen into a vial of water and wet a small cake of dried ink on his palette.

The king, flanked by his brother and the general, sat facing Nebi. Addressing him in an easy tone, Piankhy began, "Setka was my tutor—he taught me all I know about geometry and plants, and much of what I know about breeding horses. When I became king, he became our closest adviser." He easily switched between using "I" when referring to his personal self and "we" when describing his kingly self. "It speaks well of you that he trusted you. Start with who you were before you knew Setka, how you met him, and what he would have told us."

Nebi explained how his father's family had farmed in the village of Damanhur for generations. The family had choice land and was just able to afford the school for scribes in Sais. "Our fields," Nebi said, "lay next to one of the estates belonging to Lord Tefnakht of Sais. He wanted to enlarge his small army, and to attract warriors he decided to give them land in our village. His agent offered to buy our land and our neighbors'. Our neighbors said yes; we said no. We had farmed that property for nine generations. Tefnakht's agent said Egyptians had possessed the land long enough and it was the turn of the Mesh. The warriors burned our house." Nebi struggled unsuccessfully to keep his voice even. "My father ran into the house for my brother. He saved him ... but my father died."

"He died nobly," said Piankhy. "To die to save a child's life is not to die in vain."

Nebi drew comfort from the king's words. "I had to leave school. Even though Sais is Tefnakht's home city, it had jobs, so we went there. My mother found work in the laundry at the city's largest temple. The only job I could find was in Tefnakht's palace. He had no idea who I was. I was just another cook's assistant and server. I lived in the palace and gave my mother my earnings." Nebi paused. "It was at the palace that I discovered Assyria's plan."

When he uttered the word "Assyria," the others drew in their breath. Assyria had amassed the largest empire the world had ever seen. General Purem shot the king a questioning look.

Nebi went on. "That plan is to seize control of North and South Egypt, including Thebes. Then to conquer Kush itself."

"Oh, come!" burst out the bull-necked general. "Assyria is too far away to even think of such a thing!"

"Yet it keeps invading lands in our direction," said the

king's brother. "It has conquered Syria, Phoenicia, Philistia, Arabia ..."

"Also Israel and Judah," acknowledged Purem with a deep sigh. Nebi would later learn of Purem's personal interest in those two small Hebrew kingdoms. Years before, he had been among hundreds of Kushites who served as mercenaries for them in their resistance to Assyria. It was in action near Jerusalem, Judah's capital, that Purem had received his head injury.

Shabako continued. "Yes, and now the Assyrians have pushed beyond Judah. They have grabbed Gaza, the only kingdom that separates Judah from Egypt."

"But they'll never get beyond Gaza," argued the general. "Their army would have to cross the desert to reach the Nile. That's almost a week's journey, and when they arrived they would be so exhausted a much smaller army could defeat them. They cannot come by sea, either—they have no navy. This young messenger here is not believable."

The king cocked an eyebrow at Nebi. The look conveyed doubt. "Tell us the story of how you *discovered* this plan and what it contains." His stress on the word "discovered" underscored his skepticism.

Nebi swallowed hard. He shut his eyes to compose himself, and there was Setka's face, stern but affectionate, looking him in the eye. "Confidence," he seemed to say. Nebi could not let these formidable doubters rattle him. The fate of his family, even his entire homeland, rested on making the incredible truth credible.

"Speak, young man," ordered the king.

# CHAPTER 11

# PIANKHY'S DECISION

Nebi glanced at the doubting eyes of those seated across from him, leaned forward on the cushion, and began speaking. The story that he told had begun a year earlier, many months before Tefnakht's military campaign got under way. Aloud, Nebi gave only the main points, but as he spoke the story replayed itself in detail in his mind.

*An Assyrian diplomat had arrived at Tefnakht's palace. Never had the palace staff served so imposing a guest. He was a jowly man with cunning eyes, olive skin, and a square black beard that hung low over his gold-embroidered robe. He had rings on every finger, even his thumbs. He had come to Sais by ship because the overland route, across the Sinai Desert, would have aroused the attention of Egyptian border authorities. The visit was secret.*

*His host, Tefnakht, was graying but athletic. His vanity rivaled that of his guest. He favored light blue tunics to play up his blue eyes. And he had a serving girl whose only duty was to minister to his hair. She would wax his goatee daily so as to better shape it and make his jutting jaw seem even bigger. And she would plait his hair with 20 cornrows, as was the fashion among Mesh aristocrats.*

*Tefnakht welcomed the Assyrian with a nine-course dinner. When the other guests had departed, the two remained alone at the table. A dozen servants had waited upon the dinner, but only one was needed now, to keep pouring wine into the golden goblets. Tefnakht looked at the servants to see whom to choose.*

*"You!" he said, snapping his fingers at Nebi.*

*The choice was surprising, but only for a moment. It had logic. Nebi was the youngest of the domestics, so Tefnakht might assume he was the least politically aware. Also, host and guest were conversing in the Mesh dialect, a variety of Libyan, which the envoy spoke passably. It was easy to suppose that Nebi did not know the language. Having inherited his father's tan complexion and brown eyes, rather than the fairness and blue eyes of his Mesh mother, the boy looked like an old-stock Egyptian.*

*Whenever his master rang the bell, Nebi would enter with palm wine and hear snatches of a heated conversation. Much later, when the men's speech slurred and they grew incautious, he listened at the door.*

*What the envoy said so shook Nebi that, when he brought more wine, it took great effort to maintain his look of dull-eyed boredom. Anything else and he knew they'd kill him. The Assyrian's message was that his emperor intended to conquer the Two Lands and Kush. The only question, said the diplomat, was how.*

*The envoy offered two scenarios. One was that Assyria could set up a chain of supply garrisons across the Sinai Desert in order to launch an invasion from Gaza, using its own soldiers to destroy anyone, including Tefnakht, who stood in its way. The other option was for Tefnakht himself, as the strongest noble in the Delta, to take over all of Egypt in concert with other local lords. This would save Assyria the expense and casualties of waging war itself. Assyria would make Tefnakht the pharaoh and rule the Two Lands through him.*

*"So, I'd be a puppet," said Tefnakht bitterly.*

*"That," said the envoy, "is an inelegant expression. But is it not better for you to be that than to be our enemy?"*

*Tefnakht knew what it meant to be Assyria's foe. Everyone did. For cities, it could mean being burned to the ground. For*

*leaders of opposing armies, it could mean being tied to stakes in
the ground and having their skin peeled off with a knife while
alive. To discourage future opposition to the empire, the
Assyrian soldiers would assemble the vanquished population to
watch. They would then erect a pillar in a public place and fes-
toon it with the leaders' skins.*

A stunned silence followed Nebi's account.

Finally, Piankhy, his throat sounding tight, said, "What
did you do with this information?"

"At first I did not know where to go. But one day a Kushite
businessman—whom I would know later as Master Setka—
visited Tefnakht's estate, which bred beef cattle. He met with
the manager to talk of trading Kushite chariot horses for livestock. During dinner with the manager, he chatted with me
and the other servers, and later he visited the kitchens to
praise the cooks for their work and ask for recipes. He asked
what they served for really important dinner guests. The chef
proudly listed the special dishes he had prepared for eminent
people. When he mentioned the Assyrian envoy, Setka tried to
be casual, but I caught the glint in his eye. I knew he was spying. His interest in recipes was but an act.

"I approached him later and told him what I knew. He
made no effort to hide his surprise. He told me later that he'd
simply been trying to identify Tefnakht's allies in the Delta,
and he'd never expected to turn up Assyria.

"But," Nebi continued, "we had been seen together, and
Setka said I would be in danger if it were to come out that he
was spying. So he offered me a job. Because I spoke Mesh, I
could help him speak to people and collect information.

"As we traveled across the Delta, we found that Tefnakht
was forming alliances with other notables to prepare for conquest. We also found a pattern of corruption."

Tefnakht's takeover of his father's land, Nebi explained, was no isolated case. Other Delta lords too were demanding higher and higher taxes, grabbing land from peasants, and handing it to the swelling ranks of warriors.

After Nebi had described the Khmun killings and answered questions, there was silence under the canopy.

"Do you believe the messenger, Brother?" said Piankhy. To avoid influencing his advisers, he gave no hint of his own view.

"It makes sense that Assyria would do this," said Shabako, shaking his head in distress. "Thebes is the world's treasure chest. And our own goldfields have no equal. The empire would also control the trade routes."

"And you, General?"

Purem sighed. "I must admit the messenger is convincing." He had a far-off look, as if he were already considering the military implications of resistance.

"We agree, then," said Piankhy. His brow was furrowed and anxiety flickered in his eyes.

Abruptly, the king stood up. He strode to the edge of the roof and stared upward at the mountain, radiantly orange in the midday sun. Hawks glided on the air currents above.

He returned to the meeting and walked in a slow circle around the group. "Kush has never faced such danger. Nor has Egypt. Centuries ago, the Two Lands were one—a single Egypt under a single pharaoh. Now North Egypt is splintered into how many parts, General?"

"Eleven," Purem said, curling his lip in disdain.

"Imagine—eleven fiefdoms, one of them ruled by feeble old Osorkon, whom no one recognizes as pharaoh. Others ruled by petty warlords, and one ruled by a big warlord— Tefnakht." He shook his head in disgust.

"Two reports of Tefnakht's designs have come to us in recent days," the king continued. "Amonirdis told of Khmun's betrayal. And my vassal in Hensu, on the border with North Egypt, sent a message that Tefnakht was besieging his city. He begged for help. In both cases, we have hesitated to take action. Both Hensu and Khmun are far away. Neither is worth the cost of war. But now we see that they are just the beginning, and that what is at stake is the survival of Thebes and Kush."

Piankhy turned, and began circling in the other direction. "Now that Tefnakht controls Khmun, he has clear sailing all the way upriver to Thebes. Our army has one division based in Thebes, but against a coalition the size of Tefnakht's it couldn't defend the city for long. So," he challenged, "what do my advisers suggest we do?"

Shabako started to speak, but Purem cut the temple administrator off. "Your Majesty, I say we attack Tefnakht, and without mercy." His voice rang with eagerness. "What this news shows is that there is just one thing these Mesh understand—force. I say we drive the Mesh from the Two Lands and send them back to Libya, the home of their ancestors."

Piankhy had returned to his cushion. He had been expressionless as Purem spoke, and now he nodded to Shabako to speak.

"The general's idea is reckless," the king's brother said with unexpected passion. The words were hardly out of his mouth before his son, dutifully scribbling, let out a sigh. Shabako ignored him. "If we make a full-scale war out of this," he went on, "it will lead only to further chaos. If Amon wills it, we will win. The people of the North will resent us. We, as foreign meddlers, will become the permanent enemy."

Shaking his head, Shabako added, "We might also lose, clearing the way for Assyria to conquer us easily. We should concede to the enemy everything as far south as Khmun and, with Amon's help, defend Thebes."

"Be serious!" retorted Purem. "We must crush them. Pulverize them. Give those barbarians a lesson."

"Brutality," Shabako shot back, "only creates suffering and the thirst for revenge."

The king remained silent. He rose again and strode to the edge of the roof to gaze toward Egypt. All eyes were on his back as he slipped off the gold band on his right bicep. Attached to it was a tiny leather cylinder similar to Wosmol's. Piankhy opened it and consulted its contents. On a piece of gazelle leather was written, "Do right, and your father Amon will help you," Sheb later confided to Nebi.

Finally, the king returned to the group. Still standing, he said in a voice filled at once with regret and determination, "General, this is a matter of urgent self-defense. Mobilize your forces at once. Call up the militia. Commence the draft. We will need every last man. Prepare for all-out war."

Nebi whispered a prayer of gratitude.

Shabako did not say a word. He got up and stalked from the roof.

The king turned to his nephew. "Your father will not want you to be part of a campaign he opposes."

Sheb's face fell.

"You're young, still not out of officers' school," Piankhy continued, "but you have scribal skills, and no one can say you don't know how to drive a chariot. You should get military experience without entering combat. I am the commander-in-chief and, regardless of what your father might say"—here Piankhy adopted a deep, mock-official voice—"we are your king and we *command* you to accompany the army north as an aide-de-camp to the high command."

Sheb grinned broadly. Then, assuming a mock scowl, he saluted. "If you *insist*, sir!"

Nebi was struck by the close bond between them. He suddenly felt very alone. The two men with whom he had had a bond were both dead. He knew nobody here in Kush. The message delivered, he was now stranded in another country and he was without means.

Piankhy turned to him. "As for you, Messenger, what are your plans?"

The timing of the question was uncanny. Nebi had been asking himself the same thing. "I—I don't know, Your Majesty." He looked into the distance and bit his lip.

"You, too, are young," said Piankhy. "But your precocity, your loyalty to Egypt, and your physical courage are impressive. The army can use an extra scribe. Prince Shebitku would benefit from a shield-bearer if he should ever get too close to battle. It would also be good if he were to learn from you a bit of the language of the Mesh." He paused for a moment. "You would be the prince's assistant and a civilian, but you would be under General Purem's charge. Are these responsibilities acceptable to you?"

Nebi felt dazed. He could help to liberate his homeland. "Absolutely, Your Majesty!"

General Purem had stood by silently, but he could no longer contain himself. "Your Majesty," he said, "I will be overseeing a massive military campaign. That is enough. I don't need to be overseeing someone"—he shot Nebi a hard look—"so young, so useless."

"On the contrary, use*ful*. We're not going to war against ordinary Egyptians but against their misguided leaders. The young man's presence will remind us that the people for whom we're fighting are hardly fiends."

The bull-necked general glared. Working under such a severe man could prove difficult, Nebi thought. Would he be able to endure it?

The king was addressing his nephew. "With luck, maybe this young man's coolheadedness will also temper your headstrong, unruly side." His affectionate tone softened the rebuke, but Sheb gave Nebi an irked look nonetheless.

No, things would not be easy.

# PART II

# CHAPTER 12

# MAAT

King Piankhy and the Second Division's officer corps spent the next weeks seeing to the mobilization of troops. One morning, when the troops were almost ready, the king ordered General Purem to gather the 300 officers for a ceremony in a week's time, on the eve of the day the entire 7,000-man division would march to Egypt. Then he took a blanket, a sword, and two skins of water and climbed the Mountain of Purity. There, atop the mesa, the king fasted and meditated, seeking guidance for the war ahead.

On the sixth day, Sheb and Nebi arrived for the ceremony in the square. The temple, at a right angle to the palace, glowed in the light of hundreds of torches. Row after row of officers faced the temple, wearing blue capes over their tunics to keep out the chill night air. The hundreds of men snapped to attention when the king strode from the temple wearing his purple cape and cobra crown.

General Purem, standing at his side as the king took up position, barked a command that carried into the night. Instantly, the officers snapped their left legs outward and placed their hands on their hips in the at-ease position. The general turned and saluted his commander-in-chief.

"Gentlemen of the Second Division," the king began, speaking loudly enough to reach the last row, "your mission is to sweep down the valley, trampling the foe but giving help to ordinary people whenever it is needed."

Nebi was pleased that he could understand the thrust of

what the king was saying. Over the last weeks, a scribe had been teaching him Kushite, in addition to training him in army record-keeping.

"The army has two immediate targets. The first is the rebel city of Khmun. We have ordered the First Division, based permanently in South Egypt under Prince Khaliut and General Lemersekeny, to capture it."

Nebi's eyes narrowed. So Nimlot would get what he deserved.

Piankhy went on: "You of the Second Division will therefore bypass Khmun, continuing north to the loyal city of Hensu. Tefnakht's invading army has Hensu under siege. You will rescue this city."

The king's voice had lost all the mildness Nebi had heard earlier. It now rang with eagerness and authority. Many officers nodded approval of the plans. They seemed spellbound by the scope of the mission. Hensu was the farthest point in Piankhy's domain.

"As for us," said Piankhy, referring to himself, "we would like to be with you but will remain in Napata."

The surprise in the square was audible as hundreds gasped at once. The king would not share in the glory of the campaign. Instead, he would oversee the conscription and training of an entirely new division, he continued. In the event the enemy should defeat the two divisions in the north, the new unit would be there to defend the homeland against invasion.

Nebi had already scanned the assembly of officers for Wosmol's tall figure. The new division explained his absence, Nebi guessed. It seemed there was no stopping the captain's bad luck. He'd stay behind in Napata and be part of the new unit.

Piankhy went on. "You will relay this information to the troops under your command. And there is something else important you will tell them." He paused. "Some of you may feel that we should punish our enemy—that those Mesh whom we do not slaughter in combat we should drive back to Libya so that we may cleanse Egypt of their presence forever."

In the flicker of the torches, Nebi could see satisfaction on Purem's face.

"But," the king said, "that will not be our army's way." Purem stiffened. "You must make Egypt stronger, not weaker."

Piankhy paused and looked downward, as if searching for the right words.

"Egypt, Kush's brother, has drifted from Amon's ways. Laws that once gave justice even to peasants are now in tatters. Stopping the warlords will require more than battlefield might. To bring harmony to Egypt, you must also bring it back to the ways of Amon—back to *maat*."

*Maat*. There was that ancient word Nebi had learned from Master Setka. His mentor had been surprised that Nebi did not know what it meant. The same word existed in Egyptian and in Kushite. Setka said it would be the most important word Nebi would ever learn.

*Maat* meant honor, but it also meant more than that. It meant fairness. Love of truth. Righteousness. It meant things that had grown out of fashion in much of North Egypt. For farmers, *maat* meant working hard. For traders, it meant not cheating. For sons and daughters, it meant respecting parents. For rulers, it meant governing even-handedly and with justice. If the ruler allowed injustice, the nation would attract *isfet*, chaos. If an entire nation were able to practice *maat*, it would thrive in harmony and in safety. *Maat*,

Master Setka had said, was what had made Egypt great for thousands of years.

"North Egypt is now full of greed and injustice," the king was saying. "*Maat* is gone, and the empire hastens toward that void like flies to an open wound.

"The army of Kush is mighty, but not so mighty that it can repel Assyria single-handedly. After we defeat the northern warlords, we must strive to bring them to our side so they can help to resist the invasion. To convince them, we must show that Amon is truly with us. They must see that in righteousness is triumph."

Sheb leaned over to Nebi. "Look at my father," he whispered.

Shabako was standing several steps behind the king, a smile on his round face.

"This, then, is no war of conquest," Piankhy went on. "Kush needs no more land. What we seek is peace through *maat*. We will achieve this in leading by example." His voice rang with authority. The anxiety that Nebi had seen in the king on the roof had vanished, replaced now by an almost joyous sense of purpose.

"On your journey you will not strip fields of their crops and seize livestock. Instead, you will pay in gold for what you take. You will not destroy Egypt's cities. You will—I repeat, *will*—take prisoners. You will not touch women. Looters and rapists will be sent to the mines." As he made each point, the king pounded his fist into his palm. "We will light no fires of resentment.

"And there is one other thing our army will *not* do," said Piankhy. He paused. "If it is night and the enemy is asleep, you will not attack. If the enemy's soldiers are in another town, you will wait for them to reach the battlefield. If the enemy needs a day, you will wait a day. Fight when the enemy is ready."

Nebi could see some officers trading skeptical glances. General Purem's jaw tightened.

"We tell our enemy: 'Harness your best steeds, form your battle line, and know that Amon has sent us!' " the king said. "By doing this, we will show that, with Amon on our side, victory is inevitable."

To judge from the expressions of those officers Nebi could see, the men seemed to accept this. The king was the conduit for Amon's wishes, and an army that was true to the all-powerful deity would surely triumph.

But Sheb swore under his breath as the meeting broke up. "This makes no sense," he muttered to Nebi. "In war, you do anything at all to win."

"It's worth trying."

"No! Look what sportsmanship accomplished on the racetrack—we lost. It has no place in war."

Confused, Nebi did not respond. He wanted to do what was right, but he also wanted to win.

# CHAPTER 13

# AMBITIONS

With a throaty command and a touch on the reins, Sheb turned Jo-at and Jo-am sharply to the left and out of the chariot's place in the formation. The sudden movement threw Nebi, standing behind him, off balance. The vehicle cut across a row of three other chariots, enshrouding their annoyed occupants in dust. For three days the prince had kept his place in line as the army took this shortcut trail through the desert. But now he had had his fill of regimentation.

They sped in front of the chariotry squadron's captain, who was riding at the rear. The officer tightened his lips so as not to inhale the sand, as fine as flour. He flashed them a resentful look. Nebi cringed. If Sheb were not royalty, this show of rebelliousness might earn the aide-de-camp and his assistant a trip back to Napata.

"Watch the dust," muttered Nebi.

"You're not here to nag," Sheb said sharply. "If the men wanted to stay clean and dainty, they wouldn't have joined the army."

The prince flicked the reins again. The great white and black horses veered away from the six rows of chariots and toward a slope running parallel to the caravan trail. The trail pushed directly across the desert instead of following the river's winding route, saving many days.

Sheb brought Jo-at and Jo-am to a halt at the top of a sandstone bluff to the left of the trail and ahead of the march. Like all the horses, they wore broad-brimmed straw hats to prevent sunstroke.

"Let's rest them," said Sheb, jumping out of the cab. His mood had changed, and he was again friendly. Nebi had learned not to be put off by Sheb's snappish moments.

The prince swung their water skin off the hook on the chariot. He removed his stiff leather helmet and poured water into it. Nebi did the same. They held the headgear as the horses slurped.

"What a sight!" exulted Sheb, peering down from the bluff. A river of men and horses curled across the rocky desert toward them.

Purem, leading the procession, was now passing below them. A white parasol attached to the chariot shaded his bald head and bare chest. On his kilt was the broadest red stripe in the army. He not only directed his own division but, as army commander, co-ordinated the two other divisions as well.

"In Mesh, he's the *aglid*—leader," said Nebi, anxious to do as the king had said and teach the language to Sheb, a quick learner.

At that moment the general turned his head toward the hillock to stare at them. Nebi wished they could make themselves invisible.

As if reading his mind, the prince said shortly, "Don't worry about Old Bullwhip. My uncle is the *aglid* who matters." Then, back to his sunny self again, he gazed out over the panorama. "This is the life."

Following Purem was the squadron with which the youths had been riding, an advance unit of 20 chariots that included senior officers and other members of Purem's immediate staff. As officers, they wore pleated white kilts. Behind them came the professional infantry in kilts of red cowhide. Striding five men abreast, rows of soldiers passed below them. The 50-man platoon marched to the beat of the *daluka*, the two-sided drum suspended from a corporal's neck.

Bows were slung across the soldiers' chests. All wore straw caps that fitted over their heads like bowls; helmets dangled from their sword belts. A few wore bronze circular earrings so large a child could have slipped a wrist through one. Attached to their cowhide backpacks were round wicker shields covered with hide.

The men kept on coming. Two, three, then five platoons of archers marched past the bluff —a full company.

To the beat of another drum, the next company swung into view. The soldiers in the first two platoons toted short javelins; in the other three they carried copper-tipped spears as tall as a man. The spearmen tended to be heavier than the archers, their shoulders showing the effects of endless practice sessions. Here and there among the marchers, Nebi could see men whose shoulders were the same light hue as his own. They were said to be descendants of those Egyptians who, almost a thousand years before, had conquered Kush.

Behind these soldiers marched several companies of men wearing green cowhide kilts.

"Why don't they wear red too?" asked Nebi.

"They're militia or draftees," Sheb replied. "Most of them are farmers or herders. That's why most carry axes, maces, or slings—they don't need much training to know how to use them."

On and on they came, company after company, archers alternating with spearmen. One company would burst into an upbeat marching song, and no sooner was it over than the next company bellowed its own chant.

Sheb cocked his head. "Can you hear it?" A low rumble gradually filled the dry desert air.

It was the main body of the chariot corps. Nebi soon saw 40 squadrons, each composed of 10 chariots and each with banners of a different color.

"All my life I've wanted to be part of something like this," enthused Sheb. "My mother tells me—told me—that even before I could walk my favorite toy was a wooden sword."

Nebi hadn't seen Sheb's mother anywhere. "Does she live in the palace?" he asked hesitantly.

"She's dead." Sheb bit his lip. "She died about the same time you said your father died—two years ago. My father was never much with horses. He was driving a chariot up a hill. They overturned." He shook his head bitterly. "Can you imagine! Driving *up*hill. Overturning while going down a slope, that I can see—you hit a rock or hole when you're speeding. But going up!" Sheb swore bitterly.

Nebi stared absently at the tail end of the line of march, an interminable parade of lumbering wagons drawn by donkeys and horses. These carried food, spare weapons, and tents. Walking alongside were carpenters, cooks, bakers, craftsmen, and blacksmiths.

"Ever since then, I've wanted to be better than my father with horses," Sheb said. He ran his hand from Jo-am's proud tasseled mane to his powerful haunches. "I want to be better than my father in everything ... Everything," he repeated. A thought seemed to occur to him. "You're not angry with Tefnakht?"

"I don't think he even knew what happened in my village that day."

"What about Nimlot? Don't you want to get even?"

"I already have—partly." Nebi glanced down at the arrowhead. "I delivered the message."

"But don't you want to take it further? Hurt him? Kill him?"

"I think about it. But I don't need revenge. I want justice. If we win, this campaign will give me that. The king will see that Nimlot gets what he deserves."

"It takes a lot to get you angry."

"Oh, I can get angry. But I hold it in. What makes me angriest is not what strangers do to me but what people I *know* do to me. They don't have to be violent, just mean." His cheek quivered.

Sheb had shared a story about his mother. Nebi decided to tell him one of his own.

*The night after his father's funeral, voices awaken him. He, Wia, and Mosi are asleep in the courtyard of the gutted house, bundles of their remaining possessions beside them. Their reluctant plan is to leave in the morning.*

*He recognizes his mother's voice, and her tone is desperate. She is across the narrow road at the front door of the large house that belongs to the mayor. His mother is repeating one last time her earlier plea for help. She asks for a plot of land from the village council just big enough for her family's sustenance, and a loan to help cover her son's school tuition.*

*He can't hear the mayor's low voice, but his heavy wife's shrillness carries through the night. "You will never be able to pay it back! The village does not dole out charity! Go see the lord. It is the lord's responsibility to dispense charity!"*

*"But the lord is Tefnakht—the cause of our troubles."*

*"That is not the fault of the village," says the mayor's wife.*

*A door slams. His mother tries to muffle her weeping as she returns to the burned-out room. The family departs the next day.*

"Have you ever been back?" asked Sheb.

Nebi swallowed and shook his head.

"When we liberate the Delta," said Sheb, "you can get even."

"Oh, I don't think so." Nebi smiled faintly. "They have a daughter."

"Aha!" said Sheb. "Now we're getting somewhere. Is it serious?"

Nebi smiled resignedly. "You need property to marry, but I have none. I haven't seen her in two years, either. She may have forgotten I exist. And the worst thing is, she's fourteen."

"Oh-oh. In Kush, girls are almost all wed by then."

"In Egypt, too," said Nebi. His own mother was 13 when he was born, his father 18. "She'd have plenty of suitors. Her family is wealthy—they have five cows."

He blushed as soon as he'd said it. The prince would think Damanhur's elite pathetically lowly.

Instead, Sheb said, "I envy you. It must be good to have girls see you for who you are rather than for your wealth and station. That's the bad part of royalty—everyone's trying to get something from you. You're about the only person my age I know who isn't."

WHEN THE SECOND DIVISION arrived at the Nile, just upstream from Thebes, General Purem declared a day of rest. The men were to bathe and don clean uniforms, then march to the Karnak temple to receive the Divine Votaress's blessing.

Nebi pitched the tent he and Sheb shared, then waded into the deliciously cool river. He was rubbing the grime off his skin with sand when Sheb joined him. The prince had just come from one of the officers' meetings he liked to attend. But instead of splashing about, he looked rankled.

Nebi had to coax him to say what was wrong.

"It's not important," said Sheb, "but as I passed a tent, I heard the officers inside talking about me—Lieutenant Tebey especially. You know that little twit?"

"With the button nose?"

Sheb nodded. "We've hated each other since we were children. He's a very, very distant cousin. You should have heard him just now."

"What did he say?"

"That I was spoiled. Everyone agreed." Sheb's tone was indignant. "Can you imagine?"

Nebi tactfully avoided the question and asked, "How so?"

"They said I don't follow the rules. That I go to officers' meetings though I'm not an officer. That I act like a great charioteer when the only reason I was a finalist was that I had incredible horses, which others had trained."

"A few days ago you said you didn't care what the officers thought of you."

"I don't!" Sheb insisted, then added: "When I'm king, they'll look back and tell their grandchildren they were with me."

*"King?"* said Nebi. "You're going to be king?"

"I'm trying."

"Prince Khaliut is Piankhy's son. I just assumed he was next in line."

Sheb shook his head. "With us, nobody becomes king purely by birth. It can be a king's brother or son—or his nephew. The king has a favorite, and that helps, but after he dies the queen and leaders of the priesthood and army go into the temple. They don't come out until they have decided whom Amon wants."

"King Piankhy looks healthy."

"He's forty-eight." He didn't need to add that, although some people lived to be much older, 40 was considered in Kush, as in Egypt, a normal lifetime. "I need to be ready."

They waded back to the riverbank. "Who else is a contender?"

"Khaliut only *looks* kingly. He's tall and handsome, but stupid. King Piankhy is giving him a chance to shine by letting him command the First Division. The offensive at Khmun is his big opportunity to show leadership. My father is a strong contender. He has no military credentials, but he's a great administrator and he's got the priesthood on his side. Everyone respects him, and you saw how the king took his advice on *maat*.

"Then there's me." Sheb slowed down to let Nebi catch up as they walked through the tall grass. "King Piankhy hasn't told me openly, but I've got an outside chance. He lets me see how decisions are made—you saw how he invited me to that meeting on the roof. And he's sent me on this campaign to learn warfare. So, what's *your* ambition?" Sheb asked Nebi as they started dressing.

"Right now, getting my family back into our home and reviving the farm."

"For someone of your energy, that's not much of an ambition."

Nebi couldn't help laughing. "Oh, I don't know." He glanced northward. "To get what I want, we merely have to win a war."

# CHAPTER 14

# IMPRESSING OLD BULLWHIP

That evening, to receive Princess Amonirdis's benediction, all the troops lined up in formation in front of the awe-inspiring Karnak Temple. She gave them confidence that Amon would be with them in the struggle ahead. The princess had also offered some practical help. To transport them to that struggle, she had placed every vessel in her domain at General Purem's disposal. He had selected 80 cargo ships as troop carriers. He had also chosen 20 of the largest flat-bottomed barges to transport horses and chariots, plus a dozen smaller barges for supplies and equipment.

When Sheb came back from an officers' meeting that evening, he told Nebi, "Bad news. Purem assigned you and me to a horse barge. I'll be foreman." He grimaced. "Those barges will be floating manure piles."

"Purem's way of putting us in our place?" said Nebi.

Sheb nodded. "I reminded Purem that, as his aide-de-camp, I wasn't supposed to do menial work. He said that an aide-de-camp does whatever his commanding officer wants him to do, and that I was admirably suited for a barge because of my experience with horses. He doesn't want me on this campaign any more than he wants you. But I'll show him."

Next morning, Sheb supervised a crew consisting of Nebi and three non-combatants whom the army had drafted a few weeks before. Two were carpenters, a dour man and his 20-year-old son. Neither man spoke, except to each other. The third was a good-natured blacksmith, Kayse, who welcomed conscription as a way to see the wonders of Egypt.

Around his neck hung a thumbnail-sized stone amulet resembling a heart, so shaped to give its wearer vigor.

The crew took apart 25 chariots on the riverbank, then hauled the wheels, axles, and cabs up the gangplank and into what they dubbed the "sweat hole"—the oven-like, window-less storage space below deck, so low-ceilinged that they had to bend over double.

First Lieutenant Tebey made a midday inspection of the barge, while Sheb and the others stood stiffly at attention on deck. The short, chubby officer ducked into the hold to make sure the chariots were well secured. He came up half smiling, half scowling.

"Didn't anyone tell you, Foreman, to rope those chariot parts down?" he asked, plainly relishing the opportunity to chastise Sheb. "Didn't anyone tell you to tie them to the metal rings on the walls and floor?"

"No, sir," said Sheb. "Might I ask, sir, why tying them down is necessary?"

"In the army, you don't ask superiors why orders are necessary. Just this once, though, I'll tell you. If there are high waves or a collision, the cargo could slide to one side. Then the barge could capsize. So get to it!"

Nebi was shocked that someone just five years older than the prince would speak to him so patronizingly, even if he did have rank. In front of others, it was humiliating. Sheb would later explain that Tebey was a fawning sup-porter of Khaliut, but for now the prince simply glowered. He did what he was told. And that afternoon, when the charioteers brought their horses aboard, one by one, he seemed positively eager to refute his reputation as a spoiled young prince. He took the tethers himself and knelt on the grimy deck to attach all 50 horses to the rows of bronze rings. Nebi even saw him smudge some extra grime on his kilt.

At the end of the day, it was General Purem's turn to make a final inspection. He grunted that things appeared to be in order and already had one foot on the gangplank to go when Sheb said, "Permission to speak, General."

Purem sighed. "Speak."

"These horses are already tired from the desert, sir," said Sheb. "The heat on the river will be merciless. They could be exhausted by the time they see battle."

"What's your magic solution?" the general asked sarcastically.

"Sunshades, sir—canopies to cover the decks."

Purem frowned. "And where are we going to find enough covering material?"

"We already have it, sir. The troopships have sails the right size—and no one will use them." This was true. The winds were always north to south in the Nile Valley, so that northbound boats relied on the current and oars. "Why not take sails from about 20 ships, bring them to the barges, and rig them over the horses?"

The general pursed his lips.

Sheb continued: "Carpenters can install posts on the barge decks, then stretch the sails flat between the top of the posts. They'll be like awnings."

"Hmm," said Purem, rubbing his chin. "I'll tell Colonel Ameye to get on it."

By nightfall, most of the barges had their awnings installed.

The fleet sailed shortly after dawn. The morning passed quickly, as Sheb got everyone organized. Kayse lit a small charcoal burner on a corner of the barge and heated broken metal parts on the harnesses before repairing them with a hammer. Tawaki, the older carpenter, and his son Halotey replaced the worn-out rawhide rims on chariot wheels. Sheb tended to what he quickly learned to call in Mesh the *agmaren*—horses—by pitching hay and filling buckets with water for them to drink.

Nebi marked his fifteenth birthday by dumping manure into the river. When he mentioned between shovelfuls that the farmers in his village would hate seeing all this top-grade fertilizer thrown away, Sheb paused in his brushing down of Jo-at and Jo-am. He said, "You know, we *do* have a lot of manure. We have it from a thousand horses. Instead of dumping it, each barge could collect it in a corner. When the fleet stops along the shore for the night, we could invite local farmers to come and haul it away. I'll suggest it to Purem."

The general agreed that this plan could be tried. People living near where armies passed generally dreaded them, for soldiers ravaged fields and pastures for anything they could eat. The king had directed the army to compensate farmers for its needs, and Purem acknowledged that Sheb's idea might be another way to create goodwill.

The gesture succeeded that evening. Especially grateful were those poorer farmers whose fields lay above the flood plain and thus did not benefit from the deposit of rich sediment that the yearly inundation left behind. The next morning, they brought the troops baskets of warm bread and fresh fruit as gifts.

"We'll do this every day from now on," said Purem as he enjoyed a pomegranate.

Sheb had said he would show the general, and he had.

TWO AFTERNOONS LATER, taking a break from filling buckets, Sheb and Nebi sat on the edge of the barge facing the troopship that was towing them. The vast armada stretched ahead as far as they could see.

"Does going to war scare you?" Sheb asked out of the blue.

"The closer we get to it, yes."

"Same with me. What bothers me most is that everything's so quiet."

They watched a crocodile scuttle off a sandbar and knife into the dark waters.

"It makes no sense for Tefnakht to let us penetrate this far into Egypt. My uncle says that to learn strategy I should train myself to imagine I'm commanding an opposing army. So, if I were Tefnakht, I'd attack this army while it's on the river. Once Kushites are on land we are strong, because chariotry is our power. But we've no experience at fighting on water. Look at these ridiculous ships." He waved his hand at the lumbering cargo vessels ahead. "They're not for fighting."

He added: "But if Tefnakht's men do attack on the river, these old barges will be their last priority. One whiff and they'll never come near us!"

As humor, the remark was fine. As a prediction, it was terrible.

# CHAPTER 15

# THE FIGHT ON THE RIVER

"Enemy!" The cry came from the ship towing their barge.

The Kushites were in the center of the river, which was now half a mile wide. Their vessels were three, sometimes four, abreast. Sheb and Nebi, in the first of the barges, were in the middle of the armada.

Nebi drew a sharp breath. He put down the brush he'd been using on the horses and squinted downstream. He saw an array of colorful specks, sails, looking as innocent as butterflies. The ships were in neat double file, suggesting they had a careful plan. He felt the same eerie hollowness in his stomach as he had when Nimlot's gang had trotted down from the ridge.

Nebi had been issued a sword, although he had never trained. He followed Sheb's lead and strapped it on, but it was a relief to think he would not have to use it. The troopships ahead of them would do the fighting.

The enemy was coming on fast.

"I count just twenty ships, and we have four times as many!" crowed Sheb. And that did not include the barges. "This will be suicide for them."

"Maybe not," said Nebi. "Look at their hulls—high in the water. They're not carrying heavy loads like us. Their ships will be fast and nimble." Unlike Sheb, he had lived near the sea, and it felt good to finally know more than the prince about something to do with the war. Nebi thought of another thing. "Their crews will be from the Delta, too. They know all about fighting on water. Some could be pirate crews."

"Pirates? Tefnakht would work with pirates?"

"I'd see them around his palace. They'd give him a share of the booty if he let them be in their hideouts in the Delta swamps. It wouldn't surprise me if Tefnakht has told them, 'Help me conquer Egypt, and we'll split the plunder.'"

Sheb called the anxious crew members over. "We don't want the fighting to make the horses nervous. If they panic, they'll rear up. Rip some rags and put blindfolds on them. Quickly!" He ran to the stern, cupped his hands, and urged the next horse barge to do the same.

The enemy ships were now in midriver, still in double file, and heading straight toward the first row of Kushite vessels. But then they made an unexpected move. The double file split up. One line sailed to the west side of the river, the other to the east. Staying just out of arrow range, they hugged the palm-lined riverbanks, sailing past on either side of the Kushite fleet.

"Maybe they see we're too much for them," called out Halotey hopefully, as he knotted another blindfold.

The lead ships in both files kept advancing, well past Shebitku's lead barge. They were so close that Nebi could make out the forms of bare-chested, light-skinned men in the rigging and crowding the decks. Then, as if by signal, the ships displayed their oars for the first time. The oars, lined up as neatly as teeth on a comb, were poised to dip.

Even before the oars had reached the water, Sheb let loose a shout. "I understand now!" He grabbed Nebi's arm. "They're coming for the barges. If they knock us out, we'll have no chariotry. The war will be over before it begins!" He yelled to all his bargemates, "They're coming at *us*!"

He sprinted between the horses to the other side of the deck, where he bellowed across the water to the nearest barge, "Get ready!"

Nebi's stomach clenched. As he glanced around anxiously, he saw Tawaki point to an enemy ship to the right, starboard side. It had altered course and was now heading straight for them.

The sound of splashing oars grew louder, their rhythm faster.

Sheb waved for the crew to gather. "We can be safe! We'll lie down flat on the far side. They'll be shooting arrows at the horses, not us. As soon as our tow ship turns around, it'll rescue us." He paused to catch his breath. "Their plan can't work. Before they shoot more than a few horses, the tow ship will be between them and us."

Kayse shook his head. "Fire," he said flatly, as if this were as plain as day. "They'll use fire."

Sheb needed only a moment to ponder the remark. "Of course! Burning arrows!" His eyes went wide.

The enemy ship's slim hull bore down on them through the smooth waters, its oars dipping in fast unison.

"We're dead if we stay!" said Tawaki.

"Let's swim!" cried Halotey.

"No!" Sheb ordered. "This barge is my first command, and no one is ever going to say I failed at it!" Then, coolly, he told Halotey, "You and your father get your knives and cut down the awning. It'll be the first thing to burn. Throw it in the river." He pointed to two piles of hay, each as high as a man, on either side of the barge. "Nebi and Kayse—get rid of those."

As told, Nebi and Kayse ran to one stack and crouched, pushing with their hands and heads. The blacksmith was the strongest man on board; his biceps were like grapefruits. Yet the pile barely budged.

"Again!" yelled Kayse. "Let's get lower!" They heaved with all their might until, slowly, the pile slid into the river.

Just as Nebi looked up, their tow ship let fly a swarm of arrows toward the attacking vessel. First one and then two of its oars fell still—the rowers must have been hit. The immobile oars hindered nearby oars from sweeping back and forth, and the vessel advanced more slowly.

"The other stack!" panted Nebi. He and Kayse ran to it. Nebi closed his sweat-stung eyes as he pushed. This time, to his astonishment, they succeeded on the first try.

Nebi was calmer than he could have imagined. As long as he knew what to do, he could do it. He glanced across the water. The barges behind them were following their example. Men were hacking at the ropes that tied the awnings and dumping the hay.

"More buckets!" Sheb shouted, and Nebi looked around to see where he was. The prince was in the first row of horses with Jo-at and Jo-am, tying their blindfolds.

Each of the 50 wooden buckets stood in front of a horse. Nebi scrambled for those that still had water and rushed them to Sheb. Kayse gathered armfuls of empty ones and made hurried trips to the port side, away from the attacking ship, where Tawaki and his son dipped them in the river.

The operation was only half done when Nebi smelled what he had dreaded—smoke. Three arrows covered with burning pitch had struck the other side of the deck. He and Kayse sprinted to them with full buckets, but before they could put out the flames, more burning arrows fell.

At the smell of smoke, some of the horses had begun a restive whinnying. One or two that had not been blindfolded were now yanking at their tethers and pounding the deck with their hooves.

Suddenly, Nebi heard a loud, coarse voice. "More arrows!" it cried. "More!"

The words were in the Delta dialect—and the guttural voice was familiar. Nebi had heard it while he lay in the grass, pretending to be dead. It had snarled, "On your feet, cur!" He looked over his shoulder and, flinching in horror, saw the fleshy, red-bearded man, his tattooed arm waving a curved sword.

Blazing arrows pelted the barge in another flurry. Halotey yelped sharply, his eyes wild with pain. A fiery shaft was lodged in his upper arm. Shrieking, he jumped overboard. His father rushed to the side with a rope.

Nebi realized that the firefighting was futile. Even if he and the others could somehow douse every last fire breaking out on the deck, they'd never cope with the side of the barge facing the attackers. The whole length of that right side— from bow to stern—bristled with arrows. The pitch used to caulk between the hull's square-hewn logs was the first to ignite. Anyone daring to bring buckets to that starboard side would be shot in no time.

Within moments, the flames on the side of the hull rose like a deadly wall.

Sheb stumbled through the smoke to where Nebi, Kayse, and Tawaki were crouching. "Cut the horses loose!" he cried ruefully. Whether the horses could make their way to the distant shore was an open question. "Then swim to the troopship!"

Tears caused by acrid smoke blurred Nebi's vision, yet

he could see in Sheb's eyes a look of wild despair. The desperation went beyond fear for the lives of Jo-am, Jo-at, and the other horses. It was the shame of failure.

# CHAPTER 16

# CHEATER

So thick were the flames and smoke that Nebi could no longer see the attacking ship beyond them. But a harsh voice came through clearly. "Back to your oars!" yelled the tattooed man. "To another barge!"

This first barge, in the tattooed pirate's view, was already destroyed. In Sheb's view, too. He grabbed Nebi's arm. "I said try to free the horses—then swim!"

"Not yet!" Nebi shouted back. "One thing might work!" He motioned Kayse and Tawaki to come close. "Let's shift the weight! Kayse and I will push the chariots to the right side." He pointed to Sheb. "You and Tawaki bring the horses to that side too!"

"*Toward* the flames?"

"Remember what Tebey said!"

Sheb looked at him blankly. Then his face lit up. "Yes, do it!"

Nebi urgently waved to Kayse to follow. They slipped down through the hatchway into the dark sweat hole.

"You cut, I push!" cried Kayse.

Nebi drew his sword. He slashed the ropes securing the chariots and the horizontally stacked wheels. Kayse strained, shoving the equipment bit by bit toward the burning side of the barge. Choking smoke wafted through cracks between the logs. Hooves thudded on the deck above, but Nebi paid no heed. If anyone could lead frightened horses toward flames, it was Sheb.

Nebi gasped and coughed as he hacked one rope after

another. The smoke was now blinding him and he squeezed his lids closed. "Amon, give me calm," he said through his teeth. He felt his way to the next stack of wheels. Cutting the rope took longer when he couldn't see it.

Kayse grabbed his shoulder and choked out a few words: "Less smoke—floor."

Both dropped to their knees. Sure enough, Nebi could now see what he was doing. He was soon ahead of Kayse: cutting free the chariots and the stacks of wheels took less time than shoving them across the hold.

The floor began to tilt. Nebi sheathed his sword and crawled on his stomach across the floor to help Kayse push more freight. The more the vessel slanted, the easier the pushing became. Soon it listed sharply.

Kayse shouted something incomprehensible. The hoofbeats above were becoming deafening. Enveloped by smoke, the horses must be frantically rearing and trying to escape.

Kayse cupped his hands and yelled hoarsely in Nebi's ear. "How long do we do this?"

"Until we *almost* capsize!"

They hardly had to push at all now. One shove and a pile of wheels would go screeching down the hull, slamming into the rest of the freight.

Between paroxysms of coughing, Kayse managed to say, "Maybe we *will* capsize!" His voice was full of dread.

Nebi cut the ropes binding another stack of wheels. They slid away on their own and suddenly the floor was so steep that Nebi almost tumbled after them. Panting and gagging, he clung to a ring in the floor.

The pounding of hooves grew less intense.

Tawaki stuck his head down into the hatch and screamed the word Nebi had been waiting for: "Stop!" A moment later he shrieked even more desperately: "Any more and we capsize!"

Kayse and Nebi crawled up the floor on all fours and hauled themselves with the last of their strength through the hatch.

The open air had never felt more delicious. Nebi clung to a post, coughing and recovering his breath. Kayse lay on his back, his hefty chest heaving. He'd inhaled more smoke than Nebi.

Wavelets lapped gently at the very edge of the starboard deck. Only a few small flames remained, confined to one corner. Sheb was dousing them with a bucket. Tawaki had hauled his grimacing son back on board. The arrow had gone right through the fleshy part of Halotey's upper arm. Tawaki neatly snapped off the feathered end and, arrowhead first, drew out the remainder smoothly.

Nebi gazed out across the river. The last enemy sails were disappearing upstream. The troopship was now towing their barge toward a sandbar along the western bank. All the other barges were headed in the same direction. Modest clouds of smoke rose from four of them. Soldiers aboard each of those barges had formed bucket brigades.

"How many horses did we lose?" Nebi asked Sheb.

The prince winced. "Two," he said. "Flaming arrows hit them. They went berserk. I cut them loose."

"Just two?" muttered Nebi in disbelief. The success of their defense was only beginning to sink in.

"I thought we were going to lose them all," said Sheb. "I thought —"

A jolt shook the barge as it touched bottom. The sandbar was far from shore but within wading distance of a grassy island. The crew members unhitched the horses, which jumped gratefully into the shallow water. After a dinghy from the troopship came to take Halotey for medical attention, the others staggered to the far end of the sandbar. It was well removed from the bustle and perfect for rest.

Nebi flopped on the sand next to Sheb.

"Were you afraid?" asked Sheb in a low voice.

"I was scared when the ship bore down on us. Then, when I realized I could die, I wasn't scared anymore. I was too busy—it was strange."

"What scared me even more than death was disgrace. I could imagine Tebey and those other officers smirking."

Nebi's eyes closed. Just as he was drifting off to sleep, he heard a booming voice say, "Well done, Prince, well done!" It took him a moment to recognize it. He had never heard Old Bullwhip speak in a warm tone of voice.

The crew members scrambled to their feet.

The general's eyes looked neither hard nor scornful but simply relieved. "When I saw the enemy attacking your barge, I didn't give the horses much chance of surviving," he said, addressing himself to the prince. "But those on your tow ship tell me you must have anticipated they'd use fire. The barges behind you followed your example."

"Anyone could have anticipated it, sir," said Sheb modestly.

Nebi bit his lip and stood in stunned silence.

"Frankly," Purem went on, "when I saw the barge afire, I *knew* we'd lost the horses. I even saw myself having to tell Prince Shabako and King Piankhy that you had perished in battle. Tipping the barge was inspired."

"It was the only logical response, sir," shrugged Sheb.

"How old are you now?" the general asked.

"I'll be sixteen next week."

"You will come to tonight's officers' meeting. I am announcing a handful of promotions based on today's performances. You saved forty-eight horses from near-certain death, saved twenty-five chariots from destruction, and saved other barges as well, by setting an example. You're young to be a junior lieutenant in the chariotry, but you deserve to be one."

Sheb looked radiant.

"You won't have a combat role because you haven't completed military school," the general continued. "But on the rest of the trip to Hensu, you'll be foreman of all the barges. When we reach Hensu, I'll need you to handle supplies—and maybe other things. Oh, and you can keep your assistant." He nodded at Nebi without expression, then turned on his heel.

That night, the entire division camped on the spacious grassy island next to the sandbar. The retrieved awnings were spread on the beaches to dry.

The lead barge's weary crew turned in early. As he and Sheb were untying their bedrolls, Nebi could contain himself no longer. "You showed me today you're a born leader. Without you, we would have been totally unready for the attack." He was cold with anger as he delivered this compliment, and Sheb looked at him uncertainly. "But you've become an officer through fraud. 'Anyone could have anticipated they'd use fire, sir,' " Nebi mimicked. "What humility! Never mind that you did *not* anticipate it, and Kayse did."

Sheb studiously smoothed out his bedroll, as if he wasn't listening.

Nebi pressed on. "And tipping the barge—'It was the only logical response, sir!' Your real response was to tell everyone to swim for it—and let the horses die! Congratulations. Your promotion is based on hypocrisy."

"I *need* recognition," said Sheb defensively. "Kayse doesn't. He doesn't want to be anything more than a blacksmith."

"And me?"

"You don't need recognition. You just want a farm."

"I'm not against recognition if I deserve it," Nebi said hotly. "Purem doesn't even call me by my name."

The prince glared at his friend. "Every other position in life that I've had was because of my birth. This is the first I've gotten on my own. Don't try to make me feel guilty about it." He climbed into his bedroll and turned his back on Nebi. After a while he said, "I'll make it up to you."

# CHAPTER 17

# TAKING UP THE SWORD

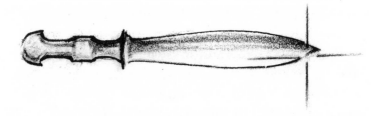

Lieutenant Shebitku had just time to call all barge crews together before the fleet set off the next morning. Wearing his kilt with the coveted pleats and the thin red stripe down the side, he cut a confident figure as he stood before his 90 subordinates. Nebi realized that Sheb was taller than when they'd met only three months before. His jaw seemed more pronounced. Many of the men in the barge crews were at least twice his age, but none appeared to resent him. His leadership the day before had saved not only his own barge but many others.

"Let me relay some of General Purem's points from last night's officers' meeting," Sheb began, speaking easily. "First, the numbers." He read from some notes. "On our side, five horse barges damaged, none sunk. Two small troopships sunk while defending the barges. Total casualties: thirty-one, with three courageous bargemen among them. We will pray for them at the end of the meeting.

"Here are the numbers for the enemy. We captured seventeen ships. Eight of these were abandoned on the riverbank as their crews fled. Casualties: hundreds. We also took twenty-two prisoners." He lowered his notes, and the hint of a smile crossed his face. "The general had them brought to last night's meeting. They expected us to throw them to the crocodiles—as they would have done to us. I will try to repeat the general's exact words." Sheb scanned the curious faces, then said, " 'You joined Tefnakht and Nimlot for gold, and so you shall see gold—more than you ever wished. You shall be miners in our goldfields for the rest of the war.' "

Sheb waited for the chuckles to subside, then continued. "Now the serious business. The general was pleased with us on the barges, but not with the fleet as a whole. The army could easily have lost more horses and chariots and been forced to return to Napata in humiliation."

The general, the lieutenant went on, was therefore ordering intensive training every evening. Javelineers, archers, and swordsmen would all hone their skills. Horsemen would aim blunt arrows and wooden javelins over their horses' heads to accustom the animals to battle conditions. Sergeants would lead platoons of draftees through marching drills. "And we bargemen," he concluded, "will get ready to be medical attendants. We'll carry stretchers." Over the next few evenings, he explained, they would cut bamboo and extra sailcloth to make stretchers and hospital tents.

Regardless of whether or not Sheb had gotten the promotion fairly, he seemed made for the role, Nebi thought as the meeting broke up. It wouldn't help the mission to hold the promotion against him.

Sheb remained on the lead barge as the journey resumed. He practiced sword fighting during the long days, springing around the deck, slashing at imaginary foes, parrying and feinting.

"You're teaching me Mesh," Sheb told Nebi at one point. "Let me teach you some moves I learned at military school."

"Medical attendants are non-combatants. I won't need to fight."

"Nebi," sighed Sheb. His tone was that of an exasperated teacher speaking to a slow-learning child. "If that human tattoo had boarded our barge and come at you with a sword, wouldn't you have wanted to defend yourself?" Nebi had to admit Sheb had a point.

Work on the barge and calisthenics with the troops had thickened Nebi's arms and shoulders. The limp from his injury was almost gone. He and Sheb kept the sheaths on their blades so as not to hurt each other as they dueled.

"Your arm is quick," said Sheb at the end of Nebi's first training day, "but your footwork is clumsy. You'll be good by the time I'm through with you, though. We'll do archery on shore, too."

One evening, Sheb returned from an officers' meeting with a pleased expression. A messenger from downriver had brought what he described to Nebi as "fine news." The First Division's siege of Khmun was going nowhere. Despite limited food supplies, the city was holding out. The division had attempted no assault on the walls.

"What's 'fine' about that?"

"Khaliut is in charge," Sheb said with a wink. "And here's good news for you: our spies have spotted Nimlot at Hensu."

"I thought the siege had penned him up inside Khmun."

"That's right. Khaliut was supposed to keep a watertight guard around the city so that no one could get out. But Nimlot escaped anyway."

"Why is this good for me?"

"Because in a few days he and you will be on the same battlefield at Hensu. Wouldn't it be perfect if you and he could resume your lovely friendship there?"

"He'd never recognize me. And I couldn't attack him—I'll be a stretcher-bearer."

" 'Couldn't,' " said Sheb. "Did you say 'couldn't'? A man can do anything he wants on a battlefield. Anything."

"I don't like this kind of talk. I've told you: I don't want personal revenge. If Nimlot survives the war, the king will punish him. That's all I want."

"Don't block your hatred. Don't pass on to others the duty of getting rid of evil. Who knows what the others will do? Do it yourself, if you have a chance."

By the next day, though, not even Sheb could make bad news seem good. The army's Theban spies had returned from Hensu with a report on Tefnakht's forces. In anticipation of the Kushites' arrival, the leader of the Delta forces was bringing reinforcements to Hensu. If they arrived in time, he'd command 15,000 troops. Excluding cooks, bargemen, and other non-combatants, the Kushites would counter with just under 7,000.

News of the possible reinforcements raced through the division like a sandstorm. So did the unease.

# CHAPTER 18

# "BE A MAN"

Nebi and Sheb were training on the barge the next morning when suddenly the fast-improving beginner put down his sword and froze.

He took a step to the side of the barge and stared at the western shore. A meadow lay between barley fields. It sloped gently up to the ridge where the desert began. The pastel green grass looked as peaceful as the sheep grazing upon it.

Sheb started to ask what was the matter, then stopped. "So," he said, "that's where it happened."

Nebi's narrowed eyes and clenched mouth did not ease until the barge had passed the scene. Then, in a low voice, he told Sheb, "The worst thing is the laughter. I can still hear it. The men were shooting at servants for sport."

"Get even, Nebi."

Nebi made no reply.

That evening, the two practiced shooting arrows at a palm tree.

"Pretend it's Nimlot," urged Sheb.

Nebi put the bow down in exasperation. "Why do you want me to kill him?"

"It's silly to be moral in a war. You're too much like my father. War is about doing everything you can to win. Nimlot deserves to die."

"The king will punish Nimlot when he gets the chance—and you know as well as I do that he'll be harsh. Nimlot not only betrayed him but killed one of his oldest friends."

"Stop waiting for justice. It can take forever. And it can make mistakes. Be a man."

Nebi flinched at the remark. He started to say something, then stopped, hating himself for feeling so flustered.

The older youth took a step forward and grasped the iron arrowhead hanging around Nebi's neck. He clicked his thumbnail against its jagged edge. "You know what I'd do if I were you? I'd stick this arrowhead on the end of a shaft and send it back to him—right between his ribs!"

Nebi knew that the fantasy Sheb had sketched was just that, a fantasy, but in spite of himself he found it delicious. For the first time since Sheb had started talking about revenge, he showed a smile. "But I'd want him to realize who I was, just before he died," he said, playing along.

Encouraged, Sheb seized the opening. "Here's what I'd do. As he's lying there, gasping his last breaths, I'd go over and introduce myself. I'd say, 'Thank you for lending me that high-quality arrowhead. But I really had to give it back to you.'"

Nebi surprised himself by chuckling. "Yes, but I'd say that in a very polite voice. Nimlot would feel the mockery—then he'd die." An oddly pleasurable sensation welled up in his gut.

THE SECOND DIVISION'S FLEET left the Nile just upriver from the city of Khmun, entering a canal that slanted off to the northwest and was the only way to reach Hensu by water. The canal was so narrow in places that the oars hit the cattails near the banks. The tall-masted ships had to stick to dead center to avoid overhanging branches. Children raced to the water's edge when they saw the ships. Farmers left their plows. Women interrupted their washing. Almost all waved and clapped.

Halotey, his arm in a sling, stood conspicuously on deck and, as an object of sympathy, soaked up particularly loud cheers. It was the first time Nebi had seen the solemn carpenter actually beam.

"They're welcoming us just the way I hoped—as liberators," Nebi told Sheb, a little surprised at the lump he felt in his throat.

"Their joy is a little premature," Sheb answered, shaking his head. "They don't know we'll be out-manned two to one if Tefnakht's reinforcements get there in time." He added bitterly, "If they arrive before we do, Purem had better not wait for the enemy to be ready."

AFTER RETURNING from the officers' meeting that night, Sheb gathered the barge workers around a campfire. "This will be our last meeting before the battle, so listen closely." Nebi admired the way Sheb, arms clasped behind his back, had perfected the clipped, businesslike manner of experienced officers. "Our besieged ally, the Lord of Hensu, has smuggled a letter to us. He says his city is starving and it will surrender to Tefnakht if we don't arrive quickly. So, from now on, we dash. General Purem expects battle three days from now—one long day's travel, one day for disembarking and readying the horses, then the fight." He paused to let the men absorb the imminence of the battle.

"Now I want to introduce the officer who will be in charge of stretcher-bearers on the field of battle, and to whom I will report. We're lucky, because he's someone with more battlefield experience than almost anyone in the army—Colonel Ameye. The reason he won't have a combat role is that, as you might have heard, he is recovering from an injury in the river fight."

A tall, gawky figure came into the firelight.

"On your feet!" barked Sheb, giving the command that accompanied any senior officer's arrival.

The colonel certainly looked unimpressive in conventional military terms. He had a skinny body and legs without calves. Hawk, as he was often called because of his sharp, downward-curved nose, wore a bandage over his right eye and around his head: an arrow had glanced off a troopship mast and blinded the eye.

Although he had never met him, Nebi knew the colonel to be among the most respected of officers. That was so for several reasons. He was a strategist and a member of Purem's inner circle. As well, the quickness and surprising power of his angular limbs had enabled him to win a division swordsmanship competition. But he was best known for his technical expertise. When he had been with the Kushites' mercenary force in Israel years before, the Assyrian invaders' rugged chariots, towers, and other engines of war had inspired him to design even better equipment. In this campaign, Purem had given the colonel the crucial responsibility of keeping all ships in working order.

"You men will be non-combatants, but you can still distinguish yourselves in battle," Colonel Ameye told the bargemen. "You will save, not take, lives." His voice was robust despite his injury. "I will give you just three instructions. First, the stretcher crews—and our one chariot, which is Lieutenant Shebitku's—will pick up every wounded man, friend or foe, and bring them to the field hospital. The king has ordered this.

"Second, all of you will receive folded pieces of white cloth that can be pressed on wounds to the torso to stop or slow bleeding. You'll also be issued cloth strips. These you'll use as tourniquets on limbs." The colonel called a man forward and demonstrated where to place the twisted linen.

"The third instruction is the one you will need to stay alive. You will take three of the white strips and tie them around your arms and your helmet. When the enemy sees those bands, they will know you are medical attendants and not to be attacked. You are authorized to bring any weapon—ax or sword—but you are not to use it except in self-defense. I repeat—except in self-defense. If any of you breaks this rule, the Mesh will see the bands as a deception and will kill every attendant in sight. I would too, in their place.

"Questions?"

A hand went up. "Have the enemy's reinforcements arrived?" someone asked. It was the question on everyone's mind.

The colonel cleared his throat. "Yes."

So they would be outnumbered two to one. Nebi found it hard to fall asleep that night. Were the men of Kush journeying toward their deaths? And would a few strips of white cloth spare him?

# CHAPTER 19

# BATTLE LINES AT HENSU

On the day of battle, the men rose in the dark. By the time the sun came up, blood red, they were already marching in double file along the cart track beside the canal. No one said a word. There was only the tramp of feet, the clop of hooves, and the squeak and rumble of chariot wheels. Each man wondered if this day would be his last. Some anxiously fingered amulets hanging around their necks. Nebi, in the chariot with Sheb near the end of the procession, wondered if the prince could hear the churning in his gut.

Jo-at and Jo-am too could feel the tension. Their ears were straight up. For protection, they, like all the horses, wore form-fitting reed mats that stretched from forehead to buttocks. Sheb had covered the mats with white cloths to make it clear that the horses were pulling an ambulance chariot.

A handful of the army's indispensable top officers had donned bronze helmets and chest armor made of little bronze semicircles overlapping like fish scales. The prince had declined an offer of such protection. The rest of the troops had leather helmets and were bare-chested.

"There it is!" called someone up ahead. Necks craned all down the line as men caught their first glimpse of the city they had come so far to save.

Hensu lay on a low ridge. Its wall, silhouetted against the pink sky, was tall and formidable. Two charred siege towers lay on their sides outside the wall. People jammed the ramparts to watch the army approach. No one cheered, though, and when Nebi drew closer he could see why. Their faces were gaunt, their eyes hollow. The citizens had paid a price for their ruler's loyalty to a distant king.

"They think we're doomed," said Sheb dryly. "That would make them doomed too."

Row upon row upon row of Tefnakht's men waited to the right of the city on the same ridge. It seemed impossible that there could be so many of them. They covered the entire slope—a daunting sight that filled Nebi with foreboding. Yet the flash of sun on armor, the flutter of flags, and the brilliance of uniforms lent an unseemly air of festivity to this place of inevitable carnage. The gentle hillside below Tefnakht's army appeared to be a vast sheep pasture—a hardscrabble sweep of stone and the occasional prickly pear. Tefnakht clearly intended it as the battlefield.

General Purem's men marched to a flat area within view of Tefnakht's troops, yet distant enough that Tefnakht could not suddenly charge and catch them unready.

Colonel Ameye drove up to Sheb's chariot. "Round up your stretcher-bearers, Lieutenant," the veteran soldier said tightly, plainly feeling the tension himself. "Have them unload the hospital tents from the wagon. Set them up where they'll be in the shade all day." He pointed to a large knoll with leafy sycamores.

Sheb issued the order to his men, supervised the preliminary work, then drove with Nebi back to where Ameye was observing the enemy's formation. The colonel slowly shook his leathery, hawk-like head as he stared at the ridge. "I don't like it. It looks as though their professionals have metal helmets and chest armor. I don't like Tefnakht's position, either." He hardly acknowledged that Nebi, a civilian, was present, but Nebi did not mind. Being within listening distance of the shrewd veteran was a privilege.

"Our men will have to advance toward them," the colonel said. "That means they'll be facing the sun." He angled his hand in front of his eye to block the sun that was low over the ridge. "We'll hardly see arrows and javelins coming at us." Colonel Ameye pointed his sinewy arm. "And look at that slope. We'll be handicapped if we march up it. Our javelineers will have to toss uphill. The enemy's throws will be downward and have more force. Our infantry will have to swing their swords upward. We'll lose power that way."

The colonel paused a moment, then shook his head in dismay. "See the rocks on both sides of the pasture?" Nebi strained to see. "Tefnakht must have put them there. Our chariots will break their axles if they try any lightning flanking movements."

"How do we get out of this?" said Sheb, frowning.

The sound of a Kushite bugle pierced the air, the signal for an officers' meeting.

"Come! We'll find out," said Ameye. He and Sheb wheeled their vehicles around and sped to the far edge of the pasture, next to a vast orchard of almond and orange trees.

Purem stood in a chariot to make himself heard by the 300 officers. His bronze helmet came low over his brow, but his eyes looked confident. So did the burly general's hands-on-hips posture.

"Tefnakht," he said, "has the high ground and the sun at his back. He thinks he's got the advantage. He is wrong. *We* hold the advantage. Look at that ridge, men. It lacks something important." The general grinned at the puzzled expressions. "It lacks shade!" He laughed. "Now, look what's behind us." He pointed. "An orchard. And look over there. A grove of tamarisks. This is a beautiful morning, gentlemen. Nowhere is it written that we must spend it fighting. The radiant sun, says the king, is like Amon himself. I suggest that we retire to the shade and contemplate those words as the sun rises in the sky."

Ameye smiled, as if he could see what was coming.

"Let us allow Amon to bake our enemy," said the general. "When his men wilt, Tefnakht will move off the high ground."

Sheb and Nebi returned to the shady knoll to help with the last of the tents. From there, they could see to their right the Kushites spread out under the trees, unit by unit, ready to spring up in case the enemy responded with a surprise of its own. Some of the officers allowed their men to rest, others gave their troops final advice or had them sharpen weapons. To their left, the Mesh were standing on the slope under a now-sweltering sun.

"The Mesh aren't just losing strength standing out there," Ameye pointed out, after he had inspected the tents. "They're also losing confidence in Tefnakht. He makes them look like fools."

It was not till late morning that Tefnakht ordered his men to march from the ridge. They moved to the level part of the pasture. Nebi, who had been caring for Jo-at and Jo-am with Sheb, watched the vast troop movements with mounting anxiety.

The Mesh were now close enough that Nebi could see what they were wearing. The professional soldiers had tan kilts, chest armor, and oblong shields; shoulder-length sidelocks dangled from under their bronze helmets. The draftees, leather-helmeted and bare-chested, held square wicker shields in one hand, axes in the other.

The Mesh foot soldiers formed three phalanxes. Each of these great rectangular blocks consisted of six rows. Each row, Ameye reckoned, boasted 750 men, and Nebi could see that all those in the front row had spears. They were the biggest and the strongest.

"When a man in the first row falls, you'll see a man in the second row take his place," the colonel told Sheb, who was listening like an avid student. "Our soldiers will do the same."

Purem had responded with three phalanxes of his own, positioned directly opposite and just out of range of composite bows. But each Kushite phalanx was less than half the size of the enemy's, with only 500 men in each of four rows. In the first row were the spearmen. In the second and third were the javelin throwers. In the last row, archers. Behind the archers was a scattering of troops holding innocent-looking cords that dangled almost to the ground—slings.

"Look!" said Sheb. He grabbed Nebi's arm and pointed. "There's your friend!" he said sarcastically. "You can see his colors."

At the very back of the Mesh forces, behind a row of cavalrymen mounted on mules, were six chariots. Each held a man with two feathers on the front of his helmet, a badge of nobility, and a second occupant who was a shield-bearer. At the far left of the cluster was a chariot whose horses had yellow and green padding. Two plumes, a yellow and a green, bobbed jauntily from the helmet of the taller of the chariot's occupants.

"Who are the others?" Sheb asked Nebi.

"That's Tefnakht in the orange and yellow plumes. The squat one next to Tefnakht must be Osorkon."

Ameye was turning his gaze back and forth between Purem and Tefnakht. Nebi did the same.

The two commanders seemed to be staring at each other with the intensity of circling wrestlers, each searching for a hint of the other's intentions. Each was playing for time, to allow phalanxes, charioteers, and cavalry to move into proper position.

The trio on the knoll watched as Lord Tefnakht of Sais abruptly lifted his right arm.

"Now watch!" said Ameye, his voice strained. "It will take him time, but as soon as he lowers his fist, his bugler will sound the attack."

Tefnakht twisted his head first one way, then the other, checking his troops and gesturing impatiently with his other hand.

Nebi held his breath, waiting for Tefnakht's arm to fall.

# CHAPTER 20

# THE TEMPTATION

Before Tefnakht could lower his fist, Purem gave his own signal. The soldier next to him beat a *daluka*, banging out a code to the waiting infantry. Instantly, dozens of other *dalukas*, one per infantry unit, picked up the beat. The broad pasture resounded with aggressive rhythm.

With a shout, the men in the first and last rows jogged away from their phalanxes and formed a two-row semicircle that faced the Mesh 150 paces away. Archers made up the second of these curved rows. They drew their bowstrings, as the spearmen in the first row lifted their shields to protect the archers and themselves. Nebi shook his head in wonderment at the tactic's precision. Those endless marching sessions during the trip hadn't been so pointless after all.

The *daluka* stopped—another signal. The simultaneous twanging of more than a thousand Kushite bowstrings, together with the whirring of scores of slings, sounded almost like a low drumbeat. Even before the Kushite projectiles could land, the Mesh bugle sounded and the air was dark with enemy arrows.

Moments later, the ranks on both sides became thinner. From where Nebi stood, so far away, the arrows' effect looked so calm and matter-of-fact. He could only guess at the pain and death inside the phalanx. He felt ill at ease being so close to where men he had traveled with were dying, and yet being safe himself. Although the knoll was within range of composite arrows, its white tents gave it immunity.

"We've got the advantage now," the colonel exclaimed. "Look, their arrows come from one direction, while ours come from right, left, and center." Sure enough, the Kushites' semicircle made defense against their barrage difficult. As soon as a Mesh soldier raised his shield against arrows coming from one direction, he was open to arrows from another.

"Look how much faster our archers reload," said Ameye, pointing. "We've trained them to inhale just once between shots." His proud tone told Nebi he had something to do with that training.

"With composite bows too, sir?" asked Sheb, his eyes glued to the fearsome double-curved weapons.

"Two breaths in that case," conceded Ameye. "Those bows take more effort to draw."

Nebi glanced quickly over his shoulder. The other bargemen-turned-stretcher-bearers were watching apprehensively, mouths open.

"You stretcher-bearers will all start work when the real fighting begins," Ameye called to them. "It won't be much longer."

Nebi touched the white bands on his arms and helmet yet again to make sure they were secure. Sheb nudged him. In a low voice, so that the colonel could not hear, he said, "Sometime during the battle, I'll drive the chariot near Nimlot. With our insignia, no one will think we mean him harm. You can get him when he's not expecting it."

"What do you mean, 'get him'?" Nebi whispered back.

"I've taught you how to use a sword."

"We're medical workers!"

"We'll rip off our insignia at the last moment."

Nebi turned away from Sheb and leaned forward to watch the battle.

The Kushite drum erupted again, and soldiers in the semicircle jogged back to their places in the phalanxes. Nebi counted only 20 Kushites down, while casualties appeared to be in the hundreds among the Mesh. He and Sheb traded disbelieving looks.

In full formation, the Kushite phalanxes started marching forward, their front row a cutting edge of slanted spears. At the same time, a jangle and clatter broke out to their rear. All 500 Kushite chariots, immobile until now, rolled forward and lined up behind the phalanxes.

The Kushite army started shooting. Unlike the foot bowmen, who arched their shots blindly into the Mesh phalanxes, the charioteers were elevated and could see their targets well; they also had composite bows. They were therefore targeting individuals—mostly officers, distinguishable by their helmets' single plumes. The Mesh charioteers now began to do the same.

The distance between the two armies shrank to a hundred paces, then half that. The advancing Kushites were bringing up their knees waist-high, and all at precisely the same time. The Mesh walked forward out of step.

Ameye's order for the stretcher-bearers to move into the tumult had to come soon. Nebi's stomach muscles cramped, and he leaned forward to ease the pain.

"It's not only how soldiers fight that's important, it's also how they march," said the colonel. Nebi marveled that the officer could sound so detached as the battle heated up.

"Everyone out there—on both sides—is scared. The green recruits especially. But we trained each of ours to lock eyes with the man opposite him."

The Kushite marchers had started shouting a chant in time to their steps. Ameye had to cup his hand next to his mouth so that he could be heard in the chariot alongside his own. "We're trying to fool the Mesh into thinking that we're *not* scared. That we're in control. If we can do that, we've half won."

When only 30 paces separated the armies, the Kushites stopped. So did the chanting. The front-row spearmen dropped to one knee. The javelin throwers in the second row took a large step forward and flung their bronze-tipped missiles over the heads of their crouching comrades. Then they too dropped to one knee.

Now the javelineers in the third row hurled their missiles. As soon as the javelineers had stooped, the foot archers in the final row, now with a clear view, let their arrows fly.

With the *dalukas* throbbing so furiously, the cramps in Nebi's stomach eased. He could feel his heart beating in time with the pounding drum. It was as if his identity and the army's were now one, and fear was giving way to exhilaration.

The *dalukas* stopped, and the entire formation stood up. Nebi heard the hoarse cries of officers up and down the ranks. The javelineers unsheathed their swords. For just a moment, all was still in the Kushite phalanxes. The Mesh had so far been oddly passive, as if Purem's initiative had thrown them off guard. They dug in their heels and awaited the Kushite attack.

A bugle blared from near Purem's position behind the troops.

The front row of Kushites held their spears in a horizontal

position as the phalanx charged forward. The battle line picked up speed the last few strides and slammed with intimidating screams into the enemy at a full run.

A roaring wave of ax- and hatchet-wielders rushed in on the spearmen's heels. The world in front of Nebi became a frenzied blur.

Ameye said to Sheb, "Lieutenant, get ready."

Sheb turned around and shouted, "Pick up stretchers, men!"

Jo-at and Jo-am must have sensed the tension in their master's tone. They took small, nervous steps backward.

"Move your chariot to the far side of the field," the colonel commanded. "The others will take the nearer casualties."

Sheb turned to Nebi and said softly, "Good—Nimlot's on the far side."

"I don't like your idea," hissed Nebi.

Sheb ignored the rebuff. "Late in the battle, when there's chaos everywhere, you might get a chance."

Colonel Ameye said, "Now's the time, Lieutenant." Then, addressing Nebi for the first time, he added in a deadly serious tone, "Keep the prince safe."

"Let's start!" Sheb shouted over his shoulder.

Sheb snapped the reins and yelled, *"Jor! Jor!"*—Kushite for "go." Jo-am and Jo-at plodded forward hesitantly. "Come on, we have a job to do!" Sheb yelled. For the first time, he unhitched the rawhide whip the army had issued him and cracked it above the horses' heads. The chariot rattled down the rock-strewn slope, with the stretcher teams jogging behind.

As the chariot looped behind the Kushite forces, the air reverberated with cries, the clang of metal on metal, and the high-pitched whinnies of frenzied horses.

Sheb's plan was to find casualties at the edge of the raging battle mass. Nebi searched the air for incoming arrows. He raised his shield to be ready.

"Look!" yelled Sheb. "There's a fallen spearman!"

Before they could reach him, a sharp smack startled them. An arrow was sticking into the floor of the chariot, nearly striking Sheb's foot. Incensed, he glared at Nebi.

There was nothing Nebi could say. He hadn't seen it. Watching arrows sideways from the knoll, it had been easy to guess where they might land. But it was different now that they were coming toward him. They were almost invisible as they flew, mere specks. As for the slingers' stones, they were totally invisible and therefore useless to worry about.

The next arrow came from the left—the driver's side. This time Nebi lurched in front of Sheb to protect him. Nebi's shield, made of plaited twigs, was two-thirds as tall as he was, yet so light he could move it quickly. He braced himself as it absorbed the shock of the arrow.

When they reached the spearman Sheb had spotted, they saw that he was dead, an arrow buried in his chest up to its feathers.

Sheb drove up next to a writhing bowman. A javelin had pierced the man's shoulder. Both youths leapt from the chariot. The Kushite was grimacing so hard that Nebi could see his farthest back teeth.

"Cover me while I put him on the stretcher!" cried Sheb.

Nebi, shield ready in one hand and the other holding the reins to steady the horses, could hear the archer pleading, "Pull it out!"

"No—it will bleed more that way," Sheb told the man. "We'll let the doctors do it."

The memory of running with an arrow in his leg flooded

Nebi's mind. He knew the heavy javelin would be even more painful. In the jouncing chariot, it would tear the man's flesh. "Pull it out!" Nebi urged Sheb.

"You can't order an officer!"

"He's suffering!" cried Nebi.

Sheb seized the javelin with both hands and pulled. The barb-less missile came out easily, and he carried the gasping man into the cab and laid him on his back.

Nebi jumped back in the chariot and reached into his bag of bandages. Grabbing a thick pad, he crouched and used his palm to press the pad on the wound.

Sheb was already whipping the horses. "You're not covering me!" he cried.

Nebi stood up, flipped off his sandal, and molded his foot around the compress while raising the shield.

At the knoll, as orderlies assigned to the tents unloaded the archer, Sheb called to Colonel Ameye, "How's the battle, sir? We can't tell."

"We've split their nearest phalanx. The other phalanxes are holding, but maybe not for long."

Sheb and Nebi rushed back to the action. Much of the fighting was now hand to hand. Men screamed to intimidate as they confronted each other. Metal rang against metal. Cries rent the air when metal bit flesh. Cruising behind the fighting were chariots from both sides, their archers mercilessly targeting enemy soldiers.

The ambulance drove past sprawled, lifeless forms, looking for one with a chance of survival. They stopped upon hearing the moans of a slender Mesh with cinnamon hair, a youthful pimpled face. He had been hacked in the back, and even before Nebi could apply a compress, the blood on the chariot floor was so deep it came up over the sole of his remaining sandal. A bubble of blood remained on the soldier's lips as he died. He was so young he must have been a conscript. Nebi surprised himself by shoving the body out of the chariot to make room for someone else. Sentiment had no place here.

By the time they made their sixth trip back from the knoll, the sounds of battle were ebbing. The farthest Mesh phalanx had been cut to pieces. The center phalanx was all that remained. Only half its men were still standing, and they had closed ranks to maintain a tight rectangle.

Sheb stopped the chariot at a safe distance, then lifted a goatskin of water and drank for what seemed an eternity. Sweat running down his torso had saturated his blood-stained kilt. He passed the skin to Nebi.

"Look!" shouted Sheb before Nebi was done. He had a wild look as he pointed. "Nimlot and Tefnakht."

The two nobles were in chariots to the rear of the center phalanx. A cluster of Mesh chariots and cavalry protected them. The warrior next to Tefnakht had four arrows in his shield.

"At least they're not cowards," commented Sheb. "I thought they'd be safely up on the ridge."

Nimlot's helmet was askew, Nebi could see, and he had lost a plume. He seemed thicker and stronger than when Nebi had seen him in Thebes. Nimlot's eyes, always intense, had never looked more so. With a regular bow, he was shooting between the men guarding him.

By contrast, Tefnakht, 30 paces from Nimlot, was cold-eyed and still, his orange cape and his plumes still parade perfect. He held his metal shield alongside his jaw so that his orders would carry over the tumult. Senior officers would ride up to him, receive an instruction, ride off.

"Now's our chance," cried Sheb. "Nimlot's guarded—but I know how to get through."

"I'm not going."

"You are! Look! There's a cavalryman." A form was lying within 30 paces of the horsemen who surrounded Tefnakht and Nimlot.

Sheb snapped the reins. He circled cautiously around the back of the phalanx. The horses' conspicuous white mats and the youths' insignia were like charms: no one paid them heed.

The Mesh soldier's severed lower leg lay next to him. His eyes stared dully at the youths as they ran up to him.

Nebi kneeled in the puddle of blood next to the man.

"Look at Nimlot!" Sheb's voice was high-pitched with eagerness.

Nebi made himself concentrate on knotting the tourniquet first, and then looked. The count was so close they could see his bloodshot eyes. He was lowering his bow after shooting a Kushite horse in the chest. The horse fell on its side, and the chariot it had pulled overturned in a tumult of screams, flying bodies, and smashing wood. "If you had a bow, this would be a perfect chance. But you have this instead." The prince grabbed the fallen man's spear and thrust it into Nebi's hand. Nebi stared at him in disbelief.

Sheb glanced at the wounded man, then at Nebi. "You'll never have a better chance! I'll help put him over your shoulder. Carry him straight toward Nimlot. No one will harm you. Even if they don't see your insignia, they won't stop you. You'll be an Egyptian carrying an Egyptian!"

A nearby *daluka* added to the din of yells, moans, and whinnying. The drummer was banging away with all his might to encourage the Kushites.

"This man will die if I carry him like that!" Nebi yelled.

Sheb shouted in Nebi's ear: "Never mind him. You wanted this war. Kill Nimlot and you'll help win it! Khmun will surrender!"

That might be true. The besieged city would likely yield if its leader were dead.

"Help me get him up!" said Nebi.

Nebi crouched so that Sheb could hoist the wounded man onto his back, then strained to stand up. Sheb grabbed his upper arm and pulled him upright.

The prince smiled the smile of one who has won the argument. He clapped Nebi encouragingly on the back of the helmet. *"Jor!"* he yelled.

With one hand holding the man on his shoulder and the other clutching the spear, Nebi staggered forward.

# CHAPTER 21

# A CLASH OF WILLS

Nebi shifted the soldier on his back to get a better footing. To steady himself, he used the spear as a walking stick. An arrow whirred overhead.

He saw the warrior in Nimlot's chariot suddenly slump, an arrow in his back.

"Perfect—Nimlot's unguarded!" yelled Sheb from behind Nebi.

The feather on an arrow grazed Nebi's ear. "Cover me!" he hollered to make himself heard over the *daluka*.

Sheb raised the wicker shield over Nebi's head, then almost collided with him.

"Where are you going?" the prince shouted angrily. Nebi was not heading in the direction Sheb had intended.

Three more steps and Nebi reached the ambulance chariot.

He lowered his burden gently to the chariot floor.

Sheb ran up. "You fool" he cried. "You don't belong in our army!"

The tourniquet on the man's leg slipped off. Nebi gasped as warm blood from the stump spurted over him. He tied a new tourniquet around the fleshy thigh. Once the gushing had ceased, he turned to Sheb. "And you, you've disgraced this army!"

The prince's mouth dropped open. "I'm your officer!"

"Purem would demote you if he knew," Nebi said. His voice trembled. "His Majesty —" He shook his head. "His Majesty would see to it that you never became king."

Sheb flinched.

An arrow slammed into the side of the chariot.

"Hurry! Drive us out of here!" Nebi yelled.

"Don't give me orders," Sheb snarled. He lifted the wooden bow off the hook and grabbed three arrows. "I'm going after Tefnakht. One shot and this war is over. I'll make my uncle proud."

"You'll make him disgusted."

"I'll say I killed him in self-defense." Before springing off the chariot, Sheb leaned over and hissed in Nebi's ear, "And you'll back me up!"

The wounded man thrashed, and when Nebi looked up from tending him, Sheb was threading his way nimbly around bodies and carcasses, headed toward the cavalry that encircled Tefnakht and Nimlot. He still wore the medical insignia.

What sounded like a roar of triumph erupted from the direction of the main Kushite force. Nebi stood to see better. The Kushites had finally broken through the front ranks of the Mesh phalanx. Two gasping Mesh soldiers ran past the chariot. They'd abandoned their bulky shields to dash for the ridge. Moments later, more men followed. If many more Mesh fled, all would have to.

"Stop!" The command, uttered in Mesh, was distant but bellowed so loudly that Nebi could hear it above the turmoil. "Stop!"

Nebi saw Tefnakht 40 paces away, driving his orange chariot sideways against his panicked troops. In vain, he tried to make them turn and regroup. Nimlot was nearby, waving his arms as if to hold the runaways back. But it was too late to prevent the stampede.

Tefnakht turned his vehicle toward the hills. From the opposite direction, Purem shouted a hoarse command: "Seize

Tefnakht! Don't let Nimlot get away!" The general's voice became desperate. "Capture them!"

An arrow felled one of Tefnakht's horses. His chariot now useless, Tefnakht and his shield-bearer leapt off. Nimlot was in trouble too, Nebi saw. The count had removed the last plume from his helmet to make himself less recognizable. He was whipping his horses, struggling to make them turn his chariot toward the ridge, but the angle of the turn was too sharp. The chariot tilted and then fell on its side with a splintering crash and a horse's terrified scream. Nimlot sprang to the ground without falling, panic on his face.

If Sheb had been waiting for an opportunity to strike at his enemies, Nebi thought, this was the moment. Yet Sheb was nowhere to be seen.

Mesh soldiers on foot and in chariots kept streaming past the two leaders. Nimlot signaled to passing charioteers to take him aboard, but they were too intent on saving their own skins to stop. Finally, the Lord of Khmun crouched below the still-turning wheel of his overturned vehicle. He reached into his chariot for his wooden bow, and nocked an arrow. The next Mesh chariot to approach had only one man in it. Kneeling, Nimlot raised his bow. Nebi saw his hatchet-like profile perfectly as he took careful aim. From a distance of 15 paces, the arrow struck the Mesh charioteer in the throat.

Nimlot ran up to the weary horses and grabbed their harness, bringing them to a stop. He bounded into the chariot, pushing the dead man out. He was just starting to pick up speed when Tefnakht clambered aboard next to him. Nimlot scowled, then whipped the horses hard. The two allies sped uphill and disappeared over the ridge.

The battlefield cleared quickly of fugitives and pursuers. Now that the din of struggle had abated, Nebi could hear eerie moans and cries of the wounded and dying left behind.

Nebi felt torn. If he left the man he had rescued and the tourniquet came off again, the man would die of blood loss. But Sheb too might need help. Behind him, he heard the clatter of an approaching chariot. He turned and saw that it carried a single occupant, the bandaged colonel. He pulled up next to Nebi.

"Where's the prince?" Ameye demanded.

"He ran in that direction, sir," said Nebi. He gestured toward Tefnakht's abandoned vehicle.

The officer jumped off his chariot, his one eye wild with worry. He dashed on his stick-like legs, making a quick check of every horizontal brown-skinned body he passed.

Near Tefnakht's chariot, Nebi saw the colonel kneel to examine a crumpled form. He heaved it over his shoulder and struggled back toward Nebi.

# CHAPTER 22

# THE "HERO"

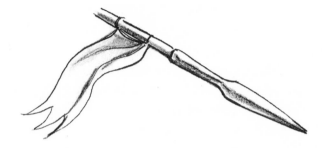

Colonel Ameye grabbed the chariot's whip and cracked it over Jo-am and Jo-at's heads. Nebi knelt on the lurching floor next to the two casualties, with one hand pressing the linen against the deep gash above Sheb's ear and with the other keeping the tourniquet firm on the one-legged man. When they reached the field hospital, bargemen carried the unconscious prince to one of the tents reserved for Kushites. They brought the other man to a tent for the Mesh.

Ameye and Nebi continued to shuttle between the battlefield and the tents. They once managed to cram three casualties aboard the chariot, soldiers from either side stacked atop each other. At one point the colonel asked, "Don't you ever get tired, Nebamon?" To be called by name was gratifying.

At dusk, after they had made more than 80 trips, the colonel left for an officers' meeting. Nebi drove Jo-at and Jo-am for the first time. Fortunately, the exhausted creatures were easy to handle. He guided them gingerly to the canal, unharnessed them and removed their protective mats, and let them wade.

He sat on the soft, grassy bank, put his head in his hands, and, closing his eyes, tried to find peace. This was impossible. Scenes of butchery that he had put out of his mind at the time now returned to haunt him. The hairy severed leg. The intestines that spilled from one torso. The mumbling, traumatized man who had stumbled weaponless across the battlefield.

Reopening his eyes, Nebi saw Jo-at and Jo-am in the water up to their haunches, drinking. He watched as they went into deeper water to let it rinse off sweat and grime. The awful day had not diminished their beauty: the brilliant and expressive eyes, the noble heads, the long and elegant necks that Piankhy had bred into them. Nebi had always admired the horses as speedy, stout-hearted engines of transport. He saw them now as loftier beings, embodiments of innocence and grace amid so much ugliness. Still, he knew the tears he felt welling up were not only because of the horses. He kept thinking of Sheb, with both anger and concern.

Finally he waded wearily into the canal. He scrubbed himself down, and washed as much blood from his kilt as he could.

Back at the field hospital, he saw Colonel Ameye crouching next to a figure at the far end of a tent that held 20 wounded men. Nebi shuddered as he made his way through the flies and the smell of filth and vomit.

He knelt next to the colonel. A bloodstained bandage was wrapped just above Sheb's glassy eyes. He looked away, as if in shame, when he saw Nebi.

Ameye made an effort to lift Sheb's spirits. "The lieutenant's a hero, Nebamon," he said, speaking softly so as not to disturb those resting nearby. "He told me how he left you and the safety of the chariot to retrieve a fallen Mesh senior officer."

"His action fills me with admiration," said Nebi, recovering quickly. He kept his tone neutral, so that only Sheb would sense the sarcasm.

"The lieutenant must have been struck from behind by an ax," the colonel speculated. "His helmet absorbed most of the blow. He risked his life in pursuit of *maat*, and Amon has spared him. I'll send a report up the line."

"The king will be so proud," said Nebi.

"*Your* performance was superb too," the colonel said. "I don't know how many men owe their lives to you." Then Ameye's expression changed. "I was just about to inform the lieutenant what the general told the senior officers. General Purem said we'd both won and lost today. We defeated Tefnakht handily, suffering relatively few casualties. But we failed in the most important task the king gave us—to remove the rebel leaders. We had them in our hands—not just Tefnakht but also Osorkon and young Nimlot. The war would be over if they had not gotten away."

Sheb shot Nebi a piercing look.

"What did General Purem say we would do now, sir?" said Nebi.

"The division will rest here tomorrow, then pursue Tefnakht into North Egypt. You and I will stay behind and work here in the field hospital. When the lieutenant gets better, he'll help. We have a lot of work to do. Three-quarters of the wounded are Mesh. Tefnakht's doctors fled when they saw we were going to win."

When Ameye had left, Nebi whispered, "You make me cringe."

"But you won't tell anyone what really happened?"

"No."

Sheb exhaled.

"But I'm not your accomplice. I'm a friend—and real friends speak their mind." He touched Sheb's shoulder. "Do you understand?"

Sullen, Sheb nodded.

"You think the war might have ended if we had killed Tefnakht and Nimlot. Think further about that. Many Mesh soldiers would have seen what happened. Word would now be spreading across North Egypt. People would be saying that the Kushites had sent assassins disguised as medical attendants. One was even the king's nephew—proof the king hatched the plot. So yes, the war might have been over, but can you imagine the resentment? Assyria would love that. Peace wouldn't last long."

"That's enough!"

"For you, this campaign is just a chance to dazzle people with your *kingly* behavior. If you thought of the campaign instead of your career, your career would take care of itself."

He couldn't tell if Sheb was listening. The prince had closed his eyes again.

Nebi stood up. "Rest well, hero."

CHAPTER 23

# STARTLING NEWS FROM NAPATA

The field hospital's chief doctor was the same bald, plump sunu who had treated Nebi at Thebes. Nebi took it as a compliment that the doctor did not recognize him at first—a sign of the height and weight he had gained. But the sunu was jovial no more. The work was too grim.

He gave Nebi many jobs. One was ordering medical supplies from the First Division at Khmun. Another was cutting out thick slices of flesh from horses killed in battle. The doctor showed him how to tie the slabs over human wounds to clot the blood. Then he directed Nebi to mix honey and olive oil and, once the bleeding had stopped, spread it over a soldier's wound to speed healing.

One of Nebi's assignments had at first filled him with apprehension. The wounded prisoners, said the doctor, were in low spirits. Doctors and nurses could discuss their treatments with injured Kushites and chat encouragingly with them to raise their spirits, but none of the medical people spoke Mesh. Nebi was afraid these men would see him as a traitor, but his fear proved groundless. Almost all resented their warlords. They were grateful to the Kushites for giving them good care.

It was on one such visit that Nebi met an 18-year-old conscript on crutches. The young man was from Kheny, a village so close to Damanhur that they shared a weekly market whose character was as much social as commercial. Nebi lost no time in asking him if he knew a Damanhur girl named Khuit.

"The mayor's daughter?" the conscript said, his eyes widening appreciatively. "I've seen her once or twice at the market. It's said her parents don't want her to become a peasant's wife, so she doesn't go to the market often."

"Then she's not yet married?"

"Oh, she might be by now. I haven't been home since I was drafted six months ago. I heard then that a rich widower from Sais was courting her."

NEWS OF ANOTHER KIND came, too. Messengers on horseback routinely stopped at Colonel Ameye's field hospital to change horses and eat a quick meal. The tough, intense riders carried letters between General Purem in North Egypt and King Piankhy in Napata by way of Prince Khaliut in Khmun. Five days after the battle, they brought news that General Purem had trounced the retreating enemy on the other side of the canal and had taken three fortified Mesh towns. Yet Tefnakht could not be found. He had fled farther north to regroup his forces in the Delta.

The messengers also said that Nimlot had slipped away in the other direction—back to Khmun. In the company of several hundred of his best soldiers, he had broken through the Kushite camp at night and re-entered his city. This was one more mark against Khaliut, Nebi knew. By returning to his city, Nimlot could rally his people and keep them from surrendering.

Two weeks later, a messenger arrived from Napata. He was carrying, among other things, two letters for Sheb. The prince had almost recovered by this time. He could walk about but had to avoid exertion. When the messenger brought his mail, Sheb was showing Nebi the technique for cleaning the insides of Jo-am's and Jo-at's hooves. As long as the talk was about horses, the two were able to get along.

Sheb examined the scrolls, both bearing royal seals. "One is from my uncle, one from my father," he said.

Having heard Sheb speak with disdain about Prince Shabako, Nebi assumed he would read that message second. But he ripped the seal vigorously, leaving King Piankhy's letter under his arm. Nebi went back to removing stones from hooves, glancing at Sheb out of the corner of his eye.

Upon finishing, Sheb said nothing for a while, holding the sheet with both hands and looking into the distance. "Here, since you're so curious," he said finally. He thrust the papyrus toward Nebi. "You know everything else about me."

Nebi accepted the scroll.

*Dear Son,* he read, *I have heard many things about you in recent weeks. You have not merely done well. You have done admirably.*

*You have done the humblest of jobs, working on a common barge and helping farmers enrich their fields—a gesture that shows we, unlike the enemy, respect the lives of ordinary people. You have also helped turn aside the Mesh attack on our army's most precious asset, its horses. But I am proudest of your work on the battlefield. You have striven to save the lives of friend and enemy alike. You have led by example. When people speak of valor in war, too often they think only of those who spill blood.*

*I praise Amon for such a son.*

Nebi handed the letter back without comment.

"I feel like a hypocrite," muttered Sheb.

Nebi did not reply. He moved Jo-am away and, as Sheb had showed him, began to check the horse's teeth for lampas and other inflammation.

He hadn't got far when Sheb came to him and held out the other scroll. "You might want to read this one too." Now he was repressing a smile. "Read right to the end."

Nebi unrolled the paper flat.

*Dear Nephew,*

*Your father and I have read with great interest the Second Division's report on your activities, and the pride that my brother feels is my own.*

*I want to tell you of a change in plans before you hear of it from your officers. We can remain in Napata no longer. We will join the campaign at Khmun and oversee this siege that so far has achieved nothing. We will take charge personally of the war.*

*I am grateful for your letter from Hensu, and I wish you a fast recovery. I am proud that the army promoted you early in the campaign to the rank of second lieutenant. You did not achieve this rank because you were the king's nephew. You earned it, just as General Purem informs me that you deserve now to be a first lieutenant.*

Here, Nebi bit his lip. Sheb's sham performance had produced another outrageous promotion.

He read on:

*I was also glad to hear from you that the young man from the Delta was instrumental in your exploit in the river skirmish and that he showed such loyalty to my principles at Hensu. The army has informed me of his brave and resolute work as a medical attendant after your injury. He has demonstrated that my trust and confidence in him were well placed. Like you, he has earned a ribbon of merit. So on this day, Nephew, I feel pride in you both.*

The letter ended with a short paragraph that Nebi had to read three times to make sure he understood it properly.

*General Purem has also written seeking my assent to a most unusual request. He would like to promote your assistant to the officer corps. Lieutenant Second Class Nebamon will become the youngest officer in my army.*

Nebi walked over to where Sheb was tending the horses.

"You wrote letters to both the king and the general," he said. It was not a question but a statement.

"I told you after the river fight that I'd make it up to you—Lieutenant. I simply told the truth, that the barge couldn't have been saved without you. They already know you're educated, loyal, unstoppable."

"I don't deserve this," Nebi said.

Sheb adopted a comically grave tone: "Are you officially doubting His Majesty's judgment? There is a penalty for that!"

Nebi felt light-headed. He was now a full-fledged member of the forces liberating his homeland.

"What's the pay?"

Sheb told him.

Nebi exhaled in a whistle. He wouldn't be able to compete with any rich widower from Sais. But his family would not be in rags. By the time the war was over, whenever that was, he'd have enough to rent decent quarters for his mother, and perhaps buy a cow and — he smiled — gifts for the twins.

Nebi then frowned as he thought of something. "Is this your way of bribing me to keep my mouth closed?"

"Of course," Sheb said. "But that doesn't mean you don't deserve this. Everyone thinks you do—Ameye, Purem, all of them. Do you know why? Because they say you're a good influence on me. My uncle was hoping for that."

"If only he knew," said Nebi, smiling weakly.

"If only he knew," said Sheb, laughing loudly.

# PART III

# CHAPTER 24

# THE TENT CITY AT KHMUN

"Well, well," gloated Sheb, halting the chariot when Khmun came into view in midafternoon. "It looks as though Khaliut's siege has achieved precisely nothing."

The lieutenants had traveled since dawn from the field hospital. In their packs were orders signed by General Purem transferring both of them to the siege.

Khmun's venerable limestone wall looked indomitable. The green and yellow striped pennants of Lord Nimlot's House of Khmun fluttered from every tower. Encircling the city, just out of the range of composite bows, were Kushite tents. This was the supposedly impenetrable ring that Nimlot and his men had burst through so easily.

Sheb said, "I can't think which is worse—failing to attack a city when you can't starve it, or letting its leader back in so he can stiffen resistance. I wonder what the king will say." He glanced at the river. "Look! He must be here already! There's my aunt's ship. My uncle must have borrowed it for the trip from Thebes." The yacht was big enough to seat 10 oarsmen on each side. Its gold trim glittered as the river current rocked it.

"This is going to be awkward," Sheb muttered.

"What will be?"

"My uncle's presence. As a horseman and hunter, he's without equal. But he knows nothing of military strategy. The real reason he stayed behind in Napata is that he didn't want to get in the generals' way. They're all veterans of wars with Assyria. Now a novice is going to tell them what to do?" He cocked a meaningful eyebrow. "It's going to be interesting."

They were greeted in camp by the sound of sword hilts and ax heads being used to hammer tent pegs into the ground. Five thousand troops of the new Third Division had disembarked with the king earlier that day. They joined the more than 6,500 battle-hardened men of General Purem's Second Division, who had arrived the day before, and the 5,000 members of Khaliut's First Division, who had started the siege.

The Second's headquarters was a long tent teeming with scribes and supply clerks. First Lieutenant Tebey issued Sheb and Nebi uniforms designating their new ranks and assigned to them a two-man tent. Then, checking a list, the little aristocrat told them both to attend a meeting of the High Command that afternoon.

"Me? Are you sure?" asked Nebi.

"All I know is that you're on the list—you're to take the notes." Tebey's snippy manner suggested he would have liked the honor for himself.

"His Majesty certainly does value records," Nebi remarked.

"Well, of course," said the supply officer in a condescending tone. "Records allow His Majesty to see long afterward who's been right, who's been wrong." He lowered his voice and added confidentially, "And there'll be some very wrong people today."

Sheb and Nebi set up the tent in the assigned spot and donned their crisp uniforms. Nebi was glad to say goodbye to the kilt the princess had given him, because it no longer fit.

"I want to look for an old friend," Nebi told Sheb as he ducked out. "I'll be back in time for the meeting."

Entering the Third Division's mushrooming tent city, Nebi needed directions. He accosted a soldier of about 20 with the unpolished look of a peasant draftee. The infantry-man dropped the sack on his shoulder in order to raise his arm in a salute.

It took a moment for Nebi to remember to return the salute. Then he said, "Excuse me, can you—" He stopped. He realized that his smiling courtesy was not officerlike. He cleared his throat and asked neutrally, "Where are the officers' tents?"

It didn't take long to find the person he was looking for. A strapping man with massive shoulders stood in a lane lined on either side by scores of two-man tents. His back was turned to Nebi as he gesticulated enthusiastically to three other officers. The storyteller's deep voice was famil-iar, but not its high-spirited tone. When the story was over, the listeners were laughing and the big man was bellowing in mirth.

Nebi tapped him on the arm and said in a grave tone, "So, Captain, when will we have that final, deciding game of senet?"

Wosmol turned to see who had asked this strange ques-tion. He looked in disbelief at the smiling Nebi, raised his face to the sky, and hooted.

"Fellows," said Wosmol, wrapping his arm around Nebi's shoulders, "let me present the second-best senet player who ever sailed the Nile."

"He must be talking about himself," Nebi told the officers. Everyone laughed.

"We'll see about that, Nebamon," said Wosmol.

"That's *Lieutenant* Nebamon to you." Nebi stepped backward so that Wosmol could take in his stripe.

"I must be dreaming," exclaimed Wosmol. "Whatever happened after I left you at the palace?"

They walked up the lane while Nebi told his story, then back again while Wosmol told his. The captain had resented the role the army assigned him in Napata, he explained. He'd had to stay in Kush and help train the Third. "I wanted to fight, not drill green recruits. But now I'll be able to show what I can do!" His eyes had their familiar droopy shape, but all melancholy in them had vanished.

The High Command's meeting took place on a low rise that overlooked more than a hundred vessels moored in the river. In the other direction were the ramparts of Nimlot's city, surrounded by a moat with a drawbridge. Sheb and Nebi stood a respectful distance from the others. There were 12— four from each division, including Purem and Ameye, who now wore a leather eye patch. As they awaited King Piankhy, all seemed anxious, General Lemersekeny in particular. He was narrow-shouldered with bags under his eyes and a bulging middle that was unusual for a military man.

A chariot rumbled toward them, bigger and higher than any chariot Nebi had seen. Three Kushite horses pulled it and there was room for six occupants, although at this moment it held just two. One was the king. His garb was imposing—a kilt made of black panther hide, a purple cloak, and a cobra crown. But it was his expression that seized attention. His tight mouth and narrowed eyes conveyed anger. The king's passenger was a man in his early twenties whose appearance matched Sheb's description of his cousin, Prince Khaliut. He was tall and blandly good-looking, although Nebi thought he had a weak chin and eyes a little too close to his nose. Right now he looked as tense as Lemersekeny.

As the chariot came to a halt, Khaliut jumped down and joined the others. Like them, he removed his plumed helmet and sank to one knee. When Nebi had first met Piankhy in the stable at Napata, he had been struck by the king's light regard for ceremony. But Piankhy now kept everyone kneeling. Finally he said gruffly, "Rise."

The king gave no look of recognition to anyone—not to his old friend General Purem, not even to the nephew he loved. He wasted no time on greetings.

"Why, General Lemersekeny, have you been unable to capture this city?"

Nebi, in his role as official scribe of the meeting, had his pen poised to jot down the response, but none came. Lines of strain deepened on Lemersekeny's face.

"Why, General, can't you take Khmun?" the king repeated. "You have been here five solid months."

"Your Majesty, no one can capture Khmun by assault. It is best to keep waiting until the food runs out." The general smiled weakly. "Khmun's walls are said to be stronger than Hensu's. Tefnakht—with more men than I—could hardly put a dent in those." Khmun's walls, he went on to say, were six paces thick, ten paces high. Nebi scribbled down the figures.

Lemersekeny explained that he had rolled siege towers close to the moat so attackers could assault the walls. "But the defenders used flaming arrows to destroy them," he said. "We built bridges across the moat for our battering rams, but they dropped boulders the size of chariot wheels onto them."

"Why, then, do you not build an earth wall almost as

high as Khmun's wall? Our men could be safe behind it and shower the city with arrows and stones. Why?"

"Commander Khaliut and I discussed that, Highest Majesty. But the earth wall would have to be very close to the city for it to be of use. As they built the wall, men would be within range of the defenders' bows. It would be suicide. Such a plan cannot work."

"Cannot. Cannot," mimicked the king. He leaned down and glared into his general's anxious eyes. "With Amon's help, we *can* do anything!"

One of the horses whinnied restlessly. Piankhy turned and affectionately slapped its haunch. Then he faced the group again. "And we must take this city quickly," he said. His voice had become strained. "Consider these facts. Almost every able-bodied man of Kush is now in the army. Three months remain before the flood, and our draftees and militia must be home soon after to plow, sow, and rebuild the irrigation channels the flood will have ruined. Without them, parts of Kush could suffer famine."

He let the words sink in, then said: "And that is only one problem. Tefnakht has blockaded the river just below the Delta—no Kushite trading vessel carrying gold or anything else can reach the sea. Without foreign commerce, we cannot pay for the war.

"So, we have hardly any time to take Khmun, then travel north—which could take a week—and engage Tefnakht. Knowing he has only to wait for the flood to force us to leave, he will not want to fight us."

The officers shifted their feet uneasily. Khaliut, hands behind his back, studied the ground in front of him. His father had spared him the treatment given to Lemersekeny, but responsibility for the delay was also his.

Piankhy continued, "How, then, will we take Khmun quickly?" He looked at the military professionals for suggestions.

Lemersekeny said eagerly: "Now that all three divisions are here, Highest Majesty, we can stage a massive assault."

"It would work, Your Majesty," General Purem concurred.

"Yes, it would," said Piankhy. "But we would take heavy casualties. Thousands."

"There is no other way, Your Majesty," ventured Purem.

"Oh, but there is," said Piankhy.

Nebi caught several officers exchanging discreet glances.

The king allowed himself the barest hint of a smile. "Last night, aboard ship, we received a marvelous dream. The dream showed us how to do it."

Everyone drew a breath. Here was hope. Dreams were important in revealing divine truths.

Piankhy was king because the gods had chosen him. Now they had sent him a message.

# CHAPTER 25

# THE CROCODILE'S MESSAGE

Pensive, the king glanced over his shoulder at the Nile for a moment and then began. "We dreamed," he said, "that as our ship arrived at Khmun, a crocodile was swimming alongside. He climbed out of the river and made his way toward the city. He said that if we followed him, we would conquer it.

"Upon awakening, we understood the meaning. The crocodile floats in the water like a ship and comes up on land." He pointed to the river. "Look at our ships and their ships. We will bring them on land. We will turn the empty hulls on their sides with their bottoms facing the city. In this way they will serve as giant shields. Behind them, our men will be able to build the earth wall."

The officers' brows were furrowed. They had not understood.

Piankhy explained. "To make it easier to move the hulls, our carpenters will build huge sleds on which the hulls will rest. Under the sleds, logs can be rolled to act as wheels. Our men will roll the ships toward the city. When they get within arrow range, they can use the ships as screens, pushing and pulling on the protected side. Then our shovel crews, safe behind the hulls, about thirty paces from the moat, will build the embankments."

Piankhy himself asked the obvious question. "Will the defenders be able to burn our ships as they burned our towers? No. The ships have been in the river for years. Their wood has absorbed much water and at first should be able to resist fire. If they dry out, we will replace them with other ships."

"Excellent, Your Majesty," said Lemersekeny in relief. "My men will start work in the morning."

"No," said Piankhy. "They will start work now. There is still time before sundown. We thank you for your services, General Lemersekeny. You may return to Napata."

The general's lips twitched. He bowed stiffly. His career was over.

"General Purem will execute the plan," the king continued without pausing. "We will work day and night, General, in three shifts. The First Division has watched the grass grow, but from now on it will work all night. Your battle-weary Second merits the coolest daylight shift, starting at dawn. The members of the Third who arrived with me today need seasoning, so they will work the hot shift.

"At the close of this meeting, each division will send its carpenters to meet with our senior engineer, Colonel Ameye, and his assistant, Lieutenant Shebitku. The lieutenant has used hoists and winches in building the new stable in Napata, and this experience will be useful in tipping the hulls. They will report to you, General Purem. Their team will be in charge of technical aspects and designing the embankment. You will bring these plans to us for approval."

"Yes, Your Majesty," said General Purem. His respectful

tone could not conceal his disappointment. He was now on the receiving end of orders. The campaign was no longer *his*.

"By nightfall," said the king.

General Purem took a short breath. "Yes, Your Majesty," he said.

"You will replace General Lemersekeny with someone of your choosing," the king went on. "To build this wall, you will require a thousand shovels. Your First Division will start fashioning them tonight. They will make the handles from sturdy branches. For the flat part of the shovel, they will have to use wood from the planks of ships. Start by cutting up Khmun's ships."

Piankhy paused. "Questions? No? Very well. After breakfast tomorrow, we expect the first ship to be out of the water."

On the way back to their tent, Sheb asked Nebi, "Did you see Khaliut's face when the king gave me my job as Ameye's assistant? He looked as though he'd been stabbed in the heart. He's out of the running for the succession, and he knows it. I have only one rival now—my father."

The camp was alive all night with the sound of saws, axes, and hammers.

At dawn, the king emerged from his tent wrapped in his purple cloak against the chilly air. He indicated satisfaction with what he inspected, and then said, "We will meet at once with the troops of all divisions. And bring to me the soldiers who have been awarded promotions for their performance so far."

The gathering took place along the riverbank. On the gentle rise overlooking the water, troops lined up in formation. Piankhy stood at water's edge. Near him, 200 decorated soldiers stood at attention, among them Sheb and Nebi.

Piankhy's deep voice carried far. "To help haul the first ship is an honor," he declared. "All those who have received ribbons will step forward." The men did so. Piankhy nodded to Purem, who directed their actions.

First the men took hold of thick ropes. With all 200 of them straining, they pulled a cargo ship that had been emptied and stripped of its mast. They dragged it from the river until its bow rested on a sled that had been rolled to the shore.

It was hard getting traction in the soft mud. At Ameye's command, some men pulled the ropes while others pushed upon the side of the hull. Palm logs lay in front of the sled, and the men struggled to maneuver the vessel up this impromptu ramp. But nothing happened. The men paused, panting, to catch their breath. The rest of the troops shouted encouragement. Nebi closed his eyes as he pushed. A few in the crowd began chanting the oarsmen's slow-beat song. Soon all were chanting, and loudly.

Slowly, the hull began to inch up the hill. As soon as it had passed over a log, men at the rear would pick the log up and lug it to the front so the ship could pass over it again.

As he strained, Nebi caught glimpses of Khmun's ramparts. They were packed with soldiers and civilians staring at what must be a baffling spectacle.

As the men parked the ship near the wall, burning arrows from the ramparts peppered the hull's other side—an exercise in futility. The water-soaked wood did not even smolder. Nebi could see Kushite soldiers already running toward the ship, wicker shields in one hand, shovels in the other. And in the direction of the river, another ship was making its way toward him. Others would follow all day.

Nebi smiled. Nimlot must be watching with alarm.

THE KING'S PLAN had energized everyone, but no one more than Colonel Ameye. Working by the river under his watchful eye, 20 carpenters took just one day to build a tower out of the ships' wet wood. After the structure was hauled opposite Khmun's gate, where the embankment was extra-high, 20 archers on the top level could look down on the ramparts. Tubs of water were at the ready to put out fires.

Sheb and Nebi saw little of this construction. Ameye had sent convoys of carts off in every direction to find ammunition, and the lieutenants led one such convoy. They were to bring back stones of two sizes: some the size of hen's eggs that would be perfect for slings, and others as big as cantaloupes. No one in the convoy knew what the latter were for: they were too big to fit in a sling and too heavy for a man to throw far.

When Sheb and Nebi returned heavily laden at the end of the day, the offensive had just started. Behind the embankment were hundreds of men. Each man clutched two pieces of twine, at the end of which was a net pouch filled with a stone. He would whirl the sling overhand, release one piece of twine, and send the stone invisibly fast into the city, about twice as far as an arrow from a regular bow could travel. Each soldier could hold stones in his other hand and feed the sling continuously, shooting every few seconds. Nebi heard an almost steady tock-tock-tock from inside the city as the stones ricocheted on streets and buildings.

Through slits in the tower's wall, archers were shooting downward onto the rampart around the gate. Meanwhile, standing on the ground behind the embankment, 40 of the strongest men from all three divisions, including Wosmol, were putting to work the larger stones the convoys had gathered. The men grasped staves that Ameye had had made from the crossbars of Khmun's ships. Each stave was slightly taller than a man, and attached to the top of each was a pouch holding one of the melon-sized rocks. The men would use both hands to swing the lever overhead and send the projectile against the wall. This throwing was hard on inexperienced men's shoulders and upper arms, and Ameye had divided the operation into short shifts so that no soldier threw more than a dozen before being relieved.

The strategy was clear: Piankhy wanted to strip the defenders of all protection on the rampart by knocking down the battlement, that low wall atop the wall which kept them from falling off and which blocked projectiles. By the end of that first day, the rocks had already pitted the limestone battlement.

As the embankment grew in length, the slingers grew in number. Unlike the hailstorm of small stones, which ended at night when people were in their homes, the barrage of the big projectiles was constant and become more intense as the men's muscles grew used to the activity.

At the end of a third day of stone fetching, Nebi climbed the tower to see the action up close. Here and there, parts of the battlement had been completely leveled— but not enough yet to warrant an attack. Archers were continually alert for defenders trying to repair the battlement. Others with composite bows trained their eyes on distant parts of the city, searching for men foolish enough to be in the streets.

Nebi watched the stave-slingers at work below. Rocks pounded either the battlement or the drawbridge itself, battering but not breaking its stout beams, while others arced high into the darkening sky, coming down on flat roofs of nearby houses. Repeated hits could cause a cave-in.

"Do we even know what we're destroying, sir?" asked Nebi.

The hawk-nosed officer shook his head. "No, but I know what we're *not* hitting," he said. "One is the Temple of Thoth—it's in that direction." He pointed. "For the king, it's untouchable." The temple, one of Egypt's largest, was the home of the god of wisdom. "The other forbidden target is the count's stable in the southwest corner. If you'd ever seen the horses his father bred, you'd know why."

As the colonel finished speaking, there was a distant, high-pitched wailing.

"That sounds like children," said Nebi uneasily.

"Can't be helped," said Ameye. He looked coldly at Nebi's shaken expression. "I don't like it either. But this is war, Lieutenant. Harden yourself." It was the first time the colonel had spoken sharply to him, and the words stung.

On the fifth day of the barrage, a putrid odor greeted Sheb and Nebi when they returned from the ridge with another load of rocks.

"Rotting flesh," Ameye said when Nebi asked. "We've blocked their access to the burial ground outside the city. I tell my slinger crews, 'Just think of it as the smell of inevitable victory.' "

In their tent that night, Nebi told Sheb, "The king said in Napata that he wanted us to do what was right. Killing innocent civilians isn't right. It's revolting."

"It's necessary," said Sheb. "It's also kinder than an assault. Storming the city would cause many more deaths, not only on our side but on theirs. And I wager we won't have to attack. Nimlot faces a revolt from his people if this continues, and he's got a gate he can hardly defend."

He was right. The next day, Piankhy sent an ultimatum

to Nimlot: surrender today or face an immediate assault. At noon, there was great commotion in the camp.

The king's crocodile had shown the way. Khmun lowered its drawbridge.

# CHAPTER 26

# DAY OF SURRENDER

A pudgy man in a multicolored tunic was the first to cross the drawbridge. Then came a hollow-cheeked soldier holding an upright spear; the helmet perched atop it signaled a desire to talk. Finally came four other haggard soldiers, weaponless, hauling two small but heavily loaded carts. Excited Kushite troops lined both sides of the way. Colonel Ameye and other senior officers yelled to a few of the men to cease their taunting and show respect.

Nebi and Sheb joined Ameye. If Nimlot yields, Nebi asked, what would become of him? The colonel shrugged. "No vassal has ever betrayed Kush, so there's no precedent. But everywhere else, it's punishable by death—with the Assyrians, by slow death."

Ameye left to walk quickly toward the royal tent, where the Lord of Khmun was headed, and Sheb followed. "Come!" he said, glancing at the leather case on Nebi's hip. "You have your scribe's kit. My uncle will want you there."

The royal tent could have held a hundred people, but just a dozen were present, those who had been at the earlier meeting with Piankhy. The level of comfort astonished Nebi. Poles rising from a rich maroon carpet held up the white linen ceiling. Strategically placed openings ensured steady air currents, making the interior cooler than outside. The light that came through the linen ceiling was mellow.

King Piankhy sat on a portable but imposing ebony throne. Each of its front legs was carved like a panther, with its head at seat level and its paws on the floor. Behind

Piankhy hung a linen sheet with two flaps; servants came and went through one of them, and the other presumably led to the monarch's private quarters.

Piankhy nodded to the guards at the entrance, and the pudgy man entered. The king's eyes were as hard as iron as the emissary threw himself on the carpet before the king, arms flung to either side in the traditional posture of submission.

"To your knees," said Piankhy harshly.

The man took a deep breath. "Most Worshipful Monarch, Lord of Crowns, Beloved of Amon, Lord of Kush and South Egypt, I am Ramose, mayor of Khmun. His Grace, Lord Nimlot, has sent me. I ask you two things. First," he said with an unctuous smile, "I ask you to accept our riches as homage. The carts that I have brought contain chests of gold, precious stones, and gold-covered clothing."

"And your second request?" said Piankhy.

"I ask for your mercy."

"We give you our contempt. While your people starve, your bulging girth declares that you eat."

"A famished leader cannot lead, Your Majesty."

"A person who takes for himself food from the mouths of his people does not deserve to lead. Tell Lord Nimlot this, Mayor: he is our vassal, not you, and we will discuss his fate, your fate, and the fate of Khmun with him alone."

"Yes, Gracious Majesty."

"Now a question for you, Mayor: what has happened to Khmun's prize horses—Gray Wind and Spear?"

Ramose appeared ill at ease. "They—they were killed in the battle of Hensu."

The king grimaced.

"Go," he said abruptly. "And bury your dead outside the city. Now."

WHEN THE DRAWBRIDGE came down again that afternoon, an angular figure crossed. Nebi's pulse raced when he saw him. The Count of Khmun's swagger was as distinctive as his hatchet nose. His once-narrow face had—like the rest of him—filled out. Chin high, he proudly wore a gold headband with a green and a yellow feather. A sword hung at his side, its sheath made of gold and sparkling with gems. Three of his officers, unarmed, followed at a respectful distance.

His eyes riveted on Nimlot, Nebi felt a surge of power, the pleasure of mastery. That Nimlot looked strong and imposing made Nebi feel even more so.

"Feeling triumphant?" Sheb asked Nebi with a smile, as they stood watching in front of the tent with the other officers.

With a touch of smugness, Nebi replied, "Doubly so."

Sheb said nothing, plainly mulling over the remark. Finally he said, "Is the second triumph a victory over me? That you were right in rejecting my advice?"

Nebi gave a slight shrug. There would be no point rubbing it in. The two entered the tent with the others to await Nimlot's entrance.

The count paused at the tent door. On the other occasions Nebi had seen him, his own stress had been intense. Now, hands on hips and almost giddy, he could study Nimlot at leisure. The count had started to grow a goatee like Tefnakht's. His brown eyes were even more penetrating than Nebi remembered. They swept the interior, pausing briefly on Sheb and on Khaliut. The count gave no sign of recognizing the young tan-skinned officer.

"Son of Kaemweset, step forward," Piankhy commanded. There was no triumph in his voice, only sadness. His reference to his friend, Nimlot's father, told why. The late count would have despaired to see what his son had become in the six years since his death.

Nimlot unbuckled the sword belt and held it horizontally in his two hands. Swirls of precious stones encrusted the golden sheath. The sword was plainly for ceremony, a symbol of rule. It must have been in Nimlot's family for generations. He took several steps forward and kneeled before Piankhy. Then, as a gesture of surrender, he dropped the sword belt in front of him. It landed with a rattle. Nimlot looked neither sorry nor respectful as he flattened himself on the carpet.

Piankhy did not command him to rise. Instead, he said, "Speak."

Nimlot raised his head so that his goatee rested on the carpet. He said in a low, resentful mumble, "Forgive me, Mighty King. Forgive me for all my disloyalty. Spare me."

"We cannot hear you," said Piankhy. "Repeat."

In a louder voice, Nimlot's resentment was more apparent.

Piankhy frowned. "Forgive you? Forgive a vassal who breaks his bond of loyalty to his king? Would your own father forgive a leader who put his personal welfare ahead of that of his people? Your appearance testifies that you, unlike your subjects, have eaten well. Now, on your knees." As Nimlot raised his upper body, Piankhy demanded, "Why should we not execute you?"

"I am like a servant to you," said Nimlot. "I will pay you all the taxes that I as your vassal should have paid long ago."

"That's the least he could say," Sheb said in a hushed tone to Nebi. "He's certainly not groveling."

The king waved his hand dismissively. "We have no need for you to *give* us treasure. We can *take* all that we desire from your palace and your city and province." He sighed. "But what strikes us most is that you want your own life spared. You say nothing about how you want your subjects treated. Your mistakes have made them suffer."

Nimlot had his hands behind his back, and Nebi could see that—despite his lofty, confident air—his fingers were writhing with stress.

"Lord of Khmun," said Piankhy, "remove your head-dress. Commander Khaliut, take it."

The prince took a long step forward and grasped the leather-lined gold band in both hands, then stepped back. The loss of headpiece signified loss of title, and all the property and wealth that went with it. Nimlot could not have been surprised. Standing rigid and expressionless, he tried hard not to show his feelings. Nebi saw him blanch and swallow hard. Nebi smiled coldly. Nimlot was now on the same level of society as he.

"Now," said Piankhy, "what do we do with this wretch?"

Nimlot did not hold Piankhy's stare as a guard fitted him with ankle bracelets. He glanced angrily at the stern faces of the dozen officers who stood near the throne.

"You show no remorse," said the king. "Explain to us, son of Kaemweset, how you can slay defenseless people and betray your lord—and yet feel nothing."

Chin up, Nimlot said, "I feel pride in having joined Lord Tefnakht."

"Pride! Explain this."

"With or without Tefnakht, Assyria decided to conquer Egypt. If, without Egyptian allies, the empire were to invade Egypt, the result would be massive destruction and carnage. Far better that Egyptians, including the Mesh, take the land and rule it for them."

"So you see yourself as a patriot—a protector of Egypt's interests?"

"Yes! And if you Kushites had not tried to prevent us, there would be less loss of life. I have looked out for the welfare of my people. You—you have starved them and smashed their bones and homes."

"A fine speech, Nimlot," said Piankhy. "But you omit what would happen to Egypt if Assyria were to control it. The emperor would sack temples and cities, make taxes unbearable, and kill or exile dissidents. In every place that the empire has conquered—Syria, Israel, Phoenicia, Arabia—life has become intolerable. You also overlook Tefnakht's other option. He could have summoned help from me. If the Two Lands and Kush stand together, we can repel the empire."

Nimlot said nothing.

"And why murder Setka and his party?"

"It was a political act. We had to keep him from alerting you." He added with a shrug, "We could allow no witnesses."

"It would seem that you took some relish in it."

"The little servant must have told you that, but he lies. Silencing those people filled me with pain."

The king glanced at Nebi with a weary smile. Then, addressing the prisoner, he said, "We need to think more about your sentence. Before nightfall you will show us your palace." Turning to two guards, he said, "Take him away." The guards gripped Nimlot's arms and led him toward the exit.

"I knew it!" whispered Sheb. "In Napata, my uncle always likes to brood before sentencing."

"It's all right," Nebi said, as if trying to convince himself. "The longer he waits, the longer Nimlot sweats."

The deposed count was almost at the tent's exit when

the king called to the guards to halt. "The mayor says that Gray Wind and Spear died at Hensu. Are their offspring well?"

"They too died at Hensu," said Nimlot.

Piankhy shook his head in dismay.

After the prisoner's departure, Piankhy turned to face Purem. "General, the physical condition and morale of our men are good, are they not?"

"They are, Your Majesty. Their morale today has never been higher."

"Good. Now that the siege is over, we must show respect for Khmun's god. We will make large sacrifices to Thoth— oxen, Shorthorn cows, fowl. Our army should still have a good number of each. After the sacrifices, have our cooks prepare a festive dinner for thousands."

"Gladly, Your Majesty. Our troops deserve to celebrate their victory here."

Piankhy smiled. "The feast will not be for our men, General. It will be for the people and soldiers of Khmun."

Purem was speechless.

"Commander Khaliut," said Piankhy, "you will be in charge of the city and province of Khmun for the rest of the war."

The weak-chinned prince looked pleased and relieved, Nebi thought. He would get another chance to show his ability.

General Purem had regained his composure. In a deferential tone, he said, "Your Majesty, if we lose the war, it will be largely because the people of Khmun have held out for so long. I am not suggesting that we loot the city, as Assyria would do in our place, but should we be rewarding them?"

"They have suffered enough," Piankhy replied. "The war is not their doing. Generosity is the best thing not only for them but for us. If we give them cause to hate us, they will someday rebel. Peace requires *maat*."

Skepticism furrowed Purem's brow.

"And here is something else," said the king. "Word will spread to North Egypt of what has befallen Khmun. North Egypt's cities will know the terrible price of holding out against us. And they will also learn of the fine treatment they will receive if they surrender. When cities hear this, they will yield."

"*Maat* as an offensive strategy?" said Purem doubtfully.

"That is an interesting way to put it," said the king.

Before he adjourned the meeting, Piankhy issued an invitation to all present. "Once the feast is under way, Nimlot will show us his palace. Those of you who wish to come may do so."

"I'm going!" Nebi told Sheb as they left the tent. "It's my chance to come face to face with Nimlot. I'd like to see his expression when he finds out what's happened to me."

# CHAPTER 27

# NIMLOT'S SECRET

As Sheb and Nebi hastened toward Khmun's palace later that day, they passed the famished crowd in front of one of Egypt's biggest temples. The smell of roast meat had replaced that of death. The rich smoke rose, mystically nourishing Thoth. Only after the god had been duly honored would the people eat.

The lieutenants were already late for the start of the palace visit, but Nebi nonetheless could not help stopping when he saw Captain Wosmol, at the far end of the temple's square, supervising the Kushite cooks. Despite the humdrum assignment, the captain wore a broad smile. No wonder— Nebi had heard that the king had ordered Wosmol's Third Division to join the Second, heading north in two days. The two divisions had a crucial assignment: they were to hunt down Tefnakht.

When they arrived at the palace, Nebi and Sheb took the front steps two at a time, exchanged salutes with the Kushite guards, and entered the vast entrance hall.

They hustled along echoing corridors until they heard voices and the sound of a chain dragging on marble. King Piankhy, General Purem, and Prince Khaliut were proceeding down a hallway next to Nimlot—in ankle chains so heavy he could only shuffle—and another man. The latter, a pale and portly Mesh, turned out to be the palace's long-time chief steward.

As the party made its tortoise-like way past one room after another, the deposed count, in a flat voice, would announce the function of each—this room for small parties, that one for banquets—and the chief steward would chime in with further details. Just as Nebi was finding the tour dragging on interminably, an incident occurred that would eventually change his life.

All the talk had been in Egyptian, the common language of all those present. Sheb, unlike Nebi, was near the front of the group and walking next to the chief steward. From behind, Nebi paid little notice when he saw Nimlot saying something to his former senior staffer, but no sooner was the remark made than Sheb stopped abruptly. Turning to his uncle, he said, "Nimlot just spoke to this man in Mesh. He must have assumed I didn't know the language. He said, 'If anybody asks to see the stable, tell them there is a deadly *tamadunt* there.' " He beckoned Nebi forward. "What does *tamadunt* mean?"

"Disease."

The king scowled as he absorbed this information. Nimlot did not even try to conceal his emotions. His lips trembled. He raised his eyes to the ceiling.

Glaring at him, the king said, "Your father was Egypt's finest horse breeder. His stallions, Gray Wind and Spear, were once the talk of Thebes. Show us the stable."

They descended a floor before coming to a door at the end of a corridor. The chief steward pulled it open. The stench of decay, excrement, and death filled Nebi's nostrils. A narrow stone stairway led into the putrid darkness.

"I will stay here," said Khaliut faintly.

Nebi followed behind the others, feeling the cool, moldy stone wall with his fingers to keep from falling. The stink grew more repellent. His eyes had adjusted to the darkness by the time he reached the bottom, and he could make out indistinct forms on the stable floor that were moving slightly. They looked too ghostly to be real animals.

Piankhy was up ahead. With the heel of his hand, he pounded in vain on a small shuttered window. Swearing, he drew his sword and smashed the shutter with the hilt. A feeble shaft of late afternoon light slanted through the cobwebs.

In the gloom, they could make out three horses lying on their sides. The animals were still. The brown head of one was facing them, and as they watched, a rat scurried over its forehead. The horse's gentle eyes did not blink.

Purem had made his way to the back of the stable. "Four here are still alive!" he called back. Moments later he added, "And two colts!"

Piankhy was on his way to join him when he spotted another form and squatted beside it. His voice was shaking with anger as he caressed the dead animal's forehead. "By his markings I know this horse. It is Gray Wind." He looked at the body of another dead horse in the next stall. "And that is Spear." There was enough light for Nebi to see that tears filled the king's eyes. "One of the finest of all horses is now food for maggots."

The king abruptly rose and strode across the stable's center aisle toward three foals that no one else had spotted. These baby horses too were lying motionless on the floor. Piankhy crouched and looked at them closely. Two were lifeless. The gentleness with which he regarded the horses jarred with the bitter tone of his command: "Nimlot, come here!"

Nimlot bent to lift his chains from the manure, then shuffled forward.

Piankhy gestured toward the foal whose brown eyes still showed life. "Who are her parents?" he demanded.

"Her grandparents were Gray Wind and Flying Rose. Her father was Akenesh."

"Akenesh!"

"My best riding horse," said Nimlot.

"I once saw Akenesh race," the king recalled wistfully. "Never have I seen a light horse with such speed or endurance. Before your father died, he had planned to present him to me as tribute. There could have been no greater show of loyalty. I would have started to build a cavalry by breeding him."

"Akenesh had a sordid end," Nimlot said indignantly. "The day a thief stole him is the day my troubles began." He spat on the floor. "Little bastard!"

The king registered grim amusement. "Ha! He's no longer so little," he said. "Lieutenant!"

Nebi stepped forward. The moment had come at last. "So I'm a thief, am I?" They were the first words he had ever spoken directly to his enemy. Nimlot took in Nebi's uniform, the thin red stripe, the sturdy physique—and then his eyes. They were burning with such contempt that Nimlot could not hold Nebi's stare.

"You!" Nimlot whispered.

Nebi hissed, "I'll see you stew in the eternal Lake of Fire." He was so close now that he could have spat in Nimlot's contorted face.

Nimlot drew back his right fist to strike his tormentor, but Piankhy stepped in to wrap a hand around his forearm.

"Enough!" the king commanded. He glanced again at the young horse, and the pain returned to his eyes. He gripped his captive's tunic with his two hands and brought his face close to Nimlot's. "I swear, as Amon loves me, what I see here saddens me more than any of your other evil acts.

Your granaries are a quarter full and have more than enough oats for your stable. You and your friends have lived well while your people have had little, and your own horses have had nothing."

Nimlot had reverted to his sullen, impassive look.

Piankhy shook him. "Do you know what horses are? They are heaven's gift to us, creatures who remind us of the world's beauty and nobility. Or do words like that only make you smirk?" The king shook his head in disgust. "General," he said, "see that Khaliut locks him in a cell until I return from North Egypt."

Nimlot took a step toward Nebi, so that they were nose to nose. His voice quivering, he said, "I will get my freedom back, and when I do I will find you."

"Excellent," said Nebi. "That would save me the trouble of finding you."

# CHAPTER 28

# LITTLE DAMANHUR

That night, Sheb and Nebi led half a platoon, bearing torches, to the stable. The men opened all the windows for air, then hauled the dead horses outside the city and, to prevent disease, burned them. Mucking out the stable, Nebi's task, took hundreds of buckets of water. Sheb saw to the feeding and watering of the survivors, making sure they did not get too much at once. The horses were far too weak to take outside; some were too weak to stand. The soldiers laid down fresh straw to provide comfort and keep the dampness from rotting hooves. They plugged the ratholes.

After midnight, Nebi alone remained. He closed the shutters to keep out the cool night air and placed blankets over each patient. He sat in the hay beside the one surviving foal, brown with a white star on her brow. The sweet smell of fresh alfalfa, heaped near each horse, filled the air. He held out a handful, and her nostrils quivered, as if savoring the fragrance. He spoke reassuringly to her as he stroked her scrawny ribs and flicked away the flies.

Looking down into her long-lashed dark eyes, he said, "You know, we have a lot in common. We both owe our lives to your father's stamina. That's what carried me most of the way to Thebes. And that's what has kept you alive so far.

"Come on," he encouraged her. "If I could survive Nimlot, you can too." He lifted her head so that she could drink from a gourd. Water dribbled down her chin and onto his leg. She gave little snorts when it got in her nose.

Nebi heard the door atop the stairs creak open. A flickering oil lamp descended. When he saw the king, his shoulders tensed. The first time he had met Piankhy, in the stable in Napata, the king had been genial and good-natured. Since then, Nebi had seen different sides of him. In his send-off speech to the troops, Piankhy had shown his official side, formal and moral. In Khmun, he had been angry and intimidating. The way he had shamed General Lemersekeny in front of others had been chilling.

"So, have you found a name for her?" the king asked.

Piankhy seemed relaxed, and Nebi relaxed too. The name came to him in that instant. "Damanhur—the name of my village, Your Majesty."

Piankhy crouched over the horse. He caressed her cheek. "What will you do if your village itself becomes free?"

"I want to give my mother, sister, and brother a home again." He hesitated, wondering what the king would think. "I'll be a farmer."

"Not finish your studies as a scribe?"

"Maybe someday. But I've seen too much destruction. Now I want to see life actually grow. Shebitku doesn't think much of this idea." He smiled apologetically, thinking Piankhy might share that view.

Piankhy returned the smile. "Shebitku thinks ambition is all about gold and glory. He has not seen yet that it can be about being useful—whether it is defending one's homeland, teaching people to do right, or raising children well." He shrugged. "In any case, I am pleased you taught him some Mesh. It has already paid off—it enabled us to find the horses. Look at this little one. Despite starvation, her tendons are like iron, her chest broad and deep." He looked Nebi in the eye. "You *do* understand why these horses are important?"

"Their offspring will be racers?"

Piankhy chuckled. "Well, perhaps. But their bloodline's main value will be for protecting your homeland. The Kushite and Egyptian cavalries are both weak. Someday, Assyria may invade and Egypt must be ready. Gray Wind and Spear's descendants are too small for chariots, but they are superior to anything the empire has for a mounted corps. I suppose that is why Nimlot lied about them. When we besieged the city, he wanted to make sure they would die before we could get to them—but he couldn't bring himself to kill them outright."

His eye fell on the arrowhead, and he frowned. Nebi remembered having mentioned its origin that morning on the roof in Napata.

"You still think of Nimlot a great deal," he said.

Nebi nodded tensely.

The king looked closely at Nebi. "I too have reason to hate certain people. But I've found that when I hate someone, he controls me—he dominates my thoughts. To find real freedom, you can't hate. Nimlot is our prisoner now. Try not to let yourself be his."

The king rose from his crouch. Sensing a return to formality, Nebi also stood.

"As you know, Lieutenant, I'm leaving with the Second and Third Divisions in two days. We're heading north for the rest of the war. General Purem has already informed Colonel Ameye and Lieutenant Shebitku that they will stay behind. The army has few men who can design buildings, and the lieutenant will work with the First Division in drawing up plans for new houses.

"You will stay here as well," the king went on. "The older horses we've rescued will never themselves be fit for cavalry, but they can breed. You'll be in charge of bringing them back to health. The little one, too."

Nebi's mouth fell open.

"I've resisted the temptation to ship the animals to Napata. They belong here in Egypt. To regain its greatness, Egypt must learn self-defense. Horse breeding is part of it. Your job is very important. You will have two grooms under your command. You will also have Shebitku to advise you. I've taught him all I know."

"Yes, Your Majesty." His head was ringing with astonishment.

"One last thing. It will take us a long time to get to the Delta. There might be battles to be fought along the way. But I will summon you to be with the troops before they get to ... to —"

"To Damanhur, Your Majesty?"

"Yes."

FOLLOWING SHEB'S DIRECTIONS, Nebi put the mature horses on a diet of kidney beans and chicken eggs mixed with wheat and barley. He learned to cook linseed with the younger horses' oats; some days he cooked them maize. After a week, all the horses were well enough to take outside. In the pasture, Little Damanhur chased dragonflies and pestered the older horses. One morning, her exuberance made Nebi laugh out loud: startled by the sudden rush of wings as a group of white egrets rose in flight, she pranced back, ears all erect, then bolted after them so fast she almost caught up. "She has her father's spark and mettle," he proudly told Sheb.

As for the mature horses, Sheb predicted it would take a year and a half before they'd be back to their old selves. "But," he said, "I wager some of the mares will soon be pregnant."

More encouraging still was the war news. Supply vessels shuttling between Thebes and the forces in North Egypt stopped overnight at Khmun and brought reports of successes in the north. The first city the army had come to over the border was called Per-Sekhemkheperre. Its ramparts bristled with defenders, but King Piankhy had sent an unarmed soldier to the gate with a message saying that, unless the city surrendered, he would assault it. If the city did yield, however, he would guarantee that no one would be hurt. The city opened its gates.

The next report came several days later. The army had left the main canal and turned eastward onto a network of huge irrigation canals just wide enough for the ships, though not with their oars. Instead, horses harnessed to thick ropes walked along the shore to pull the vessels. Piankhy had advanced until he reached the stronghold of Medum. There, he announced the same terms of surrender. Again, the gates swung open.

A week later, news came that the fleet had reached the city of Ithtowe, with the same outcome. Three cities. Three victories. And not one death or injury on either side.

Sheb told Nebi, "I know what you're thinking—that my uncle was right, that generosity is a great offensive tactic. But the next city is Memphis. We may still look like fools."

That night Nebi dreamed of a reunion with his family. He had reclaimed the old house and planted a leafy almond tree in the courtyard, and the twins were playing in its shade. It was such a happy dream that he was sorry to wake up.

He expected news any day about a victory in the north that would allow him to go home. But he was dreadfully wrong.

CHAPTER 29

# THE DEFIANT CITY

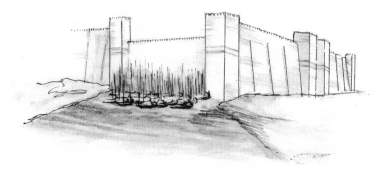

Memphis refused to surrender. The third week after King Piankhy's departure, a ship arrived at Khmun with a highest-priority message. It read: "All available officers to proceed at once to Memphis. Maximum forces needed for assault on the city."

Both Nebi and Sheb qualified as "available." The horses in Nebi's care were strong enough to be left with the grooms. And Sheb had completed the designs for most of the buildings assigned to him. As a parting treat for Little Damanhur, Nebi just had time to run to a deserted field to fetch her an armful of tasty purple lupins. He admired her as she trotted toward him in the pasture. She had powerful shoulders, a refined head, and wide-open, expressive eyes full of trust.

At dawn, Sheb and Nebi were aboard a ship with 20 other officers, including Colonel Ameye. The lieutenants were excited. Memphis was all that stood between the Kushite troops and the Delta, a day's march beyond. If the biggest city in the Two Lands fell, the troops could amble into the Delta and corner the last remaining warlords.

And, Nebi kept thinking, he would then be able to search for his family. With his earnings as a junior officer, he might be able to acquire land and livestock. Eventually, if Khuit had not married, he'd be able to start courting. The twinkle in his eyes must have given him away.

"This girl who's forgotten who you are and already has babies," teased Sheb as they stashed their bedrolls and tent aboard the vessel, "what does she look like?"

Nebi smiled. "I'm not making this up—she has one eyebrow."

"What!"

"It goes from atop one eye to the other. In the middle it's just thinner. It's nice. It calls attention to her eyes. They're huge."

After two days, the ship turned west off the river and up a wide canal that ended after a quarter mile at a harbor below Memphis's eastern fortifications. Famed for their colossal height, these walls had been made even taller in anticipation of the siege. Hundreds of cargo ships, passenger galleys, and fishing boats—a forest of masts—were moored in the harbor while their owners were safe inside the wall.

The Kushite camp was just northeast of the city, also along the canal. The king had sent all the horses to rest elsewhere for the duration of the siege; his forces here now consisted of 12,000 soldiers and support staff. As they arrived, the lieutenants wrinkled their noses, for the stench of sewage hung over the stagnant canal.

The pessimism that the lieutenants found at the Kushite camp shocked them. Soldiers tramped about the dusty encampment with long faces. On their way to Second Division headquarters, Nebi and Sheb passed through the Third Division's tent city, where Nebi spotted a familiar figure.

"There's my old bodyguard, Captain Wosmol. He'll tell us what's going on."

After introducing the big man to Sheb, Nebi pumped him for news.

"It's all bad," Wosmol said. His down-turned eyes had lost their recent liveliness. He jerked his head toward the canal. "You wouldn't have noticed it, but the waters have already started rising. The flood will be a few days early."

Swelled by summer rains in eastern Africa's highlands, the waters would surround the city within a week or two, and would not return to normal for two months. The land occupied by the Kushite camp was still dry, but the Memphites knew they had only to wait until the flood drove away the besiegers.

The Kushites, Wosmol said, had planned a desperate assault on the city. But 200 Mesh riders had countered with a midnight strike on the Kushite camp two nights before. They had targeted not soldiers but carpenters, engineers, and other specialized workers. The horsemen hurled torches into the tents where the men slept, then hacked them down as they fled. Now there were too few skilled people to construct more towers, battering rams, and other siege equipment.

"The peasants who enter the camp to sell us food must have told them which tents belonged to the workers," Wosmol explained. "The High Command says the attack was so ingenious that Tefnakht himself must have planned it. That means he can't be far away. Half our soldiers are out hunting for him in all directions. If we catch him, we could still win the war. The warlord alliance would collapse without him."

Nebi felt as if the wind had been knocked out of him. Defeat seemed so close. "We could come back next year," he said weakly.

"The cost of mobilizing the army again would be ruinous," Sheb said.

"And Tefnakht would have had a year to strengthen his defenses," added Wosmol. "The Assyrians might even be here by then. No—either we find Tefnakht in the next few days or we lose."

Lieutenant Tebey was on duty when Sheb and Nebi checked in at division headquarters.

"It's about time you got here," Sheb's diminutive cousin said irritably. "General Purem needs both of you badly. Report to him as soon as you've pitched your tent. You're the only ones who understand Mesh. He needs you to question the locals on what they might know about Tefnakht's whereabouts."

The lieutenants spent the rest of the day visiting outlying villages and questioning peasants. But they learned nothing of value.

Conditions at the camp were terrible. The drinking water was foul and flies were everywhere. By his second day there, Nebi lay curled up in the tent between frequent trips to the latrine, hoping his mild dysentery would not worsen. A quarter of the men in camp were in the same shape. Feeling as weak as a baby, he dreamed that he was in Damanhur and that his mother was urgently shaking his shoulder to awaken him. But it was Sheb.

"We need you to translate!"

"*You* translate," Nebi croaked.

"I can't understand everything. A blind peasant came into camp. He wants permission to enter the city. No one can do that without Piankhy's personal approval. We can use that as leverage for information about Tefnakht. He might know something. Come."

"I'm sick."

"Do you want to win this war or not?"

Weak and shivering slightly, Nebi dragged himself behind Sheb to where the man was waiting, Kushite guards at his side. The urchin who had led the blind man into the camp had long since left. As many Mesh farmers did to protect their pale skin from the sun from head to toe, the peasant wore a white burnoose, a flowing cloak of linen with a hood. The hood fell over his face as far as his nose.

"You are in front of a lieutenant from the Delta," said Sheb, making introductions in Mesh.

The man went to his knees. "Gracious officers—help me!" he cried in the familiar staccato accent of the Delta. "Your army is the savior of my people," the man continued. "Nobody welcomes it more than me. Because of my resistance to his tyranny, the wicked Tefnakht has ruined my life." He pointed to his face. "He has gouged out my eyes." He raised his hand toward the hood. "Let me show you."

"No!" said Sheb with a shudder.

The peasant went on to describe how Tefnakht's persecution of farmers had become worse than ever. "Now," he said, "I plead for your help, sirs. My little child is in Memphis and gravely ill. If he is to live, I must bring him this bottle of medicine." He fingered a little bottle of blue glass. "But your soldiers who encircle the city will not let me enter. Please, you Kushites who have been so merciful to the defenders of Khmun, have mercy upon my son!"

Sheb had learned Mesh well. He needed to ask Nebi the meaning of just two words—"persecution" and "medicine." The senior lieutenant then asked the peasant in Mesh: "Do you know where Tefnakht is?"

"Yes," said the man. "That king of the robbers is said to be nearing the city. It is said he wants to get inside."

"From which direction would he be coming?"

"North."

"Good," said Sheb. "I'll report all this to the king and see if he will let you go in." He took Nebi aside and said, "I'll recommend that the king make an exception for him."

"Are you sure? His story sounds too perfect."

"Well, look who's being stiff-backed," said Sheb good-naturedly. "I thought you were the *maat* enthusiast!"

Nebi skittered to the latrine, clutching his belly, and then returned miserably to his tent.

A flourish of bugles accompanied by drums woke him at the end of the afternoon. Puzzled, he sat up at once, wondering if this was some sort of new signal. His insides felt better and his limbs stronger. The joyful sound came from the direction of the city, and curious soldiers were heading briskly in that direction. Nebi followed.

As he approached, he saw two buglers and three drummers where the troops could best hear them, atop the near corner of the eastern wall. The wall there was lower than the walls on the other three sides because the harbor was directly below; it served as a spacious moat and made high fortifications unnecessary. A thousand Kushite soldiers stood just outside arrow range, staring at the musicians and asking themselves the reason for the impromptu concert. Even the king and his generals had come, staying at the back of the pack.

As Nebi made his way to the front of the crowd, the music stopped. A familiar figure in a white burnoose then appeared, the hood still far down over his face. The peasant felt his way gingerly behind the rampart, hands pawing the air. With his fingers, he found a place to climb, and as he mounted the battlement, some soldiers gasped. The sightless man seemed about to fall into the harbor. His outstretched arms were making frantic circles as if he was losing his balance.

Nebi would never forget what happened next. With a roaring laugh, the man lifted the burnoose up over his head and threw it off. Nebi recognized a jutting jaw, now shaved clean, and elaborately braided cornrows. Then, with an exaggerated motion, he placed his hand above his eyes, as if shielding them from the sun, and peered over the soldiers gathered below. He wanted to show that his eyes were fine.

He cupped his hands around his mouth and cried in elegant Egyptian, "I am Lord Tefnakht." A light breeze from the west carried his voice. "The fool who calls himself your king has graciously permitted me to enter the city. Your last hope is gone. Never can you capture me now!"

He laughed even louder, the musicians joining in. "So go back to Kush—and spare your king more ridicule!" he cried. He uncorked the little blue bottle, emptying it with a single swig.

"I drink to your pleasant journey home!"

# CHAPTER 30

# SHAME

As Tefnakht jumped jauntily from the parapet and disappeared, Nebi turned and tried to see Piankhy's reaction. He glimpsed the king's back through the crowd. He was hastening away with Purem, head bowed as if in shame.

Nebi looked away. It hurt to see the king so humiliated —and, worse, before his own men. One reason Piankhy had fired General Lemersekeny was for letting Nimlot back into his city. Now, he himself had permitted the ringleader to do the same.

And poor Sheb! He must be despairing. The king's error had been to follow his recommendation.

But Nebi's deepest grief was for his homeland and family. The war seemed unwinnable now.

That evening, Nebi's sandals squished on a low-lying path which only that morning had been dusty. The rising water already had made it muddy. He paused when he overheard soldiers around a campfire speaking in a bitter tone. As he stood in the darkness, he recognized all of them as Second Division sergeants, experienced fighting men.

The loudest voice belonged to a burly man. "The king has been too merciful all along. Now we're paying for it."

"You're right," said a lean soldier, nursing a jar of beer. "I can see why the king treated Khmun to a feast and why he didn't haul Nimlot's neck to the chopping block. He had to persuade other cities to give up. But now he's gone too far. We're losing the war because he felt sorry for that *poor peasant*." He said the last two words sarcastically. Others joined in, and their judgment was unanimous: the army needed to play by the same rules as the enemy, and Piankhy was a fool not to know it.

Nebi did not see Sheb at the mess tent. A while later, as he was about to crawl into his bedroll, one of the king's guards arrived to say that His Majesty was summoning the two lieutenants to his tent for a strategy meeting. Nebi was the first officer to arrive. As he was ushered in, he recognized the red rug on which Nimlot had humbled himself in front of his victor. Now, dark zones showed where the rising waters were starting to soak through. It was hard to believe how sharply the army's fortunes had changed.

The king held a goblet as he stared at a large papyrus sheet pinned to the tent wall. It contained diagrams of the city's fortifications. Numbers had been scrawled over many different parts of the defenses, indicating their height.

"Shebitku cannot come?" the king asked softly when he saw Nebi. He seemed to have aged since the stable in Khmun. The gray above his ears had crept upward and his forehead had deeper lines, yet his eyes, while grave, showed none of the anguish that Nebi had anticipated.

"I have not seen him since this afternoon."

"I'm not surprised. He lacks maturity. When a man makes a mistake, he does not hide."

A guard interrupted to announce the arrival of the senior officers, and the king returned to formality. He stowed the goblet in a cabinet, removed the papyrus from the tent wall, and seated himself on the same throne he had used at Khmun. The carved panthers that had before looked so fierce now seemed merely pretentious to Nebi.

Piankhy opened the meeting by asking General Purem to review the situation. The husky general stood to one side of the king, his shoulders sagging. "Our estimate is that 8,000 soldiers—well armed—are inside the city. We believe they have enough grain, cattle, and other food stocks to last anywhere from one to two years. That's their situation.

"Ours is this." He sighed. "The waters have already reached the low areas of the bank. Within a week they will be higher than this tent."

"Review our options, General," Piankhy said briskly.

"We have three," said Purem. "First, we can mount a desperation assault at once. But we have only our two good towers.

"Our second option is to continue the siege. When the waters are high enough, we could surround the city with enough shallow-bottomed ships to keep the siege going. But we'd need to send many of our soldiers home. When the waters subside, we'd be hard pressed to keep Memphis's soldiers from beating us back.

"Our last option," he concluded grimly, "is retreat."

Nebi glanced often at Piankhy during this review. The king appeared to be familiar with all that his top general was saying.

Piankhy looked at his officers. "What is your advice, gentlemen?"

The men debated the options briefly. Only one of the three, they concurred, made sense: withdrawal.

"We agree, then," said the king. "We will pack tomorrow and leave the following morning." He said it as serenely as if he were deciding on a matter of housekeeping.

Nebi could not believe what he was hearing. Everything had been in vain—his work with Setka, his mission to Napata, and all the lives lost on both sides. Apophis, the snake-god of chaos and evil, had won.

WHEN NEBI wandered back to his tent, he could dimly make out Sheb fumbling about in the darkness, grabbing clothing and stuffing it into a pack.

"What's happening?" Nebi asked with alarm.

"Can't you see? I'm going."

"Where?"

"I haven't decided. What's happening in camp?"

"It'll be announced in the morning—we're retreating. We have no other choice."

"As I imagined." Sheb's shoulders sagged. His sigh was almost a groan. "I lost the war, Nebi. Prince Perfect lost the last chance we had of winning."

True, but there was no sense in agreeing. "Tefnakht is a master of slyness," said Nebi. "There's no disgrace in his tricking you, Sheb."

"Yes, there is. You sensed something was wrong. Not me." He pushed a towel angrily into the pack. "I even dragged you to meet Tefnakht. Now that he's seen you, it will never be safe for you to go back to the Delta. I've been down by the river thinking it all out." His voice broke. "I've been a fool in so many ways."

"You'll be a bigger fool if you leave."

"No. If we're retreating, that means Tefnakht will lift his blockade of the river. I'll be able to go to some port on the Delta and take a ship to Gaza or Byblos."

"Sheb, right now, you're the only person who's ashamed of yourself. If you desert, I'll be ashamed of you. So will everybody."

"Aren't they already?"

"No. I haven't told anyone what happened. Only the king knows. He told me a man doesn't hide when he makes a mistake."

The prince sighed, then closed the pack and tied the knot. "I'm leaving."

"Desertion is punishable by death," Nebi protested.

"Only if they catch you." Sheb disappeared into the night.

CHAPTER 31

# RETREAT

In the morning, General Purem mobilized the camp to prepare the retreat. Nebi's orders were to report for scribal work on the waterfront. Muddy-footed troops were lined up there, in front of ships tied up along the canal. The men carried every kind of article—cooking pots, folded tents, coils of rope, beams of the dismantled towers. Before each loader crossed the gangplank, Nebi and another scribe would count every object and jot it down.

Captain Wosmol oversaw four platoons of these loaders. When he came over to say hello, his eyes were bloodshot and he had the surly look of a hangover.

Nebi forgot his own despondency for a moment and tried to cheer him up. "You'll see your wife and son soon."

Wosmol allowed himself a thin smile. "How about you?"

"I'm looking forward to one thing: Piankhy will sentence Nimlot on his way home."

"You want vengeance?"

"I passed up a chance at Hensu to kill him. I've been waiting for the king to pass his judgment."

"That's the best thing," said Wosmol. "But after the sentencing, what will you do?"

Nebi sighed. "I can't go home." North Egypt and soon South Egypt would be under Assyria's thumb. His voice broke. "I don't know what I'll do."

At that moment, the arrival of the irritating Lieutenant Tebey distracted him from his misery. In a high voice, Tebey relayed to Wosmol new orders from the High Command.

Tebey's eyes were level with Wosmol's chest as he said that, after the loading was done, the captain's platoons were to take dinghies onto the canal and attach towlines between the army's ships and the Memphite vessels—cargo ships and the larger fishing barks and ferries—anchored in the harbor.

Wosmol's jaw dropped. "Towlines?" he said. "Why do we need them?"

"For towing, of course," said Tebey pompously.

Wosmol glared. "But why?"

"We're taking those ships back with us," said Tebey archly.

Wosmol waited until Tebey was out of earshot, then erupted. "That won't punish Tefnakht. It will punish the boat owners. We've no quarrel with them."

Nebi shook his head in disbelief. "The king warned us in Napata against looting. Now look what he's doing himself!"

"He's betraying *maat*. Amon will punish him."

By midafternoon, the last of Memphis's ships had been gathered, poised for the trip south. All that remained was the assigning of men to ships for the return voyage. Nebi didn't see his name on any of the posted lists. He went to Lieutenant Tebey, who shuffled through his papers. The lieutenant's eyes widened.

"General Purem, Colonel Ameye, Lieutenant Shebitku, and *you* are to travel on the king's own ship," he reported.

"Oh no!" Nebi blurted.

"What!" huffed Tebey. "The former servant is invited to travel on the fanciest ship afloat and he's still not happy?"

Nebi sighed and said nothing. When the king didn't see Sheb, he would surely ask where his nephew was. The last thing Nebi wanted was to be the one to break the news that could bring the royal family dishonor and scandal.

Lugging his gear, Nebi trudged dejectedly toward the royal flagship. He glanced up and down its polished cedar deck, but he hardly noticed the splendor. He saw the angular figure of Colonel Ameye at the stern, chatting with the skipper in the shade of a gold-encrusted canopy. The steward said King Piankhy and General Purem were conferring inside the deckhouse. Covered with a pattern of ivory and lapis lazuli, it appeared to be about 20 times the size of the cabin on the ship that had carried Nebi to Napata.

Nebi went to the deserted bow, scanning the dreary landscape of flood and dikes. "Sheb," he said through clenched teeth, "where are you? Don't be an idiot."

The sound of distant jeering came from Memphis. Thousands of people were crowding the wall that faced the harbor, shouting and making obscene gestures as the first Kushite troopship lifted anchor, pulling a local trading vessel toward the center of the broad canal. It was the flagship's role to lead the fleet, and the troopship waited for it to go ahead.

The flagship's skipper cried out orders, as 20 oarsmen took their places in the pit. Riggers climbed the mast, poised to unfurl the sail.

"Wait—we've got to wait. We're missing one passenger," Nebi told the skipper in desperation.

The skipper looked vexed. "His Majesty's orders were to leave as soon as other ships were ready, and I'm not about to interrupt his meeting." He eyed the deckhouse warily.

"But it's Prince Shebitku—we can't leave him behind!"

The skipper shook his head in annoyance. "I'll wait just a bit," he said.

After four more Kushite ships rowed into the canal, the skipper could wait no longer. Two crew members hustled to the shore and untied the flagship.

The ship had already pushed off when Nebi caught sight of a broad-shouldered figure in the distance. He was carrying a bulky satchel and sprinting awkwardly along the top of a dike toward the canal.

Nebi hurried to the skipper and pointed. "Our passenger!"

On the skipper's order, the oarsmen paused their stroke, their raised oars dripping, while the helmsman edged the great vessel near the bank. Sheb waded through the water that overflowed the bank until he was waist deep. Then he hurled his bundle, which landed on the deck with the clatter that a sword would make, and began swimming through the stinking water to the ship. He grabbed the rope Nebi had dropped for him and hoisted himself up on deck.

Sheb sat on the deck, panting, arms around his knees— plainly as embarrassed as he was exhausted. When he had his breath back, he looked up. "Don't ask me anything!" his expression seemed to say.

The rowers dipped their oars. The great purple-trimmed sail came down. As the people on the ramparts saw the king's ship departing, they chanted goodbye, blew sarcastic kisses, and waved handkerchiefs. Their musicians played a jubilant serenade.

Sheb stared at the deckhouse in anguish, as if knowing all too well that its walls could never keep the sound of disgrace from reaching his uncle's ears. He put his head in his hands. As the mockery reached a crescendo, he covered his ears. Nebi sat down beside him. There was nothing to say.

# CHAPTER 32

# A DESPERATE PLAN

The helmsman muscled the tiller sharply to one side, and the flagship turned to leave the canal and join the Nile. The river was twice as wide as when they'd last seen it, and it would get wider still as the waters rose. They were sailing against the current now. The skipper stood at the tip of the bow, signaling to the helmsman how to steer clear of uprooted trees that the floodwater carried toward them.

The water here was clean at least, and Sheb poured a bucket of it over his head, washing off the sewage. As if he were purifying himself, he did so again and again, rubbing his scalp and his skin until Nebi feared they would become raw.

General Purem emerged from the deckhouse. He spoke briefly to Colonel Ameye and then headed for Sheb and Nebi. "His Majesty wishes your presence," he said, and returned to the deckhouse with a light step.

Nebi and Sheb exchanged startled looks. Purem had been smiling.

The deckhouse had two rooms: one, a bedroom to which the door was shut, and the other, the chamber they entered now. The low sun's mellow light made the mahogany walls rich and warm.

At the sight of the king, seated behind a desk, the three visitors sank their knees into the thick multicolored carpet. "Be seated," said Piankhy, indicating the cushions behind them.

"The war," the king said, "is not *quite* over." He folded his hands in front of him. "For security reasons, we have waited to reveal the plan until we were all under sail. General Purem has just heard it, and he has been helping this afternoon to refine it." Purem, standing behind and to one side of the king, nodded approvingly.

"Colonel Ameye, you have been invited because the plan depends on engineering skill. With the lieutenants' help, you must make certain modifications on the ships we have seized—or, rather, borrowed."

Sheb's face glowed with cautious hope. Maybe the war he had helped to lose was not lost after all.

"Now," said Piankhy, "I will tell you how our men will reach the ramparts." He opened a scroll and smoothed it across the desk. It had the same diagrams that Nebi had seen in the king's tent.

Step one of the plan, Piankhy had told them, was to prevent any suspicion by Tefnakht that something was afoot. The Mesh leader, as a prudent commander, would send monitors to keep an eye on the retreating fleet's movements. Upon learning that it had stopped, spies would try to ferret out what tricks were in store.

That night, all men were ordered to stay aboard their ships when the fleet halted for the night. There was nothing suspicious about that: floodwaters made camping on shore impossible. As darkness fell, Nebi went by dinghy to a troopship anchored nearby. Concealed inside his bedroll were an ax and a crowbar. He handed the skipper a scroll on which General Purem had dictated a brief message. Nebi read the message aloud to the wide-eyed skipper in a corner of the deck where no one else could hear.

"This is the strangest command I've ever received," said the skipper, shaking his head.

At midnight, while men slept on deck, Nebi crept past

the soldiers on watch and made his way quietly into the dark hold of the troopship. He lit an oil lamp and unrolled his blanket. Using his ax blade like a knife, he dug into the hull quietly, so that the guards would not hear. He made a hole the size of an orange. Perfect. Water gushed in.

Nebi returned to the deck and dozed in his bedroll until a guard sounded the alarm. The ship's crew jammed a rolled-up tent into the hole in the hull as a temporary measure until daybreak. The morning light revealed the troopship lying low in the water, tilted slightly to one side. Nebi looked over at the nearby flagship and saw that it too was listing. Sheb—still aboard—had done his job. Anyone watching from shore might assume that, during the night, the two vessels had collided.

Other ships towed the disabled pair to a field that was not yet flooded. Soon the area was teeming not only with workers repairing the damage but also with curious out-siders, mostly people from nearby villages. It was only a matter of time, Nebi knew, before spies would arrive to mingle with them.

It took two days to bail water and fix the hulls. Ameye made a convincing display of impatience as, hands on hips, he stepped about the work site on his birdlike legs. In fact, delay was what he wanted. The waters of the Nile kept rising but were not expected to reach maximum height for another three or four days.

Piankhy kept out of sight. The first day, Purem let it be known that the king was ill with fever. The squalid condi-tions in the encampment outside Memphis made this all too plausible. Word was put out that, because of the repairs needed on the flagship, the king had been transferred to the ship General Purem had used on the northward voyage; that much was true. On the second day, the generals planted rumors that the disease—the plague, no less—was spreading to other ships and that the fleet's journey would be delayed until the sickness could be brought under control. Tefnakht would understand why the army wanted to prevent bringing an epidemic to Khmun, Thebes, and Napata.

The crew on Purem's original ship had been dispersed to other vessels. The only people now aboard it were the king and the four officers who had been aboard the flagship, including Nebi and Sheb. The morning after the "accident," the four met with the king inside the spacious cabin that Purem had ceded to His Majesty.

"Now is the crucial phase," said Piankhy. "The colonel here will be in charge. He'll need carpenters, at least a dozen. Finding them may not be easy—so many were killed or injured."

Nebi winced at the memory. Kayse and the older of the carpenters, Tawaki, had been among those killed in the enemy's raid on the Kushite camp.

"How many are still with us?" asked the king.

"Only four, Majesty," said Purem.

The king grimaced. "We need at least eight more men who are handy with tools and with ropes, who know something about knots."

"Five men helped me build the tower at Khmun," said Ameye. "They'd do."

Piankhy nodded. "Good. We need three more."

Purem knew of two.

"Now we need just one," said the king. There was a long silence.

Nebi broke it. "Your Majesty, I know a former army rigger and carpenter who's with the Third Division—Captain Wosmol."

Purem whistled. "A rigger who worked his way to captain!"

"Find the twelve men and bring them here without telling them why," Piankhy ordered Sheb and Nebi. "And have them bring their tools."

Once the 12 carpenters were on the deck of General Purem's ship, Sheb ushered them into the cabin. Nebi closed the door behind them. Colonel Ameye looked at each of the men as they entered, nodding approvingly.

"Only we in this room will be privy to this plan," the colonel began. "We can't tell who will be watching from shore, or who among our troops might trade information for gold. This is a plan to win the war, to save Egypt, to protect our homeland.

"As you came aboard this ship, you might have noticed that all the vessels we towed from Memphis are clustered just to our starboard." He nodded to the small window on the right side of the cabin. "They are in midriver, distant from the rest of the fleet. Your job will be to work on them. There are fifty ships, big and small. But they have one thing in common— high masts."

All the carpenters save one looked puzzled. The exception was Wosmol. He stood at the back of the group, a head taller than anyone else. At the word "masts," Nebi saw his old friend's weary eyes come alive.

"In three days, perhaps four," the colonel continued, "the flood should crest. When that happens, Amon willing, we will be at Memphis, and we will, shall I say, return these vessels." He allowed himself a mischievous smile.

"You will remember that one of Memphis's four walled sides is lower than the others—the eastern wall, facing the harbor." The colonel paused and the men nodded. "The peak flood level will bring the top of these vessels' masts even with the ramparts. Your job is to modify the masts so that our men will be able to climb them at top speed and storm the wall."

The carpenters worked until after sundown, then slept on the vessels where they were working. When Nebi, Sheb, and Ameye rowed to them at dawn to bring breakfast, the men were already at work. Wosmol had them organized. They were making ladders from pieces of the siege towers, and had finished that by the end of the morning.

"The next step," said Ameye, "is to build platforms atop the masts. These platforms will be like crow's nests on sea-going ships, only they'll have to be bigger—big enough for two soldiers to stand on after they've climbed the ladder."

The men finished the platforms that night by moonlight, then gathered on one ship. "Tomorrow we'll do the final step," said Ameye as they sat around him with jars of beer. "It's tricky. Once our soldiers are on the platforms, they'll be at the same height as the ramparts. But even if our hulls are scraping the wall, the masts will still be three, maybe four paces from the rampart. It'll be too far to leap. If we just sling a plank bridge between the platform and the rampart, the plank will wobble when the ship rocks and men will fall. So we've got to build plank bridges with railings."

"Build them strong, boys," Wosmol interjected, "I'm going to be crossing on one of them!" The big man was the only soldier in the group. He waved an imaginary sword. Nebi had never seen him with such fire in his eyes.

# CHAPTER 33

# THE FORLORN HOPE

Their timber supply ran out the next day, so the carpenters tore up the deck of a surplus Memphite ship and used its planks for bridges. They completed the last bridge that afternoon. After darkness had fallen, General Purem sent messengers to rouse every combat officer in the fleet. They were to gather on the flagship at once.

Nebi and Sheb strapped on sword belts and joined the officers. The mood was serious and subdued. Most officers assumed the reason for convening them was to inform them of a bad turn in the king's health. When everyone had arrived, General Purem came out from the deckhouse.

"There will be no cheers, men, no noise," he told his perplexed listeners.

Piankhy then emerged from the doorway, wearing his cobra helmet and purple cloak. In the dim moonlight, the officers stared hard before accepting that this sturdy person was the king. His strong voice reassured them of his robust health. "Tomorrow, Amon willing, we shall have our biggest victory."

Piankhy explained to the officers that by the time they returned to their own ships, the carpenters and riggers would already have started installing ladders, platforms, and bridges on each of the vessels from Memphis. The officers were to have their men prepare their battle gear—all with the utmost quiet. The fleet would set sail in the pre-dawn light, and each ship would tow one Memphite boat.

"We cannot take Tefnakht by surprise without speed," Piankhy told them. "It will take us time to load our men on the Memphite boats and get under way, time that spies could use to race toward Memphis. Our oars must churn the water white."

The Kushites' own ships would not assault the wall, he went on to say. Oarsmen would take up too much space; there'd be too little room for the fighting men. Since the towed ships would have no rowers, they'd be able to carry standing-room crowds. Because the wall had room for only two ships at one time, the soldiers must debark swiftly.

"Choose archers as your oarsmen," Piankhy added. "After the attackers debark, the archers should remain near the wall and rake the ramparts with arrows.

"Once in the harbor, I will oversee the landing at a distance. Arrows will be coming from the rampart—a high angle—so my shield man must be tall." Piankhy's eyes swept the crowd. They fell on a towering man in the rear. "Step forward," said the king.

The man took a few moments to respond. Then, dutifully, he advanced, officers parting the way for him. The king brightened. "I know you. Colonel Ameye has been praising you for your work on the masts."

Many officers would have rejoiced in Wosmol's place. It was an honor to defend the king and a chance to advance one's career. Yet the captain's mouth tightened. Nebi remembered the anger that had once exploded aboard the Napata-bound ship and sensed that he was concealing an even greater frustration now. Batting down occasional long-distance arrows would be no test of his ability.

The king gave further instructions on maneuvering the vessels at the city's wall, then invited Purem to deal with the assignments. At the word "assignments," the murmuring in the crowd stopped.

"Each of you will command a different boat. But I won't assign anyone to either the first boat or the second." His voice had become grave. "I'm looking for a *volunteer* for each of those. Those two boats will be the Forlorn Hope." The last words prompted an uneasy shuffling of feet. "I'll give you a little time to think."

Nebi whispered in Sheb's ear, "Forlorn Hope—what's that?"

"It's when those leading an attack face almost certain death or injury."

"Some of the oldest among you," Purem went on, "have served in Israel, Judah, and Philistia. You have seen how the Assyrians attack walled cities. They used prisoners of war or court-martialed soldiers as their Forlorn Hope, forcing them forward at the point of a sword. That is not our way. We send in those who love valor—those who have stomach for battle, who cherish the cause."

He looked at the faces before him. "Each towed boat will carry sixty to a hundred men. When the first towed boats arrive at the eastern wall, the rampart might be packed with the enemy. Boulders can fall on our men's heads while they're still on board. As they climb the masts, they'll be as near the enemy archers as you are to me."

He let the words sink in, then said, "Who will go?"

A shout came almost immediately. "I will!"

A solemn, stocky colonel shouldered his way through the group. Nebi recognized him as one of the few First Division officers who had not remained at Khmun. A respectful murmur rippled through the officers. The colonel was clearly trying to redeem himself in light of his division's past timidity.

"And I!" said another. A fresh-faced young lieutenant

with tribal scars identical to Purem's stepped forward. He was also from General Lemersekeny's discredited corps.

The two stood before the king and Purem. Heads high, they looked not like doomed men but like proud standard-bearers at the head of a parade. The king addressed them and the group as a whole: "Those men who get into the city should find streets that will take them to the North Gate. Taking the gate and lowering it will be crucial. Floodwaters will have reached it on the other side, and many boats will be waiting there, filled with troops waiting to pour in."

Purem told the two Forlorn Hope officers that they should seek volunteers from their own division to accompany them. He then proceeded to assign the order of later boats. At the end he said, "Now for the medical attendants—they'll be busy. Because Colonel Ameye has other duties, Lieutenant Shebitku will replace him as head. Lieutenants Tebey and Nebamon will assist him. Lieutenant Shebitku?"

"I am here, sir." Sheb stepped into the torchlight.

"Inform the men who served as stretcher-bearers at Hensu that they will repeat tomorrow."

After the meeting broke up, Sheb sent Nebi and Lieutenant Tebey to row separately around the fleet, alerting the men and distributing compresses and bandages from the supply ship.

It was long after midnight when Nebi finally got back to the flagship. He hoped to snatch some sleep on deck before departure, but a loud voice from inside the deckhouse distracted him. It was furious, and it was the king's. Whoever Piankhy was arguing with was speaking quietly.

Only once were the king's words intelligible. "No! I forbid you to be part of the Forlorn Hope!"

Nebi spread his bedroll on the moonlit deck as far from the noise as he could.

Presently the door creaked open. Sheb came across the deck and spread his bedroll next to Nebi.

Nebi whispered, "What happened?"

"I volunteered for the first ship."

"That's suicide!"

"That's what my uncle says. He ordered me to go on a later ship."

"So will you?"

"No."

"He's commander-in-chief. You can't refuse his order."

"I told him he was ordering me for family reasons, not military ones. I told him that being his nephew didn't entitle me to a safer assignment. You know what his response was?" Sheb sighed. "He said he did not want Kush to lose a potential king."

"That's what you've always wanted to hear."

"Not anymore. I told him I wasn't good enough to be king."

"What did he say?"

"He said, 'You've learned something at Memphis that every good king needs—humility.'" Sheb shrugged. "I don't know about that. All I know is that I'm responsible for the stretcher-bearers. If I didn't take the first ship, someone else would. Then he'd be the one in danger."

"You won't be alone." The words were out of Nebi's mouth before he could weigh them. "I'll be in the second boat."

# CHAPTER 34

# THE HORROR INSIDE THE WALLS

The fleet was under way by dawn. Nebi stood in the bow of the second towed boat. Fighting men pressed so tightly around him that he could not turn around. Now the river was at its fullest. Foaming current and the straining oarsmen of the towing ship made the boat race as fast as his pulse. No one spoke in Nebi's boat. The air began to reek with the smell of the soldiers' cold sweat of fear. The spearman next to Nebi leaned over the side and vomited from tension. Several others followed, Nebi among them. He had never done that before the other battles.

Sheb's white-swathed helmet was barely visible in the towed boat up ahead. Nebi wondered yet again why he had so impulsively elected to follow his friend on this assault. Maybe it was a wild belief that he'd live forever, no matter what risks he took. Maybe it was loyalty gone too far. Maybe it was the guilt he would feel if he stayed in the rear and Sheb were to die.

Off to the right, Nebi caught sight of the king's flagship. Powerful Wosmol was helping the helmsman keep a straight course. Nebi's thoughts strayed back to the night in Napata when the king had addressed his officers. He had told them never to attack the enemy when it was not ready. Now Piankhy himself was leading just such an attack. Nebi tried to push the contradiction out of his mind.

As they came within sight of the canal, the two lead towing ships slowed, drifting as the rowers rested on their oars and caught their breath. The real test was about to start. Once the vessels had entered the canal, any sentries stationed on the city's ramparts would be able to see them and send for reinforcements. The rowers had to reach the wall before these fresh troops arrived.

Conspicuous in his purple cloak, the king raised his sword, paused, and then slashed it down. The flagship held back, but for the other ships the sprint was on.

They made a sharp left turn into the canal. The great wall loomed ahead, but the distance and the dim morning light prevented seeing who was on the rampart.

The oarsmen in the towing ship sat facing the boat they were hauling. Their faces were contorted in effort, eyes almost closed, teeth clenched. To inspire the rowers, some men near Nebi began chanting to the beat of the coxswain's thrashing arm. From the middle of the towed boat came the tense voice of the earnest young lieutenant with the scars: "No noise!" Now all that could be heard was the rhythmic splashing of oars, the creaking of oarlocks, and the grunting of rowers.

Halfway up the canal, Nebi could see only four defenders. Two were on the harbor wall, one was on the tower just to the right of the wall, where Tefnakht had pranced, and the fourth was on the tower just to the wall's left.

"Where *is* everyone?" a soldier asked elatedly.

"Hungover from celebrating our retreat!" came the reply.

Small whirlpools made by the oars kept swishing by at the same superhuman pace.

The sentries on each tower ran off. They must have gone to sound the alarm.

The first towing ship was now close enough to the wall for the key maneuver. Its helmsman pushed the tiller with all his weight to starboard, while the starboard-side rowers plunged their oars as close to vertical as they could. The vessel slowed and swerved. Sheb's towed boat swung off toward the left like a stone at the end of a string. Its own helmsman brought the hull's port side thudding against the wall. Perfect.

The urgent voice of the colonel commanding Sheb's boat carried across the water. "Shields!" The men who hadn't done so already lifted their shields over their heads so that they formed a roof offering shelter from arrows, rocks, and falling comrades.

"Climb!" yelled the stocky colonel.

Men swarmed up the ladder.

"Faster!" The colonel roared oaths like lashes over the climbers' shoulders.

Nebi saw a Kushite slam down on the deck an arm's length from Sheb, an arrow through his throat.

Amazingly, this was the only casualty he could see for that entire Forlorn Hope unit.

At the top of the ladder, the Kushites drew swords and axes. Like a cloudburst, they rained onto the rampart. Though trained to scream as they charged, they were now silent, a sign that there was no one left to intimidate. Nebi could only hear feet thudding along the plank and faint cries of alarm from within the city.

Nebi's boat now approached the wall. Its first troops were already atop the mast by the time the hull made contact. Meanwhile, Sheb's boat was already being towed away from the wall to make room for a third boat. The prince leapt into Nebi's almost empty boat.

Bells within the city started pealing urgently. "They're summoning men from the barracks—let's go up!" cried Sheb, scrapping the original plan to stay aboard to tend the wounded. "That's where the real fight will be!"

Clutching their stretchers and carrying bandage-stuffed packs on their backs, the young lieutenants followed the last soldier up the ladder.

When Nebi reached the rampart, he turned to his friend and gasped, "I can't believe it."

Everything looked so tranquil. Nebi and Sheb looked down on a spiderweb of empty streets, the attackers having disappeared into the city. The friendly smell of charcoal rose from early-risers' courtyards. Except for two defenders and one attacker in the weeds at the foot of the wall, obviously dead, it looked like a normal morning.

"Here comes Hawk!" said Sheb.

Colonel Ameye, leading the troops from the third boat, sprang nimbly onto the rampart.

Distant shouts had erupted from the right. Then, the clash of metal striking metal, and more shouts. The noise was coming from the direction of the North Gate. The colonel didn't let that distant crisis distract him. Despite having less vision, he had spotted what the lieutenants had not: three or four men had just reached each tower flanking the wall and were stringing their composite bows, a two-man operation.

A sergeant was right behind Ameye. The colonel pointed with his sword at the right tower. "Take ten men and hit that tower," he told the sergeant. "Do it fast. The flagship's within range." Nebi had never before heard such urgency in his voice. When, moments later, another sergeant jumped over the battlement, he sent him off with a squad to the other tower.

Then Sheb said, "The other problem is there, sir," as he pointed inside the city in the direction of a clanging bell.

The colonel crouched next to Sheb and squinted at a broad paved plaza near the center of Memphis. The bell was in a tower in the plaza, and around the plaza were many two-story buildings—evidently barracks, for troops were now pouring out of them. They started to line up in formation.

"They'll be rushing the North Gate in no time," said Ameye.

He watched the plaza until the last of his men had joined him on the narrow rampart. Then, speaking loudly so all could hear, he said, "Get ready for the fight of your lives, men. I see maybe 1,800—even 2,000—of their soldiers, led by chariots, about to rush to the North Gate. That's where we're going. If we don't want to be outnumbered eight to one, we'll have to open the gate before they arrive. Let's go!" He raced down the stone steps and disappeared up the street, the 60 men at his heels.

Sheb peered down at Ameye's boat. It was about to be towed off, even though one man remained aboard.

"Lieutenant Tebey! Come up here!" Sheb yelled. As a supply officer, Tebey had received little training for combat and had been made a stretcher-bearer.

Tebey shook his head. "I was told to give help *on board*. I'm staying!"

Sheb bellowed, "Get up here, you mouse!"

Tebey put his foot on the first rung.

"And don't forget your stretcher!" shouted Sheb.

When Tebey had joined them, Sheb said, "Three boat-loads of our men are at the North Gate—maybe 250 men. That's where we're needed. Check that your insignia are tight." He felt the bands around his own helmet and arms. "Come on!"

Tebey looked terrified. He pointed to the plaza. "Look at that horde heading for the gate! They've even got chariots! It'll be a slaughter."

"Follow me or I'll see you court-martialed," Sheb warned. He was about to put his foot on the first downward step when anguished cries came from the harbor. Turning, they froze.

Three men on the flagship were crouching, and a purple cape was visible between them. It lay horizontal and was splotched with blood.

"The king's dead!" cried Tebey.

"It can't be!" gasped Nebi. He glanced at Sheb. The prince had tears in his eyes.

Tebey said out loud what Nebi was thinking. "You could become king," he told Sheb. Then he added desperately, "But not if you get killed there." He eyed the North Gate with horror.

Nebi thought Sheb would lash out at him for, in truth, thinking of himself. Instead, he put a comradely hand on Tebey's shoulder. "We have a job to do. Let's go."

The three scrambled down the steps.

Swords slapping at their thighs, they ran along a street just wide enough for a wagon to pass. Getting to the gate was easy. They only had to follow the sound of shouting and clanging.

They stopped at the last house. Sheb peered around the corner to his right, then motioned to the others to follow. Nebi stepped forward, and the sight cut his breath short. Piercing screams, rallying shouts, and the ringing of metal reverberated in the small square. It was lined on three sides by houses, and on the far side by the coveted North Gate, which consisted of a raised drawbridge with protected towers on either side. Scores of men from both armies lay sprawled on the cobblestones. The 200 or so Kushites still standing were struggling to reach the gate, and about the same number of Egyptians blocked their way, many barefoot and wearing only the loincloths in which they had been sleeping.

Kushites from a fourth boat poured into the square from the same street the three lieutenants had taken. The melee now engulfed the whole square except that side where Nebi, Sheb, and Tebey crouched. To give medical help in this chaos was out of the question.

Despite being fewer, the defenders in the square held the advantage. Rocks were dropping from the towers and ramparts on any Kushites who approached the gate. Twenty Egyptian archers were also atop the fortifications, picking off Kushites who were out of range of the rocks. Some Kushites fought awkwardly while holding shields above their heads.

"*This* is the Forlorn Hope," whimpered Tebey.

A boulder the size of a cartwheel crashed into the center of the attackers. It landed on a soldier who had been in Nebi's boat, then rolled thunderously toward the three lieutenants.

"Watch out!" cried Nebi.

Sheb leapt out of the way, but the boulder splintered his stretcher.

Turning again toward the square, Nebi saw Ameye. With his conspicuous feather and eye patch, the colonel seemed an easy mark. But the champion swordsman was in his element. Holding a shield overhead as if this was a natural position, he dipped and bobbed on his long, spry legs, almost dancing as his sword parried and slashed at a brawny foe. Suddenly Ameye's leg lashed out, hitting the man's knee and knocking him off balance before the colonel drove the blade into his abdomen. Then, instead of moving to find another adversary, he paused. Nebi quickly saw why. The colonel kept a Kushite sergeant to his right to protect his blind side, the two forming a unit. Only when the sergeant had dispatched his own opponent did they both whirl to take on others.

"Fall back!" someone shouted near the medics. It was the fresh-faced lieutenant. He raised his sword. "We'll regroup and rush the gate all at once." Fifty Kushites gathered around him, ready to hurl themselves at the horde of defenders. But the next moment the lieutenant lay on his back on the cobbles, a sniper's arrow in his heart.

"The Egyptian reinforcements must be almost here!" Sheb shouted anxiously.

Ameye, on the other side of the square, had seen what had happened to the lieutenant. With the sergeant glued to his right, the two hacked their way toward the cluster of now-leaderless Kushites near the lieutenant's body. Yet another boatload of Kushites ran into the square. "Over here!" cried Ameye in his reedy voice. The men joined his group rather than dispersing around the square.

Nebi could not hear what Ameye told the men, but the colonel was pointing to a sturdy wagon that had been abandoned at the edge of the square. The soldiers raced to it, some lifting it to their shoulders, others crouching beneath it, the remainder getting behind it. The wagon became the point of a wedge. This formation began smashing its way toward the gate. A flurry of arrows struck the vehicle, and four of the men carrying it fell, but others rushed to take their place. A giant of a man on the rampart raised a huge boulder over his head and aimed for the wagon. It smashed through the wagon's floor but still did not slow the vehicle's progress.

Nebi whirled as he heard a clatter of hooves behind him. A Memphite cavalryman had entered the square from one of the four streets that fed into it. He was not there to fight—his sword stayed in its sheath. Looking over the surprised stretcher-bearers' heads, he took in Ameye's gradual advance, and the hundreds of soldiers who stood between the street and Ameye's wedge. Then he wheeled around and galloped back up the street.

"Nebi!" Sheb gestured urgently to his fellow medical attendant to squat next to him. He grabbed Tebey's arm and pulled him down too.

"He must be a scout for the reinforcements," said Sheb. "He'll report there's only one way for them to reach the gate before our wedge does. Their chariots need to plow into the square at high speed" —he smacked his fist into his palm— "and scatter everybody."

"We'd better leave before they get here!" cried Tebey.

"No! We're going to slow the chariots down!"

Tebey looked at Sheb with alarm. *"We?"*

"We'll get in the horses' way," Sheb explained.

Tebey dropped his stretcher with a clatter and fled up the street they had arrived on, his chubby legs churning.

Sheb turned to Nebi. "We don't need him. We need *this*." He reached for the abandoned stretcher. "Look behind you at those two side streets. Both come from the direction of the barracks. The reinforcements will take one of them."

Nebi nodded.

"I'll take this street." He motioned toward the one the horseman had taken. "You take the other. Don't let them see you. Stay in the square, hug the wall, and peek around the corner. When you see a chariot coming, wait till the last moment. Then swing the stretcher across the street and hold it chest high."

As he spoke, Sheb tore the white band from his helmet and ripped off his armbands.

"The stretcher's only made of bamboo and cloth," said Nebi. "The horses will brush right by it."

"Maybe not. I know horses. Go!"

Nebi ran to the farther street, Sheb to the other. Nebi too yanked off his insignia. They stood facing each other 20 paces apart, breathing hard, peering around their respective corners.

They were just in time. Nebi heard clattering on the cobblestones. Coming around a curve was a two-horse chariot. Behind was a second chariot. After them rose a forest of spears.

Nebi jerked back his head so he couldn't be seen.

"They're coming!" he yelled.

Sheb scrambled to Nebi's street, staying on the other side.

"They've got two chariots," Nebi told him. "But they're going slow."

"That's because the infantry has to keep up with them. But the chariots will speed up at the end. That's the only way they can create havoc. Get ready!"

They held the stretchers vertically over their heads. They heard the charioteer's whip and his cry to the horses to charge. Soon the sound of the hurtling steeds was almost upon them.

"Now!" cried Sheb.

They abruptly brought the stretchers down horizontally, presenting the illusion of a blockade.

"Hold strong!" Sheb yelled.

Two horses, two reactions. The horse on the left tried to stop, skidding on the cobbles. The other ignored the stretchers and kept going—or tried to.

The world exploded in deafening noise. The chariot careened to the right into the side of a building and blocked the street. The horses of the next chariot were too close behind to stop. As they whinnied desperately, their legs and chests collided with the perpendicular lead vehicle, knocking it over and sending its horses spilling into the square on their sides.

A writhing mass of horses and charioteers sprawled amid the splintered vehicles. Under it all lay Nebi.

# CHAPTER 35

# WOSMOL'S CHANCE

When Nebi opened his eyes, he was staring at a white ceiling. For a moment, he thought he was back in the infirmary in Thebes. Then he saw that wounded men lay on either side of him.

A passing orderly told him he was in the Memphis barracks, which had been turned into a hospital. He'd been in and out of consciousness for two weeks. The orderly said he would inform Colonel Ameye that the patient had awakened. The colonel, he added, was now in charge of Memphis.

Nebi fingered his body and head for bandages. He was relieved when he found none. He seemed to have only a tender spot on the back of his head. He felt very weak, though. And anxious.

"Sir, what happened?" Nebi asked Ameye that evening as the colonel set his lean frame down on a stool. "How is Shebitku? And the king?"

"Most of the news is happy," said the colonel. He smiled. "The lieutenant went north with most of the rest of the army. And His Majesty is well—very well. In fact, he has never been better, as I will explain in a moment."

"That must mean we've won the war." Nebi found it tiring to say even a few words.

"We've won it for now."

"For now?"

"You and Lieutenant Shebitku held up the enemy's reinforcements long enough for us to take the gate and open it for our troops. We might have been able to do it anyway, but your action saved many lives on both sides. You and he have both won the Medal for Prowess. It's a formidable distinction. The only thing higher is the Medal for Valor."

The colonel dangled the medal before his startled face.

The back of Nebi's neck tingled. He shook his head in wonderment. It was an honor for him, but for Sheb it was much more. Just when the prince had given up on himself, and put the success of the campaign ahead of his ambition, this.

"And I should tell you who came by your mat to award it to you," Ameye continued. Emphasizing every word, the colonel said, "The Pharaoh of North Egypt."

"*North* Egypt?" Nebi shot Ameye a puzzled look. "Osorkon? He's our enemy."

Ameye grinned. "Osorkon gave up his foolish claim to the title last week. North Egypt has a real pharaoh now— Piankhy. The coronation was at Iunu."

Nebi leaned back on his pillow and stared at the ceiling. After a few moments he said, "I never thought he wanted glory."

"He doesn't," the colonel said. "But to keep Assyria out, all Egypt must be united. That means having one ruler. Piankhy is now King of Kush, Pharaoh of South Egypt, and Pharaoh of North Egypt. He fought the war in Amon's name and showed he is Amon's chosen one. The people will follow such a pharaoh. Tefnakht's allies, including Osorkon, have surrendered to His Majesty. All ten lay on their bellies before him last week, pledging enough tribute to rebuild Egypt's damaged cities and to pay our soldiers."

"He hasn't sentenced Nimlot yet?" Nebi asked anxiously.

"Not yet."

"Good. I want to see that."

An orderly brought Nebi a cup of broth. Ameye took it and helped raise Nebi's head from the pillow, allowing the patient to take several sips.

Ameye sighed. "Yet despite the enemy's surrender, I am not sure we have won—*really* won."

Nebi gave him a questioning look.

"The problem is your old master, Tefnakht. Between the time our fleet left Memphis and the time we returned to attack it, he had left the city. We fooled him only too well— he thought the war was over. Purem chased after him into the Delta. But he vanished in the coastal swamps."

Nebi groaned. He knew the swamps were like a deep jungle, impenetrable except to pirates and their friends.

"We couldn't track him, but he sent His Majesty a message: 'Dread of you is in my body! Illness is in my bones, my head is bald, my clothes are in rags.' He said if King Piankhy sent priests to a meeting place, Tefnakht would vow allegiance. And he said he'd send homage of treasure and horses. But he refused to come to the king to do this in person."

Nebi frowned.

"It was the best deal we could get, so we agreed," Ameye continued. "The problem is that his surrender has less weight than if he had made it directly to the king. Some say I'm too pessimistic, but I fear Assyria could link up with Tefnakht again when he gets back on his feet. But at least that won't be for years."

"The ten other chiefs aren't a worry?"

Ameye shook his head. "They all begged His Majesty to his face for mercy, and he gave it to them. Their loyalty oaths were made before the gods and unbreakable. He allowed them to keep their titles and lands."

"Strange," Nebi commented.

"Not really. If His Majesty had ousted them, he'd have had to name replacements, who would be seen as occupiers. If Assyria does threaten to invade in future, the existing chiefs will be better able to raise good armies than outsiders could."

"But what if any of them abuse their power?"

"General Purem will be in charge of the Delta. The chiefs will lose their titles if Purem reports that they stray from *maat*—if they become corrupt or exploit their people. They also have been ordered to return to peasants certain land-holdings that Tefnakht's warriors snatched from them!"

Nebi closed his eyes. "My mother will get our home back!"

Ameye's expression became grave. "Before I go, there's something else I must tell you. Captain Wosmol was standing next to His Majesty when five arrows came at once from two directions—two towers. He stopped three with his shield and flung himself to stop the other two with his torso. He landed on top of the king to protect him from more." He shook his head admiringly. "It was Amon's will. No one knows how he could have done it."

Nebi turned his head away as tears rolled down his cheeks.

"You were his friend," said Ameye. "We thought you should have this." He placed the leather cylinder containing the amulet in Nebi's hand.

The young lieutenant was too distressed to mind if the colonel saw him sob.

Ameye put his hand on Nebi's shoulder. "He received the Medal for Valor. His Majesty said it was the single most heroic act of the war."

"His family won't need medals." Nebi's voice was shaking.

"No, but the captain's widow is being invited to live in

the princess's palace in Thebes. His son will attend the same schools as the royal family."

The colonel rose to leave. Nebi raised the amulet. "I'll see that Wosmol's son gets this someday." He paused, smiling now. "Wosmol wanted to make his son proud, and he got his wish."

# PART IV

# CHAPTER 36

# NIMLOT'S FATE

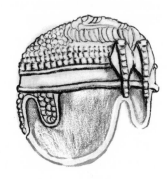

"Hurry! It's about to start," urged Sheb at the entrance to the grand hall of Memphis's palace.

Back to full strength after six weeks' recuperation, Nebi followed Sheb as he shouldered his way through spectators standing six deep along the walls. On one side of the hall were a hundred Kushite officers, including Ameye, now wearing the broad stripe of a general. On the other side, separated by a wide, open space, were an equal number of North Egyptians, including the reinstated leaders and their families, courtiers, and senior officials. They had come to learn the fate of the final member of the pro-Assyrian alliance.

Nimlot was the only South Egyptian among the leaders, a stranger to this region. Yet interest in his sentence was intense. His *sepat*, or province, was unusually large and prosperous, and it lay at the geographic center of the Two Lands. The spectators knew that the delicate business of keeping Egypt unified would depend on making the *sepat* of Khmun loyal to the pharaoh. The new pharaoh's treatment of Nimlot would signal what kind of ruler he would be—strong or weak, just or cruel.

"Let's get closer," said Sheb. He wove his way to the front of the hall. Nebi followed, eager to witness Nimlot's reaction to the sentence.

At the front of the hall, a herald in a blue tunic knocked a ceremonial spear three times on the marble floor. Until the crowd suddenly hushed, Nebi had not realized how much noise it was making.

Everyone bowed as the new supervisor of North Egypt, General Purem, strode out. His deep black skin and tribal scars seemed exotic in this Mediterranean land. As if to reflect the fact that Egypt was now at peace and that he desired to fit in, he wore a civilian tunic in the striped local fashion.

"We are no longer divided," he told the assembly in reassuringly perfect Egyptian. "We are one people, the people of the sacred river, standing together against invasion, against *isfet*. It would please His Majesty our Pharaoh when he enters this hall to see us reflecting this unity. I want every other Kushite to stand on the other side of the hall, and every other Egyptian to take his place."

As an Egyptian, Nebi stayed where he was, next to Sheb, who whispered, "To think that back in Napata he wanted to drive most back to Libya."

When the mixing of the crowd was done, Purem called out, "Bring in the prisoner!"

Stern guards marched in, holding Nimlot by his forearms.

Nebi's hands tightened into fists. A series of images passed before him—the count's amused sneer as he yelled *"Run!"* to the servants, the Mesh charioteer's startled eyes as his leader's arrow struck his neck, Nimlot's innocent look as he lied about his horses' whereabouts.

Ashen-faced, the former Count of Khmun shuffled forward in leg irons. He had lost none of his recent musculature, which suggested that he had been exercising in his cell, but his face was drawn, his eyes empty of hope. The last traces of bravado had vanished. His only clothing was a prisoner's drab gray kilt.

A herald announced, "His Majesty Piankhy, Beloved of Amon, Uniter of the Two Lands." Nimlot flattened himself on his stomach. Everyone else in the hall fell silent and, head bowed, dropped to one knee.

Nebi studied the marble floor as he listened to King Piankhy's heavy footsteps. He was anxious to look up and see if he had a new aura. Before the war, Piankhy had held the title of Pharaoh of South Egypt, but he had been a distant and passive pharaoh, ruling through his sister; now he had saved the South and conquered the North. Truly, he had to be the beloved of Amon. Indeed, during the coronation, in the most sacred chamber of Iunu's main temple, Amon had recognized Piankhy as his son, and the god's life force, his *ka*, must have flowed through Piankhy and become one with the pharaoh's *ka*.

With a word from the herald, the spectators lifted their heads and beheld the Pharaoh of the Two Lands. Piankhy's face looked much the same—perhaps a little more grave—and he wore the same kind of diaphanous tunic over a gold-embroidered kilt and chest straps that Nebi had once seen him wear in Napata. What caused a tingle up Nebi's spine was his new crown. It consisted of a helmet-shaped covering made of gold that fit snugly over the top of his head, the back of his neck, and his cheekbones. Embossed on this thin layer of gold were decorative circles evoking the curly hair underneath. Circling this covering was a diadem, a headband made of thicker gold, and from it arched not one cobra, but two—one for each land. No one, Nebi knew, had been entitled to wear a double-cobra crown in a very long time. Later he would learn it hadn't happened in three centuries, not since the days of the still-revered Rameses and his dynasty.

While those in the crowd remained on one knee, the pharaoh nodded to a priest, who had a leopard skin over one shoulder and had been shaved of all hair, even his eyebrows. The priest recited a prayer that noted that His Majesty was Amon's living likeness and that he ruled on Earth by Amon's principles. The implication was clear: the prisoner's sentence would express Amon's will.

As the spectators rose to their feet, Piankhy surveyed them. He seemed as curious about his new subjects as they were about him. For a moment Nebi thought that when Piankhy's eyes passed over him, the pharaoh inclined his head almost imperceptibly. No, it wasn't possible; he must have been looking at Sheb.

"Rise," he told the prisoner.

Nimlot stood up and hung his head.

"Read out the accusations against you."

An official handed Nimlot a scroll. In a low voice, the former count read out his offenses: withholding tribute from his lord, taking arms against his lord, ordering the murders of six people in the province of Khmun, and plotting the fatal poisoning of a man in Thebes.

"I am guilty of all these," said Nimlot.

"Young man," said Piankhy, "we cannot understand you. Oh, your *treachery* we understand. We can see why you joined Lord Tefnakht. I had rejected you as a husband for my niece. By going over to Tefnakht's side and becoming Assyria's servant, you thought you'd amass more land, more riches, more power. You thought it was easier to collaborate with the empire than to resist it.

"These things we understand: resentment, greed, fear. But what we cannot grasp is your cruelty, your abuse of what is innocent in this world. What we saw of you at Khmun was an example of this. While you and others in the palace ate well, you let your subjects starve. You let your horses starve. Do you regret anything?"

"I do," Nimlot murmured.

"Speak up!"

"I do! My heart cries out in shame! I should have seen that *maat* prevailed."

Piankhy said, "Already you have promised us abundant tribute. Whether your remorse is real is for the gods to decide on Judgment Day. But before announcing your sentence, we will deal with a preliminary matter.

"In uniting the Two Lands, our goal is to make Egypt strong against invasion. That is being done. We will return to Napata and leave General Purem in charge here. We hope this return will be permanent."

A murmur of astonishment rippled through the chamber. No sooner had he been crowned than the man-god was leaving the seat of absolute power. As well, he was relinquishing the splendor to which Egypt's pharaohs were divinely entitled. Comfortable as Napata was, it could hardly compete with either Memphis or Thebes in terms of luxury.

Yet everyone knew that Napata was not just a city. The Mountain of Purity was Amon's home. A pharaoh was responsible for maintaining *maat* throughout the realm and thus repelling chaos. At this time of danger, a pharaoh could be in no more strategic place than at the abode of his divine father, where he could honor Amon properly through ritual and deeds.

"In our absence, we are calling on others to help defend the Two Lands. This defensive effort will have many aspects." Piankhy went on to describe several, the most notable of which was Purem's role in seeing to the new vassals' military preparedness.

The king then looked directly at Nimlot again. "Another aspect concerns your father's horses. Only eight survive— two stallions, three mares, two colts, and a filly. It will take years for their seed to produce the great herds of cavalry horses that the Two Lands need. We must have someone to care for these thoroughbreds properly.

"Lieutenant Nebamon, step forward."

Nebi was not sure he had heard correctly.

"That's you!" Sheb whispered, nudging him.

Nebi strode to a spot about the same distance from the pharaoh as from Nimlot, bowed, and sank to one knee.

"We are transferring these horses to the lieutenant. We will lend him our best breeding expert and grooms to help him start up. He can sell the animals on our behalf to any friend of Egypt."

Nebi was stunned by his good fortune. His life would be transformed. In principle, the horses would be the pharaoh's, just as Khmun or any other part of the realm belonged to him. But in practice, Nebi would be the master of the horses. Although he had never aspired to wealth, he knew the animals would be worth as much as the combined property of all Damanhur's families. He would be able to return to farming while helping in his country's self-defense. If not for the solemnity of the occasion, he would have whooped for joy.

Nimlot was staring at him, he realized now, and Nebi stared back. He saw only cold points of darkness.

Nimlot's lips trembled as he turned again to face the pharaoh.

Piankhy nodded, and Nebi went back to where Sheb was standing, trading excited looks with him.

"Now," said Piankhy, addressing the prisoner, "your sentence."

The pharaoh said nothing for a moment as he searched for the right words. "After a cobra makes an intruder run, it does not pursue him. We seek to restore harmony to Egypt. If Khmun is unstable, the Two Lands will be unstable. If we yield to vengeance and execute you, this heartland will be hollow, bereft of leadership. Your family has ruled diligently for generations, and any outsider with whom we replaced you would stir resentment."

Nebi whispered to Sheb in alarm. "Where is this logic leading?"

"You are still young, Nimlot," Piankhy went on. "Your people are still loyal to you, if only out of respect for the memory of your father. You have had power at too early an age and have wreaked evil. But without the influence of Tefnakht, the potential exists for change.

"If we give you amnesty, if we give you back your title and land, will you give us undying obedience and loyalty?"

It took Nimlot a moment to recover from his surprise. Then, his voice ringing with amazement, he cried out, "In Amon's name, I will!"

Piankhy signaled to the priest, who read aloud an oath of loyalty in the name of the gods; Nimlot repeated it word for word. As he did so, a scene flashed before Nebi. The count was in Thebes, beseeching Amonirdis to believe him as he swore to Amon that he was loyal to her and to the king.

"Count of Khmun," the pharaoh said, "we grant you mercy. It is a time for healing. As soon as the guards remove your chains, you are free to go."

Face quivering, Nebi rushed from the hall and out onto the palace drive. Expediency had routed justice. Anger flooded his being.

# CHAPTER 37

# THE ARROWHEAD

Nebi had taken only a few steps on the crunchy gravel drive leading from the palace when Sheb caught up with him.

"Where are you going?"

Nebi was trembling. "I don't know." He'd controlled his emotions long enough. He couldn't anymore. He felt betrayed by the man he trusted most, Piankhy. "I can't believe this injustice!" he shouted.

Sheb pointed to Jo-at and Jo-am, tethered in the shade of a grove of stately palms. "Let's go for a ride." He took Nebi's upper arm to steady him.

"The pharaoh not only forgave him, he reinstated him!" Nebi's voice shook.

"He forgave me," said Sheb. "Forgiveness can change people."

"Nimlot didn't make a mistake by accident—he killed people by design! But murder doesn't seem to matter anymore! Where is the *maat* in this?" He stopped and faced Sheb. "Where is it?" he shouted.

"Nebi. You're supposed to be the cool-headed one. Which do you want—revenge or *maat*? You can't have both."

As they resumed walking, Sheb tried to defend his uncle. "He has to work with the people in place to keep Egypt from flying apart. A victor can help himself by showing mercy."

"*Mercy!* You're talking like your father."

Sheb shrugged. "I've started to respect him."

Nebi turned to see if his friend was serious and realized he was.

"If Piankhy can forgive me," Sheb said, "I can forgive my father."

"Piankhy said Nimlot could change, but he's evil. Evil can't change."

"He's young. I changed."

Nebi hadn't seen Jo-at and Jo-am for weeks, and they greeted him by tossing their big white heads. While Sheb untied them from the rail, Nebi nuzzled them. "Anyone who lets creatures like these suffer is —"

A sharp thud interrupted him. An arrow had burrowed deep into the trunk of a palm an arm's length above his head.

Nebi whirled in the direction from which the arrow had come. A lanky figure in a gray kilt strode toward him. The person was too far away for his face to be recognizable, but Nebi knew it was Nimlot. After leaving the palace, he must have taken a composite bow, already strung, from one of the chariots parked near the steps.

"Hello, Thief," the reinstated count shouted. "I said I'd find you."

Nebi grabbed Sheb's wooden bow from the chariot. But the arrows were on the other side, next to Sheb. "Hand me the arrows!" Nebi ordered him.

"No!"

"Give me them!" Nebi was frantic with rage.

"Nebi, let's drive away. He won't shoot you if you're unarmed. He knows Piankhy would execute him for that." Sheb grabbed the arrows in his fist and backed away from Nebi's fury.

Nebi heard the wicked smack of a second arrow. This one had penetrated the chariot's cab up to its feathers.

"That's my last warning shot," the count snarled. He was close enough for Nebi to see his vengeful leer, and he was getting closer. "When I swore loyalty to the pharaoh, my oath said nothing about you!"

Nebi threw down the useless bow and drew his sword.

Sheb dropped the arrows and ran to Nebi. "If he kills you, there'll be no one to care for your family."

"Out of the way, Shebitku!" Nimlot yelled, but Sheb held Nebi by the shoulders as he struggled.

Panting, Nebi looked over Sheb's shoulder. Nimlot was steadily advancing. He was five steps away when he stopped, close enough that he couldn't possibly miss. Nimlot was even smirking, plainly enjoying this dispute that had played to his advantage.

That smirk had a sudden cooling effect on Nebi. It told him that rage would not get him out of this. He had to think.

Nimlot had lowered the heavy bow during the struggle with Sheb. He had already nocked an arrow, but to let it fly he would have to raise the bow again. To draw back the string of a composite and shoot, Nebi remembered Ameye saying, took longer than for a regular bow.

Nebi, still nose to nose with Sheb, swung his foot behind Sheb's leg and pushed, hard. Sheb fell.

Now there was nothing between Nebi and his enemy. Raising the sword, Nebi sprinted.

Nimlot was still drawing his bowstring when the sword struck the weapon from his hand. Nebi kept on going, slamming his head into Nimlot's chest. Nimlot fell heavily on the gravel, the breath knocked out of him.

Now Nebi stood over his enemy, ready to ram his sword down, down, down into Nimlot's neck until it hit gravel.

The count's eyes were terrified and Nebi felt a wild surge of pleasure at the sight. He gazed down at the arrowhead around his neck. He grasped it, poised to return it with a cleverly phrased goodbye.

Suddenly Nebi shuddered. Nimlot's habitual snarling expression must be on his own face now. Was defenseless Nimlot dragging him down to his own despicable level? If he killed Nimlot now, would Nimlot's evil live on in him?

Raising his eyes, Nebi recalled Piankhy's words in the count's dimly lit stable: "To find real freedom, you can't hate." The pharaoh had been true to this belief in his treatment of the vanquished warlords. What was true for Egypt's freedom must be true for a man's. Wasn't hatred the real enemy?

Nebi took his foot off Nimlot's chest and slashed the bowstring, then turned and walked unsteadily past Sheb. After sheathing his sword, he unhitched the horses.

Sheb drove the chariot. As they left the palace behind, Nebi felt cleansed. The tightness in his gut was gone. The struggle to free Egypt of disharmony was over. And so was his own.

Gripping the arrowhead that hung from his neck, he gave the thong a good jerk. The leather snapped, and with a flip of the wrist he sent the piece of iron spinning into the bushes.

# CHAPTER 38

# THE RETURN

The day after Piankhy's triumphant departure at the head
of his Napata-bound convoy, Nebi set out to search for his
family. He held out the slim hope that, once Tefnakht had left
the Delta to make war, his mother had somehow been able to
return to Damanhur. If she had not, perhaps people in the
village might have heard of her whereabouts. But he was not
traveling alone.

As supervisor of North Egypt's reconstruction, General
Purem needed staff members familiar with the language of
the Delta, and his first decision had been to appoint
Lieutenant Shebitku as his personal assistant. Nebi had a
few days' leave coming to him before his military discharge,
and when he told Sheb he was leaving the next day for
Damanhur, Sheb requested time off to come along. For security, they had brought along three Kushite soldiers.

They made the journey in three chariots. Nebi, accompanied by a corporal, drove the lead vehicle, thundering
down familiar roads. Nebi had first traveled them on foot as
servant to Master Setka. Now, with his brilliant blue cape
flung over his shoulders, he was returning in the uniform of
the army that had whipped the area's despot. Someday, he
hoped, he'd go cantering down these roads on a full-grown
Little Damanhur.

"How much farther to Damanhur?" Sheb asked when
they stopped to rest the horses.

"Not far," Nebi said. His heart was beating faster. He
was thinking of his mother and the twins, but also of Khuit.

He was unsure if she would even remember him, and unsure of his own feelings.

The first sign they saw of Damanhur was wisps of smoke curling from the mud-brick houses' courtyards. The evening meals were cooking on charcoal fires. The village looked smaller to Nebi than it had once.

A swollen creek separated the village from the charioteers. Nebi put up his right arm, signaling to the chariots behind him to stop. He got out and strode back to Sheb. He took off his helmet, sword belt, and cape. "Could you carry these for me? I'm going to swim across like I used to. Why don't you and the others wait a little while before driving into the village? There's a bridge up ahead."

Sheb nodded. "You want some time alone. There's no rush for us."

Barefoot and wearing only a kilt, Nebi crossed a field and came to the creek where he had often splashed as a child. He dove into the cool water floating with white water lilies. Coming out on the other side, he walked up the muddy bank and through the reeds. He entered the village's narrow main road, just wide enough for a wagon.

The sight of his old house was jolting. Gutted, with black fire stains on the once-whitewashed adobe walls, it was in even worse shape than when he'd left. The walls were crumbling, and doves strutted in and out of the front door. He'd build a new, larger one, he told himself, and set it farther back from the road.

Three little boys, none of them older than five, eyed him suspiciously. They looked ready to flee if he were to make the slightest movement toward them. Nebi realized he must look like a suspicious stranger. He stood in the road dripping wet, with hair streaming down over his forehead, with muddy feet and a long piece of reed stuck to his chest.

Nebi knelt down. Speaking the Delta dialect, he gently asked the oldest boy, "Do you know what happened to the people who lived in this —"

Before he could finish, the frightened child dashed across the road to a door, seized its handle with both hands, and disappeared inside, yelling, "Khuit! Khuit!"

It was the largest house in the village. It belonged to the mayor and his wife—that habitually cross, arrogant woman who had scorned Nebi's family. The village snobs. Khuit's parents.

Nebi looked in the other direction. The two other youngsters had also fled.

"Well, well," said a voice behind him. The voice was cautiously friendly, with a touch of teasing. "Look who's back."

He turned. In the doorway the boy had entered stood a girl with her hands on her hips. No, she wasn't a girl. She was a young woman, with large, intelligent eyes. Her glossy black hair was parted in the middle and pinned loosely, elegantly, behind her ears.

"Am I going to get a greeting from the shyest boy in the entire Delta?"

"The shyest in all Egypt," he corrected.

They both laughed.

"You've changed!" he said.

"Not as much as you. You're much taller. And your voice is much deeper."

They both grinned. "What have you been doing?" Nebi asked.

"I've been caring for children. About a dozen of them. Most are war orphans. I'm going to help set up an orphanage."

She stopped. Her face showed concern. "You're looking for your family."

"Where are they?"

Khuit frowned. "I heard that your mother works in the laundry of an estate somewhere east of Sais—in Sebennytus, I think." She shook her head. "That's a day's walk from here. That's all we know."

Before Nebi could ask more anxious questions, Khuit's mother—plumper than ever—appeared at the door. She was carrying a tall stack of earthenware. The smell of delicious supper came wafting through the door. Her pinched expression as she looked at him signaled that he would not be invited in.

"It's Nebamon, Mother," said Khuit. "He's back."

"So you're the boy who dropped out of scribe school." She scowled. "You abandoned the education that your parents were saving up so hard for. Just when Lord Tefnakht's people caused us trouble and your poor father died, what do you do? You disappeared! Now that Amon has sent us a real pharaoh to free us from tyranny, you drift back. I can see, young man, you're here for the good times, not the bad."

Khuit blushed. "Mother!"

The frowning woman turned to her daughter. "While young people like you care for their community, off this boy goes at the very first sign of trouble. Keep away from riffraff like this!"

At that moment the trio of chariots rumbled single file up the little road. Careful not to tip the pile of dishes in her arms, the woman leaned out of the doorway to get a better look at these extraordinary visitors. "Now, Khuit dear, *these* are the kind of people we can depend on. They're here to help."

The soldiers reined in their horses, stopping them at the doorway. Sheb must have recognized Khuit by her continuous eyebrow. He flashed Nebi an approving grin.

A swarm of barefoot children arrived out of nowhere, a mixture of timidity and admiration on their thin faces as they beheld the rare horses. The presence of soldiers in their bright dress uniforms dazzled them all the more, and when Sheb spoke to them in their dialect, their faces lit up with pleasure. One bold youngster asked the names of his horses, and Sheb answered, "This is Jo-am, and this is Jo-at. They ran in the Napata championships."

That was too much for them. Many of the children scattered, returning minutes later with disbelieving parents. Khuit's brother returned with the open-mouthed mayor in tow. Soon the soldiers were mobbed. Nebi, standing up the road away from the mayor's wife, chatted with Khuit. When the crowd thinned enough for the chariots to advance, Sheb drove up to Nebi.

"Are you soldiers looking for this young man?" said the mayor's wife, following the chariot. "Has he done something wrong? Is he a criminal?" She seemed to enjoy the thought. "I knew it."

Sheb and the soldiers looked at each other blankly. Then they saw Nebi roll his eyes. They grasped the situation.

"Unfortunately, madam, we don't have any chains or leg irons," Sheb said. "But these belong to him. Here, Lieutenant," called Sheb, "catch!" He tossed a jangling sword and sword belt.

The mother gaped, not comprehending. Khuit put her hand over her mouth and smothered a delighted laugh.

The poor mother looked as though she was ready to drop the stack of plates in her arms. As Nebi fastened his cape to his shoulders, her bulging eyes were caught by the row of small ribbons and one gleaming medal on the cape. "What are those?" she said.

Nebi glanced at his shoulder. "Oh, just baubles."

Sheb snorted. "Those, madam, are awards for heroism in the face of overwhelming odds. My uncle awarded him the medal personally."

Nebi swung up onto his chariot. Out of the corner of his eye he caught the woman's expression. She looked even more startled than before. He called to Sheb, "We ought to be leaving. My family was last seen in Sebennytus. That's east of here."

"Let's go!" cried Sheb.

Nebi saw Khuit beaming.

"I'll come back," he promised.

But the mother had one last question for Sheb before they drove off. "Excuse me, young man. You mentioned your uncle. Just who *is* your uncle?"

Sheb hesitated a moment. "The pharaoh," he said. "The lieutenant had a lot to do with his coming here to the Delta." He winked at Nebi and snapped the reins to signal to Jo-at and Jo-am that they were off.

The rumble of the chariots and horses was loud in that narrow street. But far louder was the clatter of the dishes as they hit the ground.

# AFTERWORD

Remarkable though his achievement was, Piankhy (sometimes also called Piye) is little known today. His conquest laid the groundwork for the 25th of the 31 dynasties that ruled pharaonic Egypt in the course of its 3,000-year existence. Prince Shabako would become that dynasty's second pharaoh. Eventually, as a grown man, Prince Shebitku became pharaoh himself.

This novel is largely based on Piankhy's own account of his military campaign; it was chiseled in Egyptian hieroglyphics on a block of granite, or stela, which archaeologists discovered at Napata in the 19th century. Piankhy's detailed narrative begins by telling of the arrival in Napata of an unnamed individual who informs him of turmoil in Egypt; in the novel, the bearer of this news is the fictional character Nebamon. Piankhy then goes on to describe the actions of Nimlot, Tefnakht, Lemersekeny, and each of the warlords. Additional contemporary records tell us of other people who appear in the novel, including Amonirdis, Shebitku, Shabako, and Khaliut.

Since this is a novel, I have taken numerous liberties in the presentation of characters. I have, for example, altered some of Nimlot's particulars, including his title and age. I have also omitted some minor elements and invented others, including the chariot race—a way to present Piankhy's documented devotion to horses. The novel as a whole, however, honors the historical core of the campaign. Its depiction of Piankhy's strategic genius and moral code, including his orders on how to deal with the enemy if it is not battle-ready and his treatment of the vanquished foe, are

true to the stela. The presentation of Amonirdis as a powerful ruler also reflects the fact that women enjoyed a more
elevated status in Kushite society than in most other contemporary civilizations.

Piankhy's account makes no overt mention of Assyria.
My reasons for seeing the Assyrian threat as the subtext for
the campaign are described at length in my non-fiction book
*The Rescue of Jerusalem: The Alliance between Hebrews and
Africans of 701 BC*.

English translations of Piankhy's 5,000-word account
are available in several scholarly works: Henry Breasted,
*Ancient Records of Egypt*, vol. 4 (University of Chicago Press,
1906); Miram Lichtheim, *Ancient Egyptian Literature*, vol. 3
(University of California Press, 1980); and *Fontes Historiae
Nubiorum*, vol. 1, ed. Tormod Eide et al. (University of
Bergen, 1994). (Readers may find discrepancies between the
novel's and the stela's place names. For the sake of accuracy,
I have tried to use the names that people at the time
employed, such as Khmun and Hensu, which the translations
do not always do. I have retained some other anachronistic
names such as Thebes and Memphis, however, since these
are now in general usage.)

In the end, Piankhy's conquest of Egypt turned out to be
the warm-up for a direct collision between the 25th Dynasty
and Assyria. That struggle shook the ancient world, and
Shebitku would be at the center of it.

—H.T.A.

**HENRY T. AUBIN**, a Harvard graduate and former *Washington Post* reporter, is a columnist at the *Montreal Gazette*, where he has won three National Newspaper Awards. He is the author of an acclaimed non-fiction book for adults on the Kushites. *Rise of the Golden Cobra* is his first work for younger readers. He and his wife have four children and live in Montreal.

**STEPHEN M. TAYLOR** is the illustrator of several books for children, including *The Story of Kwanzaa*, *Music from the Sky*, and *One More Border* which was shortlisted for the Red Cedar children's choice award. He lives in Toronto.